About the Author

Once an English and business studies tutor, Diana Jackson is now living in Fife and at present enjoying writing and semi retirement. Her other passions are social history, gardening, travelling and more recently walking The Fife Coastal Path. *(The Healing Paths of Fife)*

'MISSING, Past and Present' is Diana's fourth novel and was inspired whilst walking around the lanes of Bedfordshire where she used to live. It is the second book in her *Mystery Inspired by History* series, following her successful murder mystery, *'MURDER, Now and Then'.*

Over the years Diana has volunteered at a soup kitchen in Luton and more recently at a local foodbank, thus her strong social conscience is reflected in this novel.

Diana says,
'If you enjoy reading *'MISSING, Past and Present'* I would really appreciate you telling your friends about it, giving it a star rating and writing a review on Amazon or Goodreads, to help spread the word.
Heartfelt thanks!
Diana'

D1465194

MISSING,

Past and Present

by

Diana Jackson

This novel is fiction. All characters, both past and
present, are fictitious, as is the town of Drumford and the
village of Canbury. Other locations such as Bedford and
New Lanark are factual.

A CIP catalogue record for this title is
available from the British Library.
ISBN 978-0-9932608-7-2
Published by Eventispress in 2020
Printed by Biddles Books Limited

Dedication

To all my friends and family, new and old, who have encouraged me to tap the keyboard once more.

Acknowledgements

Heartfelt thanks go especially to my editor Marcus Webb and my proof reader Brenda Webb, who have both given me so much enthusiasm for the project as a whole and took me on a walk giving me my initial inspiration. Many thanks also to my Beta readers, authors Felicity Snowden and Rose English, who gave valuable feedback and encouragement along the way.

Thanks to the authors at Eventispress for their continued support and Les from Germancreative for the great cover design.

I am also grateful to all my family, friends and followers on Facebook and Twitter for keeping faith.

The Prologue

I HAVE VIVID memories of feeling restless one evening early in the autumn of 1985. My husband, Gerald, and I had recently been through fertility tests and now we knew that I would never be able to birth children naturally. Instead of reflecting on what next, Gerald threw himself into his work. On the other hand I felt lost; numb by the enormity of the realisation that I would never set eyes on a tiny life conceived in love, or have the privilege to watch our child grow. I took to strolling down into Belmont Park in the evenings after work.

On one particular occasion as the sun was setting and a full moon, already traversing on its arc through the sky, peered from the glassy stillness of the lake. The tiny island of scrubland fronted with birds' nests protected in the shallows, was now in shadow. I sat on a bench where my eyes were led over undulating grassy slopes on the far bank towards a stone folly. This structure of four external Roman columns held a green domed roof which covered a sandstone building. Alcoves at regular intervals protected statues of gods, some preserved, a few damaged and several missing. This was the only reminder of Belmont House, once a grand palatial mansion, now in ruins. Only part of its footprint was still visible, rising raggedly between shrubberies, sometimes forming irregular backdrops to the planting. Three towering oaks, must be four hundred years old at least, formed a circle to my left; sentinels watching silently over me.

Beneath these majestic trees a pin prick of dancing light caught my eye. It seemed to settle a while on a leaf of the nearest tree before somersaulting across the grass towards the ruins. There it hovered, as if searching for something. I was mesmerised, a tingle of emotion seeping through my body to the tips of my fingers as it flew to the top of the folly's dome and vanished upwards.

A trick of the light maybe? A moth, whose fluorescent pattern on its dark wings was caught in the moonlight - another plausible possibility? A firefly? Whatever the truth in the matter my eyes were drawn further upwards to a row of familiar larch trees, behind which was the house I called home.

That day I followed the path of the 'moth - beetle', paused a few moments under the trees, ambled through the ruins and then stood on the steps of the folly, my eyes turning back towards the town of Drumford; the River Dee and Canbury Woods in the far distance.

It was years later, when my life imploded, never to be the same again, that I remembered that strange light. Looking back I wonder, does life follow a planned destiny or is it full of chance encounters; just like *a throw of a dice*?

CHAPTER 1

I DISCOVERED A dice in the hedgerows yesterday whilst foraging for blackberries. I was about just before sunrise, eager to be the first to reach them before the hoards of WI jam makers. A burnt orange hue dappled the horizon. I smiled. This scrubland was like a hidden nature garden, allowed to grow wild in a bowl of tall grasses and native flowers. The sight of cowslips, foxgloves and even bee orchids at certain times of the year lifted my positive energy levels. Butterflies and bees hovered in abundance. Two ancient trees, an oak and a magnificent horse chestnut marked the boundary between this sanctuary and a field of oats, bristly from the recent harvest. In winter, the fingers of their bare branches contrasted with even the greyest of skies, reaching ever outwards. Occasionally, on balmy summer nights I've slept in this haven out in the open, glimpsing stars through the leafy canopy. At times like those I must admit to feeling fortunate to be relieved of the trappings of modern life.

Last night though, I was huddled in an abandoned shed which I had adopted for my late summer home. Pulling my coat around my shoulders I sat for a while glancing across allotments towards the village of Canbury, the Victorian stone building of the primary school visible through the bushes, and I imagined the community shop on the village green closing after their long day. To my left across the valley the town of Drumford, familiar to me from childhood to the present day, lay in the evening mist quietly brooding. Pushing the ill fitting door to, I sighed, shutting out the sights but not the memories.

There in the quiet of the shed, chapters of my life that I'd blanked out for the last two years as I had learnt to survive from day to day came one by one. Trying the distraction of food I dined on two stale cheese sandwiches, made more palatable by the dandelion and young honesty leaves I'd picked from under the brambles, followed by a dessert of fresh ripe blackberries, some juice escaping unhindered down my chin. I rolled the dice absentmindedly. With each roll a scene arrived as vivid clips of movies in my mind.

In life I don't think that I've thrown a *six* more than once or twice. What would a *six* have been, I pondered? Maybe if I'd ever had children of my own it would certainly have been a *six*. I can imagine holding the tiny mite in my arms for the first time, my whole body glowing with the sheer bliss of the moment, in the aftermath of the pain of birthing. Unfortunately I have not been blessed that way. I revelled in my imagination for a while before a scratching brought me out of my reverie. I smiled as a tiny field mouse, which I had recently elected as my closest friend, nibbled at the crumbs I'd dropped, before scampering back into its own hideaway. My eyes rested on a crumpled copy of The Complete Poetical Works of Thomas Hardy, found in a charity shop a few months previously. Thoughts came unbidden of my calling. I was a librarian for years but I fancy that a position at the Bodleian Library at Oxford would have been a *six* for me too. This dog-eared copy would not have graced the shelves of any library in its current state, let alone the Bodleian, and yet it held words I dearly treasured. As I stroked its cover, I knew it was no coincidence that the volume fell open at *The Vagrant*.

When I married Gerald full of love and hope was a *six*, though in truth most good marriages are probably *fives*. For shame on you I can hear you romantics cry. I am a realist you see and believe that, as time drifts on, a *five* probably sums up most of our dreams for marital bliss; that comfortable partnership rooted in a deep trust, formed over years of loyalty, friendship and yes, love. We also had our difficulties because my background was Jewish but Gerald's was Church of England. I agreed to attend his church and that was that. I found the scripture puzzling at first, but church attendance and the overall message it relayed was quite comforting, in its own way.

A *five*? When, at the age of three Beverly appeared, complete with cot at my bedside on Christmas morning. Ironic that my favourite doll was the closest I came to nurturing my own offspring. Then there was being accepted for my first real job at Drumford Library. The thought of a lifetime in the presence of books - thousands of novels by authors I revered and many deliciously unknown. And I was going to be paid too. Incredible! Or there was a time I had some savings in Premium Bonds – it seemed safer than the lottery to me. At least I felt I wasn't throwing my money away each week. I won £5,000. Wow! It felt like a million dollars at the time. It wasn't life changing. I couldn't buy a yacht or a second home in Greece. We did have a holiday in Corfu though, the last but one break abroad Gerald and I ever enjoyed together, bringing memories of the sun's miraculous glow, the vivid blueness of the Mediterranean Sea and the ambience of Greek Tavernas. On the other hand I recall that Gerald was distracted – always on his mobile or furtively sneaking his laptop down to the bar where there was Wi-Fi while I was in the shower, thinking I didn't '*have an inkling*'.

A *four*? Yes there were numerous *fours* in our lives and I should be content with my lot. Anniversary celebrations? What about the one where we had a meal floating along the Thames and then on the London Eye we watched London and Big Ben move ever so slowly towards the setting sun. It was a perfect day and would have been a *six* if we hadn't arrived home to find our heating had packed up. I reflected on how quickly an event can alter in value on a scale of *one* to *six*.

There was the occasion; bored with life and depressed by the unsatisfactory conclusion of infertility treatment – a *one* almost certainly became a *four* when I had an illicit affair with a man just over half my age. He'd been studying in the library. What was his name now? Must have been nearly twenty five years ago. A quarter of a century. Max! How could I have forgotten Max? Max was a *four* certainly. I couldn't handle the subterfuge and soon put an end to it. He haunted me in the library for a while after that. I'd be putting some books away and turn and he'd be standing behind me, or I'd be at the main desk and he'd come to make an enquiry, just as an excuse to talk to me. I had none of it. It was my own stupid fault. He soon gave up, out of boredom probably, and went to pester someone far more interesting.

Oh yes. Max was at least a *four* while it lasted. Possibly a *five*. Gerald never knew, or at least I didn't think he did at the time. Twelve years later when I was fifty, call it a mid life crisis, I decided that it was time for a change. I'd worked in the library for over thirty years, since I was sixteen, initially doing voluntary work in the summer holidays before working full time when I was eighteen. I hadn't regretted a moment, apart from my indiscretion maybe.

I picked up a leaflet about short term fostering and over the next six months left it in different places around the house. I occasionally mentioned it casually to Gerald, dropping subtle hints in the quiet between us.

'Did you know that the Jones's down the road have started to foster children?'

and

'I'm not sure that I could cope with a toddler now Gerald, do you?'

I never got much response. Just a grunt over his tea cup, until one day at breakfast he lifted his eyes from The Financial Times and announced, as if it was all his idea, 'Why don't we think of fostering children Dot? We've got plenty of room here, which is a waste. It might be good for us to breathe a bit of life back into our lives. We could take teenagers. They may be a challenge but that wouldn't be such a bad idea, would it?'

He spared me with his thoughts on our stale marriage. Much like the sandwich I was eating - only just palatable but it kept us alive. I was so excited.

'What a fantastic idea Gerald?' I held my breath, smiling at the power of female wiles. Leaving the *ball clearly in his court* I continued, 'Shall I look into it? See what's involved and we can have a discussion over supper at the weekend. 'Maybe that moment of triumph was a *six*. I'm not sure.

After the intrusive initial assessment when Gerald nearly gave up on the idea, but I held on to the hope, we were graced with numerous children through our care. I'll always remember the first two, a twelve year old brother Michael and his sister Emily who was only nine. Their mother was in hospital long term and so it was comfort and stability they needed. I took them to see their mother regularly, a single parent who had been coping really well until the big C struck. Most unfair. Anyway Emily, the bossy one, and her brother looked upon me as a kind of aunt. They were no trouble at all and when their mum went into remission they were fortunate to go home to her, but she's always kept in touch. They moved to France where she remarried a chap from La Rochelle, but we always got a card and an up-to-date photo at Christmas. Lovely really.

We had some characters too. Teenagers almost out of control. Gerald always laid firm rules before we agreed to have them and after some bolshie patches they usually came around to treat us pleasantly and, more importantly, to respect themselves.

Then, just five long years ago, Jamal and Ahmed came into our lives. They were refugees from Syria - asylum seekers, one sixteen and one seventeen. No-one else would take them and their social worker came to plead with me one day.

'They've lost their parents in the war,' she said. 'The Red Cross rescued them from the refugee camp in Lebanon and for three months they've been in a detention centre for assessment, but it's no place for them. There's a children's home but what chance in life will they have, barely time to be educated and integrated into society before they are out of our jurisdiction?'

'But we only ever have children for up to six months at a time,' I argued, thinking that Gerald would be furious. He was sympathetic about the plight of the poor souls fleeing the war, just so much as it was seen behind a TV screen.

'Yes that's true. It would be a longer term foster than you are used to - until the boys are eighteen. For Ahmed that'll be less than a year but for Jamal nearly two. They desperately need stability Dot, to encourage them to do something positive with their lives. You'd be perfect with your experience. Why don't you just meet them? No promises. They are delightful, polite lads, you'll see.'

'Why hasn't someone of their own kind offered then?' I said stalling, visions of these two unwanted lads settled in the oh so empty rooms upstairs, already creeping up on me. 'Surely it would be better for them.'

'We have nobody suitable on our current team of foster carers Dot, and anyway, they need to learn English and fast. I do think a totally new environment would be best for them and I've seen how you treat those in your care. You're a blend of sensitivity and firmness, which could go some way in alleviating their trauma. You're kind but you set clear rules and above all you have time to spend with them. Your records also say that you taught English-as-a-Second-Language as a volunteer in the evenings before you were married. You would be ideal.'

Gerald didn't particularly like the idea but then he was never home. He worked long hours in London so we talked little in the evenings. I saw him at weekends but when he was not in his office upstairs he was mowing the lawn, washing his car or out playing golf. So that was that.

CHAPTER 2

JAMAL AND AHMED became my whole life. I encouraged them to go to their mosque. I was a high days and holidays type of church goer. After all these years of hearing familiar stories I believed, but I did not feel that Christianity had the exclusivity of all the perfect answers, especially with my Jewish background. They both came with me to the Christmas service and occasionally to other Sundays too, because like myself it was important that they integrated, but I also believed that it was vital that they held on to some of their roots. It was a balancing act which was not always easy. I'd been to see the local Imam to explain - a lovely chap who told me that Mary the mother of Jesus was mentioned more in the Koran than she was in the bible. I still don't know if that's true, but certainly his hospitality was welcoming and he agreed to keep an eye on Jamal and Ahmed and keep in touch.

My life with the lads oscillated between a *five* and a *one*. We had brilliant times when they were learning English and I'd help them every evening after school, then they'd eat supper with me. The best times were when we went on outings to Brighton or London. You should have seen their faces when we walked along Brighton Pier in the sunshine. They'd never seen the sea before. We ate fish and chips out of paper and they thought that it was really 'cool!' Happy days.

It was a *one* when I caught Ahmed smoking pot in his room. He knew the rules and that he was likely to be thrown out, but he'd had a tough time at school and got in with the wrong crowd.

'You've got no right to stop my allowance,' he yelled. 'It's mine, not yours.'

'You have forfeited your rights Ahmed, by breaking not only our rules but you've broken the law. I should turn you in to the police.'

'Go on then,' he goaded, blowing smoke into my face. 'I dare you.'

I was so angry that I walked away, afraid that one of us would say something we'd regret, but I could hear Jamal arguing with Ahmed upstairs. They'd been with us for four months by then and if Gerald knew about the incident they'd be out immediately, no second chance. Then I heard heavy footsteps on the stairs and the front door bang. Jamal came into the kitchen.

'I'm so sorry Auntie.' The lads called me that out of respect and I must admit that I quite liked it.

Jamal continued, 'I've opened the window in Ahmed's room and sprayed with that nice air stuff from the bathroom. I'm sure he'll come and apologise when he's calmed down. You won't throw us out will you?'

I looked at Jamal. He was the younger but by far the wiser of the two brothers, but then again he'd probably witnessed far fewer atrocities that Ahmed, I reasoned with myself.

'Sit down and we'll have a cup of tea,' I said, watching Jamal relax, his shoulders dropping almost an inch and his contorted face losing some of its frown lines. I made the tea in a daze, almost borrowing time from the moment to calm myself. Putting the mugs on the breakfast bar in front of us, I sighed.

'It's the last thing I want to do ... to throw you out, but you must understand that I cannot have pot smoked in our house. I don't know what Mr G would do if he knew. Apart from breaking the law, how does Ahmed know that it's safe stuff. You hear such stories of skunk, do they call it, bending people's minds or even worse. He's my responsibility while with us. You've got to understand that.'

'Oh I do,' said Jamal, the emotion dripping from his voice, 'and I'm sure Ahmed does too, but can't you make allowances for the life he's had? Please give him another chance Auntie.'

Jamal looked so distraught that I just wanted to hug him but knew that it was inappropriate. I couldn't help but wonder if either of the boys had experienced genuine love in their lives.

The phone rang me out of my reverie. It was the Imam.

'Mrs G. It is the Imam from the mosque here. I have just had a chat with Ahmed who came to me almost in tears, thinking that he was about to be thrown out of your house. Is that true?'

I had to think quickly here. I couldn't be seen to rescind too easily but I did wish for the Imam to know that I was compassionate and not unreasonable.

'And did Ahmed tell you why I was angry with him?'

'Yes, he told me everything. I cannot make excuses for Ahmed. What he did was very wrong, to smoke pot in your house when it is forbidden. He knows the rules and he is also aware of the law, but'... and then he paused for a second or two. 'It is hard for the young not to be drawn in by their peers and in some quarters, even within our religion, smoking mild drugs like cannabis is not seen as anything wrong. It is a bit of a culture clash but I understand your concern and I'm sure Ahmed does too.'

There was silence for a few seconds as I tried to digest this information.

'If you were me, would you give Ahmed a second chance? He knows the rules and he is also aware of the consequences. You are a tough religion. How do you treat people who break your rules?'

There was another pause.

'Well, I know what you are saying, but we have a lad here who will be eighteen in eight months time. He needs your firm care to show him the best path to follow. I'm not sure what he would do if you refused to keep him, now that he is settled with you. He's been doing so well.'

I thought about all that had been said but grasped for time. 'I'll have to think about it and decide whether to tell my husband.' I paused. There was silence and I could hear my deep breath echo in the earpiece. 'Tell Ahmed that he can come home, but it's on the understanding that he never smokes cannabis in our house again.'

'Thank you so much Mrs G. I know that Ahmed will not let you down again.'

'My head is muddled at the moment. In a week's time ...'

'I'm sure you are doing the right thing Mrs G.'

'No promises,' I answered as I put the phone down.

The next week Ahmed was subdued but his behaviour was exemplary. He even helped me out in the kitchen by loading and unloading the dishwasher, which I knew he felt was women's work, far beneath him, but it was as if he was holding his breath at times, waiting for sentencing.

At the end of the week I couldn't stand the tension and Gerald was beginning to get suspicious. I hadn't told him the full story, just that I'd found Ahmed smoking, a habit I know Gerald abhors. I was surprised that Saturday when it was Gerald who made the final decision by asking the lads if they'd like to have a go at playing golf. I winked at Ahmed as he left the kitchen and he smiled, the warmth of which said a heartfelt thank you, without words.

Ahmed never smoked anything in the house again to my knowledge. I was sure he still took the drug now and then by his occasional glassy bloodshot eyes. A couple of times he would not look at me and headed straight to his room, but by the morning, to my relief, he'd be normal again. On the other hand Jamal covered for his brother by continuing with the chores of the dishwasher, long after Ahmed had lost interest. He would also sit drinking tea with me telling me vivid tales of their fraught lives until they were rescued, and happier memories of life with his parents before they were lost in a bombing raid, their bodies never recovered. I hoped with all my heart that this was helping Jamal to heal. It was the least I could do to listen, but it certainly opened my eyes.

CHAPTER 3

BACK AT MY tumbledown shed it was good to daydream about Ahmed and Jamal because that was the last time I experienced any sort of normality in my life, until things changed. Nearly two years later they had moved into a flat of their own but we kept in touch, especially Jamal. Both had found steady employment, Jamal in a warehouse and Ahmed was involved in something at the Mosque. I didn't ask too many questions but was just relieved that, whatever it was, it was paying the bills.

I threw the dice again. I had nowhere in particular to go, so it passed the time.

Perhaps most people's life experiences are *threes* and *fours* - on a law of averages; everyday existence, neither good nor bad, blending into half forgotten snippets of memory. Work, shop, walk, eat and sleep. I mused that the mundane *threes* could become *fours* in a moment - noticing the first snowdrops peaking up their white heads whilst pegging out the washing on an unusually mild winter's day - seeing a new line in fresh sauces on the supermarket shelf turning a bland fish dish into a gourmet meal - spotting a hawk hovering above the verge whilst driving to a hospital appointment at nearby Bedford, and being struck by its magnificent poise as it sought for its prey. So many *threes* could become *fours* if only we kept our eyes open to opportunities, or the unexpected.

Then there were the *twos* in my life. *Twos* are such irritating happenings, like my headteacher telling me that my handwriting was so small that I must have something to hide, or the Christmas I didn't get that lovely ballerina doll which sat in the middle of the toy shop window in Drumford High Street, tantalising every young girl in the town. You see, I've lived in Drumford all my life, boring I know. Maybe that's a *two* too! It was even worse the day after Boxing Day when I realised that my best friend Madeline had been the fortunate recipient.

They were *twos* more recently when each of our foster children left us for something more permanent. My desolation in the following weeks made me question our decision to be short term carers, but time and time again since then I have gained much pleasure at giving youngsters a brief period of stability in times of need. It has been so rewarding and a privilege to give young people a refuge and let them go on to the next stage in their lives, knowing that I'd been an important stepping stone. Oh, there have been lots of *twos*, far too mundane to list here, but you get the idea.

That brings me to the *ones.* The day I was knocked down in a town car-park and broke my leg. It was the endless time it took to recover which was the most painful, literally; learning to be patient and to depend on others, initially even to go to the toilet. Sobering times eh. The day I heard that my best friend Madeline had died in a skiing accident was a big *ONE*. At least, months later, after the initial grief and loss had waned slightly, I reasoned that she had died doing something she loved. Not many people can say that. The day my father died was undoubtedly a *one* for me - I found that oh so hard. I told Jamal about it the day he shared the story of his parents' demise with me.

'My father died when I was only fifteen too,' I said. 'the same age that you were.'

'Oh Auntie, I didn't know.' Jamal's concern brought a moistness to my eyes. He was obviously waiting for me to explain.

'It was a long time ago Jamal, but I know that it is an impressionable age to lose a father. I was so angry and hurt that he should leave me. I didn't really consider how my mother felt at the time. But at least I still had her.'

Jamal nodded. A mixture of empathy for me and pain at his own loss etched in his eyes.

'I think she only coped because she focussed on supporting me, but it must have taken its toll on her health too. She was never well after that. It was my mother who gave me away when I got married. We became so close.'

'Where does your mother live now Auntie?' Jamal asked looking puzzled.

'Oh Jamal, that was a long time ago. When my mother died it was expected. She'd been ill for some time and, in a way, it was a relief for her to go. I could celebrate her full life but my God I missed her. I still found myself looking for a birthday card for her years on and beginning to dial her number before I remembered. I would replace the handset, feeling a trifle foolish.'

There was silence between us, of poignant moments shared.

'We both have good and bad memories Auntie, but it's great to be able to tell them, even the bad ones. I'm so happy to be with you.'

A little embarrassed at this outburst, Jamal made an excuse to go to his room to do some homework but I knew, from that moment on, wherever Jamal's life might lead him, our relationship would be special to both of us. I was yet to find out how precious. At the time I just hoped that he'd want to keep in touch.

CHAPTER 4

I SMILED AT the thought, but then immediately frowned, wondering if we would ever speak again. So much had happened since we last met that it seemed like another life – so far away from my current situation. I wiped my mouth with an old hanky which I stuffed in my pocket, making a mental note to myself to exchange it next time I visited The Ark in town. After all, I had to keep up some standards, didn't I? It was comforting to know that it was only an hour's walk away from my dry, albeit dilapidated shed, in which I'd chosen to shelter when the weather was on the turn.

It was nearly dark. I threw the dice a final time. A *zero*. I call it a *zero* when the dice balances on its edge, maybe lodged by a wall or a leg of a chair. This time it got stuck between a couple of old boxes of junk and I had to prize it out with my index finger. *Zero* for me was when life as I knew it ceased to exist and strangely enough it happened at the end of Gerald and my last trip together to New York City. This was a couple of years after our holiday in Corfu, when Gerald had been so preoccupied. Until *it* happened I would have called the holiday *'a five,'* verging on a *six*.

We seemed to be in love again, Gerald and I, strange after nearly thirty years of marriage. He didn't switch on his mobile phone or his lap-top once during our stay. It was a very cold February break. We were like children, dancing in the snow in Central Park in the spirit of Ginger Rogers and Fred Astaire in 'Shall we Dance', then pretending we were part of a school party going up the Empire State Building. As dusk approached and New York was covered with a million twinkling lights we acted like the young lovers of 'Sleepless in Seattle' falling into each other's arms as if for the first time. I didn't understand the connection when Gerald dragged me towards a taxi outside the United Nations building shouting out 'the lady's ill' as he pushed a man aside who was about to get in. It wasn't until I was on my own after ... you know ...*The Happening* ... that I watched 'North by North West' - Gerald had left a copy beside the TV. I realised that, for once in Gerald's life, he had been wrong and the scene in the 1959 movie had been outside another building entirely. My eyes were so blurred with tears at the time that I can't even recall which it was.

The oddest and most out of character behaviour Gerald revealed on that holiday was his preoccupation for women's lingerie. He made me rummage through the underwear at Macy's and he couldn't pass a shop window without making some remark about buying me something for Valentine's Night. At one point I remarked,

'Anyone would think that you were looking for a younger model Gerald,' as I eyed the bra and panties in his line of vision. They barely existed - literally! 'I wonder if the price goes up as the quantity of fabric decreases.'

'You're missing the point entirely,' Gerald put on a hurt expression as I marched him by yet another alluring shop window.

'But, for all we know it might be a sex shop in the back,' I reasoned.

'Well?' grinned my husband.

Exasperated, I huffed as I strode purposefully on to the relative safety of 35th Avenue.

For the rest of our stay we were enlightened and entertained by several tour guides to visit places like the Theatre District, the Meat Packing District and Brooklyn Bridge. I can recommend every one. On the latter I was impressed to learn of the crucial part Emily Roebling played in the bridge's final construction. Apparently she relayed instructions from her sick husband Washington, who had got the bends whilst diving in the contraption they used to build the pillars underwater. I think that was what the guide said, but if you are interested I will leave you to research the story at your leisure. I always have a hankering to discover great women of influence in history, feeling a bit of a mouse myself.

It was on our last day that I called Gerald's bluff and it happened to be Valentine's Day. Each day we had passed his favourite shop, Victoria's Secrets, and so, instead of walking past making some flippant comment as I usually did, I marched to the door. Gerald followed in my wake, his expression more than a little shocked. Now let me set the scene here. I was a fifty eight year old, wearing walking boots, a pink woolly hat and at least three layers of coats, looking as if I was about to hike in Iceland rather than to walk into a classy underwear shop in down-town Manhattan.

With glee I led Gerald, a sixty two year old equally unsuitably clad man, from display to display asking his opinion, watching his face turn shades of pink. The choice was breath-taking and I had to admit quite alluring, from subtle pastel shades to animal prints, from glittery chiffon to pitch black or post-box red satin.

In the end I picked up a black number with flesh coloured lace. Undeterred by the image I must have given to the smiling shop assistant, I asked, 'I wonder if you could help me to find a 34DD please,' in as perfect Queen's English as I could muster.

'The lady rummaged in a drawer below and found the article; filling the details in on a card before directing me to a fitting room. I grinned wickedly at the thought of Gerald waiting for me while I tried it on, but 'Victoria's Secrets' was even prepared for embarrassed husbands. They provided a cushioned waiting area screened from the main shop. Jammy!

Gerald sank down, suitably relieved, as I was shown into a cubicle. This was just as well because by the time I had taken off the five layers of clothing and tried on the bra I realised that it wouldn't fit. I groaned. Pressing the bell provided, a lady called Dee could not have been more helpful as she handed me a variety of bras to try on until, eventually, we located the perfect size, but I'm not going to tell you what it was. No way!

With bra in hand I picked up a relieved husband and led him back out to the store.

'I need to find some panties to go with this bra,' I asked, smiling at the assistant who was totally unfazed. 'What is a size 14 in American do you think?' I added.

Looking me up and down I could see the young lady trying to judge my size - quite difficult through my layers.

'What style would you like madam? We have those,' she said pointing to the modest but adequate knickers on the stand in front of us, 'classic briefs, or bikinis which are smaller, thongs or even g strings like these?'

'Oh those I think,' I said, trying but failing to imagine myself in panties the width of less than a strip of sellotape. The thought of thongs horrified me too.

'What do you think?' I said, turning to Gerald with a cheeky grin.

He just shook his head, totally speechless.

'Now which size? Here's the large size,' The shop assistant held up a pair of pants big enough to go around me one and a half times. Seeing my face she dropped them in the drawer and chose another. 'Medium?' She said, her lilting voice rising a notch or two.

'Yes, those look just right thank you.'

The lady pointed to the check out desk and I turned to Gerald.

'Yes, I suppose I'd better pay, hadn't I, but only if you say you'll wear them tonight,' he said.

That night we dined in an Irish bar close to our hotel called O'Reilley's, which was both lively and friendly. I tried some Guinness and must admit to becoming quite partial to the black stuff.

I won't describe what happened in the hotel room that night to spare both of our blushes. Suffice it to say that we danced around our suite like teenagers – it was only about eight o'clock and so I don't think we disturbed the guests below, and, with a music channel playing on TV to hide our modesty, we giggled like new lovers as I was stripped of my new garments, which fitted perfectly as it happened.

Oh such happy memories! Maybe my only true '*six*' in life to date.

The trip home the following day was uneventful. Our stay had been so action packed that it seemed far longer than five days, though it was almost seven with the travelling either end. It was at Heathrow Airport that things started to go decidedly wrong. We'd collected our baggage and decided to take turns to go to the toilet, but when I came out of the Ladies there was a pile of my luggage still on the trolley but Gerald and his luggage had disappeared.

Somehow, after feeling a little foolish reporting him missing to the airport police and sitting for hours waiting to fill in forms and answer questions, I found my way home on the train with a taxi from the station. The house seemed decidedly empty. No husband and no foster 'children' in our care. After Jamal and Ahmed had left we'd decided to have a break and reflect on whether we were getting too old for the highs and lows of fostering. It was eerie. The clock in the hall struck FOUR.

I went upstairs and ran a bath, soaking for half an hour. Empty headed, I found it difficult not to doze, only just aware that it would be dangerous to do so. With barely the energy to towel myself dry, I changed into a brushed cotton night dress and sank into bed.

I awoke disoriented and confused as the hall clock chimed twelve, my hands fumbling for the nearby switch. Light filled the room, the empty bed next to mine coming into focus. We had long since reverted to using single beds, Gerald and I, sleeping better that way. Wrapping my thick cream dressing gown around me I visited the bathroom, before stumbling downstairs. My luggage, still in the hall-way, jolted me to action. Taking one with me to the kitchen I emptied its contents on the floor, sorting out the coloureds to put in the washing machine first. The new underwear slipped through my fingers and on to the cold tiled floor. Glancing up I caught my reflection in the glass door - a watery smile prompted by satin memories of that extra special night.

Once the machine rumbled, busy for both of us, I sipped a mug of cocoa. Should I contact anyone? My sister-in-law Charlotte maybe or my friend Karen? I glanced at the clock, confused by jet-lag. Stupid me. It was only just gone midnight. It would have to wait until morning. Surely Gerald would have turned up by then. I swallowed a sleeping tablet and took the remainder of my drink back to bed. Soothed by the normality of the sound of the washing machine downstairs and the pill, I was soon fast asleep.

CHAPTER 5

LIFE WAS A blur for the next few days, like looking at the world without glasses. The police called at 8.30 the next morning. I was up and dressed, fortunately. There was a man and a lady – I forgot their names the moment I was introduced.

'Hello, Mrs Gibbons isn't it? Dorothy Gibbons?' I nodded as they flashed their ID cards at me and I gestured for them to come into the house. They followed me into the kitchen where I instinctively put the kettle on. It was good to busy myself with a mundane task.

They both must have been in their late twenties or early thirties. I remember thinking how sweet this petite young police officer appeared with her black bobbed 1960's hairstyle and pale oval face. The young man, although slightly older, had that 'boy next door' sort of image about him and they both looked upon me with concerned faces as if they were humouring their aged grandma. Until, that is, it occurred to me that I probably *was* the age of their grandmas.

The lady started to speak and my eyes returned to focus on her lips, trying to decipher what she was saying from the muffled sounds reaching my brain. Do we have the ability to blank out words we don't want to hear to protect our sanity, I wondered. I think Gerald certainly did that. I shook myself back into reality.

... 'Pardon,' I muttered. 'What did you say again?' I passed them cups of coffee.

'Ah thanks,' the lady said, 'What I was saying was, we have received a report from the airport police, but since we are your local force, we are working with them to investigate the disappearance of your husband.'

'Oh yes I understand. What did you say your names were again?'

'I'm DC Cathy Peterson and my colleague is DS Tony Brown. We're from Bedford Police Station but are working from the small satellite branch at Drumford as part of the new 'Close to the Community Initiative.' They sat down on bar stools and the lady, Cathy Peterson gestured for me to join them. I sat opposite feeling the security of the breakfast bar, firm and unyielding between us.

'First I must explain that usually a missing person's case would not be a priority so soon after the MISP has been reported.'

'Oh,' was all I could say.

'Usually they turn up in the first forty eight hours.'

'I see.' My puzzled expression showed that I really didn't see.

'We usually only need to make a report at this stage, unless anyone's life is in danger, or we have sufficient suspicion that a crime has been committed.'

'Oh,' was my feeble response.

'But the airport police wish the case to be pursued. A false passport may have been used for example.'

'Identity fraud,' I stated matter-of-factly. I'd read my crime novels in proliferation.

'So please can you start from the beginning Mrs Gibbons.

I took a deep breath. 'Well, I had enjoyed a break with my husband in New York City. It was the best holiday we'd had together by far. My husband had recently been very preoccupied you see. Business problems I expect. He never shared them with me. Anyway, after our last foster children left us - well, they are nearly adults really; he surprised me when he booked up this break. It was wonderful - as if we'd found each other after searching through a foggy night - such a relief.' I blushed.

'Did anything happen during the journey home Mrs Gibbons?' Cathy Peterson prompted.

'Nothing really. We slept and talked a bit, excited about what we'd seen. What was most unusual during the whole trip was that Gerald didn't check his laptop or his phone once. Normally he'd be glued to the things, in anticipation of returning home I suppose.'

'What happened next?' Tony prompted.

'We came through passport control; no problem at all. Then we waited for our cases, but before coming through customs we both decided to go to the loo. I went first leaving Gerald looking after the luggage but, when I came out, both Gerald and his cases had disappeared.'

'What did you think had happened?' Tony asked.

'I didn't know what to think. I waited for about twenty minutes in case he appeared - perhaps caught short - you know - couldn't wait. Then I asked a passing gentleman if he'd check in the toilets and call out Gerald's name or see if he was ill or something. Nothing. Then I went to customs and asked what to do and they said to report it to the airport police. It took about two hours before they were happy for me to go. They could do no more. He had not booked on a different flight. There was no way of checking the buses or trains without lengthy looks into CCTV images, so they suggested that I take the train home, thinking that my husband might have turned up here. He hasn't as you can see, so I phoned the number they gave me to let them know and sank exhausted into a bath - then bed.'

'You didn't phone anyone then Mrs Gibbons, your son or daughter maybe?' Cathy asked.

'Please call me Mrs G. That's what I'm used to.' I took another breath, reticent to continue. 'I've not had any children. I've only fostered children and teenagers - never had any of my own I'm afraid. My only brother Jeff lives in Ealing sixty miles away. He wouldn't know what to do and anyway, we've not spoken for a few years now. My sister-in-law Charlotte and I speak occasionally, but I didn't really want them to be troubled for now.'

'So you have no one you could contact to be with you?' Cathy asked.

'Not really, no. I have a good friend but she's disabled and housebound and, to be honest with you, I thought I'd wake up and find Gerald with some story about work. He was never very good about telling me things or sending me messages. I'd often have to second guess if he'd be home for supper - but fostering kept me occupied,' I added, my eyes misting over.

'I know you gave all the information you could remember to the airport police but could you write down your husband's workplace and any key people you think we should contact. He's in sales isn't he?'

I nodded, writing the address of Gerald's company on the proffered piece of paper and the name of his boss, Peter Snow. I couldn't remember the telephone number so had to check on the phone. I knew Gerald had saved both his extension and Peter's as 2 and 3. We had the fostering agency as no 1. I fiddled with the phone as I spoke. 'Yes, he travels around the country, sometimes staying away for a couple of nights. I'm not sure what he sells - some kind of computer systems I think.'

I frowned and tried pressing some more buttons. 'That's strange. The numbers have been deleted I think. Shall I check in Gerald's Office upstairs?'

'Yes please,' said Cathy Peterson. 'I'll go with you if I may.'

The constable followed me upstairs to Gerald's office and watched while I rummaged through Gerald's papers on his desk and in his drawer. I was getting frantic now. There seemed to be no record of either his workplace or Peter's phone number. I began to check again, getting extremely flustered. Tears ran down my cheeks blotting the papers in my hand.

'Let me take those,' said DC Peterson gently. 'Would you like us to look through them for you? You're suffering from shock - not to mention jet lag. It's not surprising that you can't find anything.'

I collapsed into Gerald's office chair, the papers I'd held falling to the floor.

'Why don't you have a nice hot cup of tea and sit downstairs for a while. What do you think? We don't have a warrant to search your home but we can go ahead with your permission.'

I nodded the affirmative, afraid to open my mouth. The kind constable led me back downstairs, made me a cup of tea and sat me in the lounge, switching on the TV. I sat staring through the BBC morning news while I heard rummaging and whispering upstairs. I felt helpless.

About ten minutes later they came down with blank faces. They'd found nothing.

'Don't worry Mrs Gibbons, we'll set an officer on to the task of trying to trace Peter Snow and this computer or technical firm. It shouldn't be too difficult. When did you last use either of the numbers?'

'I'm not sure officer. They were for emergencies only and I didn't like to worry Gerald unless I had to. I don't think I've used either number for at least two years and then I couldn't speak to Peter Snow. I was trying to arrange a 60th birthday party for Gerald and wanted to invite Peter and his wife but I reached a lady who said he was far too busy to be contacted. They never did come and Gerald was mad at me when he'd heard I'd phoned for anything so trivial.'

'So Gerald Gibbons, your husband is 62 years old?' asked Tony Brown. 'Is this him? We found the photo on your landing.'

'Yes, that's him. With the new rules he has another four years before he's officially an OAP and can claim his bus pass.' I tried to smile.

DS Brown raised his eyebrows so I explained. 'Gerald hated the thought officer. He even refused to travel with Saga, even though they have good deals for the over 55's. Odd really because he was always careful with money.'

'Talking of money, if you are up to it, the first thing you should do is visit your bank, especially if you have a joint bank account. Ask if there have been any odd transactions in the last week or so and if your husband withdrew any money at all yesterday. It might also give us some idea of his whereabouts. Here is my direct extension number.' I held out my hand for the card Cathy was offering and nodded. She held my gaze for a moment, her eyes conveying compassion. 'Please can you give me a call, especially if you find anything suspicious?' she continued. 'Yet again we can carry out checks through our channels, but it would be quicker if you looked into it first. It's nearly 9.30 and the banks will be open. Would you like us to drop you off in town and wait for you outside?'

I gathered my thoughts. 'A lift would be helpful, but you don't have to wait. I'll catch the bus back. I'm not too proud, even if I do have to pay for my fare.'

As they walked out of the house, I paused to set the alarm, then changed my mind thinking of Gerald's irritation if he arrived flustered and it went off by accident.

As an after-thought DC Peterson asked, 'Have you checked your mobile for messages recently?'

'That's something I'm pretty confident there won't be. I don't think Gerald has ever sent me a message since he bought the thing for me. He would call if he needed anything.' I retrieved the mobile from my handbag and squinted down at it without my glasses on. 'No', I said. 'I've had no calls or messages. You can check for yourself.' I waved the phone under DC Peterson's nose. She fiddled with the buttons. Click, click, click.

'Here's Gerald's number. Do you mind if I write it down? We couldn't find one upstairs and assume he has his mobile with him.'

'Go ahead if it helps.'

Cathy Peterson jotted down the number and handed the phone back to me. 'Let's go,' she said.

I sat in silence in the back of their police car and said a quick thank you as I was dropped off outside the bank.

'Phone us when you get home Mrs Gibbons and let us know what happened. You've got my direct number,' Cathy Peterson smiled reassuringly.

CHAPTER 6

AT THE BANK I waited in line at the only remaining counter. Progress, I thought.

'Can I help you?' a lady asked, coming from the information desk just inside the door. Do you have money to pay in or out, because you could use the self service machines?'

'No thank you,' I bristled. 'I need to speak to someone about my account, but it is a matter of some urgency.'

'Please tell me about it and I'll see if I can help you.'

'I'm afraid I will need to talk somewhere more private,' I said, my face colouring.

The lady looked back towards the information desk where there was another customer waiting.

'Please sit down and I'll try to find someone to help you,' she said.

From my vantage point I observed the comings and goings. Twenty minutes passed before a gentleman came and ushered me into a screened off area.

'Take a seat,' he said, 'and what can I do for you?'

'My husband and I have a current account with you, a savings account and two ISA's. I need to know the balance of them all and if there's been any unusual withdrawals recently. Here's my Debit Card. There should be around £50,000 in total as far as I can remember my husband mentioning.'

The young man, Joel Mathews by his name on his lapel, took my proffered card and tapped the number into his PC. He clicked a few screens, his youth unable to hide his dismay and confusion at what he saw, despite trying to mask it with polite conversation.

'You've been to New York recently I see.'

'Yes,' I said feeling naked, as if all our actions on holiday were flashing before this young man's eyes on his screen.

'You returned home yesterday afternoon,' he added.

'How do you know?' I asked stupidly.

'This is the last entry for your current account,' he said turning the screen towards me. 'A withdrawal of five hundred pounds at Heathrow Airport by your husband.'

I could see the item he was pointing to but my eyes had skimmed down to the bottom of the screen where, to my horror, I could see that there was only fifty pounds in our account. 'That can't be right,' I said. 'I'm sure there was over £10,000 in it. What about in our other accounts?'

Each account told a similar story. Over the past month my husband had withdrawn all but £50 out of each. What I thought should have been a combined £50,000 nest egg for our retirement emergency fund had dwindled to almost nothing. I was horrified. I had always left the accounting to Gerald but, when I gave up my job and began foster caring, Gerald had spent some time reassuring me that we would be fine financially. That was five years ago. All the transactions had taken place on line.

'You didn't think to consult me,' I stuttered. 'After all, these *were* joint accounts.'

'We only need one authorisation I'm afraid, unless we are talking about a huge amount and it has happened over such a long period of time that no one questioned it. Actually there have been no withdrawals or transfers of more than £1,000 at a time. Anything over £2,000 in our bank would have flagged up an alert. I'll print out up to date statements for you.'

'Can you give me details of where the money has gone to then?'

'I'm afraid we are not at liberty to do that, although you must have access to your accounts on line. The statements will show reference numbers for you to check yourself. They might give you the information you need.'

'I've never had anything to do with the finances Mr Matthews. My husband always dealt with them. I have no idea where to start and since you never send paper statements anymore how could I have known. This is outrageous!'

'I do apologise, Mrs Gibbons, I think we need to issue this as a formal complaint to be investigated. I'll just write a few notes down and get you to check to see if you agree.'

While Joel Matthews was tapping on his keyboard I sat there stunned. I glanced down at the statements on the desk in front of me. Doing a quick calculation I realised that, at one point in the last six months we had amassed over £200,000. Now there was next to nothing left. How, I had no idea. I could feel the colour drain from my face. My whole life had imploded and I was not sure who I was anymore. I shuddered. What else was I to find?

'Do you mind if I make an urgent phone call while you're doing that?' I asked.

'Not at all,' Joel replied looking on me with embarrassed sympathy. How was he to know, with his whole life ahead of him, that mine had just literally fallen apart?

I dialled Cathy's number.

'Cathy Peterson speaking, are you all right Mrs Gibbons?'

Swallowing the temptation to ask how she knew it was me, I blurted out my depressing news. 'He's emptied all of the accounts. Every single one of them. There was nearly £200,000; I had no idea. Gerald was always hinting that we had to be careful with every penny. That was until the uncharacteristic generosity on holiday. Where on earth did he get such a sum and where has it all gone to?'

It was a rhetorical question but DS Peterson missed the nuance of my phrase and she answered, 'I think it's time you booked an appointment to see your solicitors to see if they can *shed any light* on the matter Mrs G. Do you think you could manage that? We will set our experts to glean as much information for you as we can, to assist us in our investigation.'

Snapped back to the present, as if an old video tape had come to an abrupt end, I sat hunched in my little shed, my memories suddenly seemed as far away from my current reality as New York. I smiled and pulled down a piece of sacking which I had appropriated to use as a pillow. The final glimmer of light, as dusk approached, was visible from under the poorly fitting door. I didn't dare leave it open though, for fear of being found. I rested my makeshift pillow against an old box, closed my eyes and relaxed. My mind raced with a rerun of the end of the conversation as if it were yesterday.

'I knew we should have come with you Mrs Gibbons,' I heard the DC say. 'Hang on there and I'll be over shortly and then we'll find a quiet cafe to have a chat.'

'OK,' I said, my voice barely reaching my unfamiliar mobile phone. 'CALL ENDED,' the phone read, which suddenly seemed very final.

'Can you read this please?' asked Joel, turning his screen towards me once more.

I bit my tongue as I wanted to correct his grammar to ask '*would you read this*?' instead. Of course I *can* read it, but this was no time to be a pedant. I agreed with his wording. I was too stunned to do otherwise, and then I was ushered back to the chair in the lobby. The young man had to give me support because my legs nearly buckled. Once settled I sat staring, unseeing, out of the bank window. Through the slit of clear glass a banner exclaimed,

'We are the Friendly Bank, the Bank you can Trust.'

It was only five minutes before Cathy arrived, since the temporary police station was only just over the road. Her partner Tony was guided back into the screened off area to talk with Joel Mathews whilst Cathy, after a short word with the bank clerk, persuaded me to follow her out of the faceless building and down to Rose's Corner Cafe on the junction of the High Street and River Road.

We sat down and ordered coffee. Cathy put a large spoonful of sugar into my cup and stirred it, seeing yet again that her charge was in an acute state of shock. I didn't protest as I sipped the sweet drink.

After pausing a while she began talking.

'It appears that your husband must have been planning this for a while Mrs Gibbons. The airport authorities have just phoned to say that they've found his missing phone on a seat near the luggage carousel where you last saw him. That's a shame because we could have followed his whereabouts if he still had it on his person.'

I listened silently as Cathy continued, her words barely registering. I watched her lips moving as if mesmerised.

'However, if he has used the Internet since then we will still be able to track him, although this has a lower degree of accuracy. We do, however, have the power to check any accounts he has placed the money into and he *will* have left a trail, I assure you.'

She seemed oblivious to me as she rambled on.

'They are still going through CCTV footage at the airport.'

I tried to look surprised.

'Maybe your husband has had some kind of break down,' she continued, 'but if so we will try and investigate why and what has caused this.'

I was thankful that she didn't use the words *'just a missing person's case.'* She was professional and ever sensitive to my needs. I nodded but in truth I was barely taking her words in. I was sure that Cathy was aware of this, because she began to ask direct questions. I felt that this was almost certainly to engage with me rather than to glean much useful information.

'Think, Mrs Gibbons. Has your husband mentioned anything recently that might point us to where we might find him?'

No, I shook my head.

'Has he had any visitors of late that were unfamiliar to you?'

Again I shook my head. Gerald never encouraged either his friends or his acquaintances through business to call at home.

'Has your husband enjoyed good health recently, as far as you know?'

I nodded in the affirmative.

'Has he got any hobbies?'

'Oh yes,' I replied, making a sound for the first time in this one sided conversation. 'Golf. He loves golf.'

'What course does he usually play on?'

'Drumford Golf Course - just as you go out of the town towards Aylesbury,' I replied.

'That gives me a place to begin while Tony continues to check with the bank and investigate your husband's financial situation.'

'Our financial situation,' I added firmly.

'Yes, of course.' The Constable's normally unfazed demeanour coloured momentarily. 'I think it's time I took you home to rest. Maybe you could ring and make an appointment with your solicitor later. Are you sure there is no one else you can call?'

'I think I'd rather keep it to myself for now if you don't mind. I'm still feeling a bit woozy from the flight and just need to sleep. Maybe I'll phone my best friend Karen tomorrow, after a good night's sleep and I should let Gerald's sister Charlotte know. I'd hate her to hear it on the media. Maybe Gerald will have turned up by then with some explanation.'

'I can only hope so,' said Cathy Peterson, with what can only be described as a look of pity in her eyes, as if to say that the chances of that were now slim.

She ushered me into her car across the road outside the station and we drove off in silence.

'You can drop me off here,' I said, maybe a bit too loudly because Miss Peterson brought her car to an abrupt halt just beside the entrance to Belmont Park, a Capability Brown inspired few acres of rolling grassland, interspersed with mature indigenous trees and the occasional spinney, leading down to a lake in the distance.

'The path leads across to my street on the other side of the park, obscured by those magnificent oaks. I could do with some fresh air and exercise to try to clear my head before I sleep again, if you don't mind.'

'Are you sure you'll be OK?' Miss Peterson asked.

'Don't worry about me. I'm sure you've got a lot more urgent cases to deal with than a middle aged lady's woes. Thanks for the lift.'

I got out of the car and walked off before she could change her mind and as I walked I watched her drive slowly away out of the corner of my eye. I sighed and then breathed deeply, filling my lungs with the cleansing air.

It was only a few minutes down to the lake, so instead I took a detour through the winter gardens; hellebores nodding and snow drops pushing their heads through bark mulch. I wasn't eager to get home. On the way I watched a mother whose toddler was feeding the ducks and swans. There was also a young boy who was trying to master his remote control sailing boat, much to the impatience of his elder brother, who longed to wrestle the controls from his sibling and tell him how to do it. Giving the lad his due, he resisted temptation and grinned when the youngster finally managed to control the boat to circle the lake.

This reminded me of Ahmed and Jamal, although I felt that it was Jamal who was always the wise one, standing back hoping his elder brother would learn to adapt to his surroundings and achieve something with his life. Should I phone Jamal? No, I decided. He was working and doing well for himself. He didn't want my problems.

I continued along the path beside the lake looking over towards the island where there was a monument to St Francis of Assisi, the patron saint of ecology. I stared at St Francis for quite a while seeking inspiration.

It is only now, in my recent itinerant state, that I have understood what a wonderful thing it is to wander about and to gain pleasure in talking to birds and animals.

Next I took the long sweeping path which headed back up the hill towards the larch tree line, visible from our home. I paused at the top to catch my breath. I remember thinking that maybe I was getting old before my time. Maybe Gerald was fed up with me. Maybe he *had* found a younger model, as we had joked about in New York.

The phrase Jest Ye Not, filled my mind as I opened the door to my home and stepped over a couple of letters. I picked them up absentmindedly and headed straight for the kitchen to put the kettle on. The envelopes were addressed to both Gerald and myself but I wouldn't normally have opened them. Today was different. To my horror both said the same thing:

Dear Mr and Mrs Gibbons
We are writing to remind you that you have not paid the gas and electricity bill for the last two quarters and the outstanding balance is now £357. We have noted that you have also cancelled your direct debit.

If you do not settle this bill or do not contact us within ten days then we may have no option to avoid cutting off your utility supplies. If you are having difficulty paying the full amount then please ring ... bla bla bla

I tore open the other envelope from BT, already guessing correctly as to the contents. I sat down on the kitchen stool with a bump, the boiling kettle forgotten. The phone rang. I let it ring. It rang again. I ignored it. It must have been a full hour that I sat in the silence of my kitchen, unaware of even my loud grandfather clock chiming in the hall.

Dazed, almost on autopilot, I finally made a cocoa and taking my sleeping pills with me I pulled myself upstairs, clinging to the banister before falling into bed. Taking a couple of tablets with my drink I slipped into oblivion.

CHAPTER 7

I CAME TO my senses to the sound of loud banging, oblivious to the doorbell. Massaging my temples whilst stumbling downstairs in my dressing gown, I barely considered what a sight I was. It was DC Peterson. I sighed and let her into the kitchen, always the hub of our house. Without words I passed the letters to her, to which she nodded, not looking the least bit shocked. Before she could comment I heard the post drop on to the mat once more, heralding another night passing me by. She went out to the hall while I poured the tea and when she came back another letter was in her outstretched hand. It was addressed to me; only to me, and I recognised Gerald's handwriting immediately.

'I think you'd better sit down before you open it,' said Cathy, her intuition telling her that it would be more bad news. 'Do you recognise the handwriting?'

'It's from Gerald,' I said in a voice barely audible. My hands were shaking so much by the time we were both in the lounge that Cathy offered to open it for me. She slid out a single sheet of paper and handed it to me, still folded.

I read:

Dear Dot

I'm not sure how to say this but I think by now you have realised that we are in a big financial mess. Over the past year I've tried to deal with it in my own way and not worry you, but we've got into so much debt that I've gradually eaten up virtually all of our savings in order to pay them off. The last two were the utility bills which I've now paid in full, so please ignore any red reminders. I've made sure that there is nothing outstanding for you to worry about. A blank page. I must explain.

A year ago our company went bust. At first I thought I'd get another job but I'm just too old. Time and time again I was rejected but instead of talking to you I started gambling, big time. You were keeping us afloat, just by your fostering, but I didn't feel part of your world. It was only near the time when Ahmed was to leave us that I began to get to know him and after he'd gone he didn't want to know me. You were the one who was close to Jamal.

Oh Dot, I'm very sorry. You deserve so much more than this. The worst thing I did was remortgage our home and then, when you were visiting your friend Karen a month ago when she was ill, I found a buyer for our house. How I've kept all this from you I shall never know. You are so trusting and kind. Well, apart from that fling you had all those years ago. Yes I know about it, but I don't blame you.

You'll need to move out by the end of the month and our solicitor has all the details. I'm afraid that I am too chicken to face up to all of this with you and so, by the time you read this, I will have taken my own life. My aim is that you will never really discover how, but I also hope that in time you can learn to forgive me, like I forgave you for straying. I also wish for you to make something worthwhile with the end of your life. You are far stronger than I, so I am confident that you will.

I won't close with the word 'love' Dot. Our love for each other was replaced by a sort of deep affection long ago, but I wish you a happy life.

Yours Gerald

If I had been stunned by any news so far in those short three days since we arrived home from New York, I have no words to describe the utter desolation which descended upon me, like a huge black shroud. I wanted to be swallowed up. I wanted to die. The letter drifted from my open sweaty hand on to the carpet and DC Peterson reached down to pick it up. All I could do was sit with my head in my hands and sob, until I could cry no more.

I could hear the police woman making several phone calls, but had no understanding of what was spoken until a person was let in the door, a locum from the local doctors. Fortunately Dr Shalwar knew me and was able to administer another sleeping draft before I was helped back to bed. As I slipped into sleep I could hear talking and I thought I could hear Jamal's voice but I wasn't sure.

CHAPTER 8

BACK AT THEIR small office in Drumford, DC Cathy Peterson and DS Tony Brown sat staring at each other in thoughtful silence. It was part of a converted chapel used for various municipal purposes, including the current local policing initiative. Talk about ideas going in cycles.

Cathy Peterson broke the silence. 'What do you think? Do you think he's really committed suicide?'

'We've traced an account that some of the money initially went into and a great deal of it seems to have been swallowed up in paying off debts. So far he was telling the truth. There are just a couple of large amounts which I can't track forward. There could be different on-line betting companies of course, which come and go with each passing day, but I'm not sure. Any luck in looking for any unidentified bodies found recently in the UK?'

'Nothing. It's frustrating. All the obvious spots for suicide have brought a big zero. That doesn't mean anything though. He could have gone anywhere. The weather in Wales and Scotland has been atrocious. It may be that the body just hasn't been washed up or found as yet.'

'He took £500 with him from the airport. Is there a chance that he's changed identity and got on another plane somehow?' Tony asked.

'Unlikely. The airport police put out a description within the hour of him going missing, unless he already had his ticket and we have no record of that from his credit card statements.'

'And CCTV footage appears to be inconclusive.'

'Yes, they were standing under a camera when he went missing. He can't have just vanished though!'

'Yes, bags from a flight from Mexico were on the carousel next to the one from New York. Several men appeared in those cheap sombreros and sun glasses – a stag do maybe. It's possible that Mr G slipped in amongst them.'

You mean dark glasses and a Mexican hat?' Cathy raised her eyebrows.

'Yes, something like that. The CCTV cameras identified four of them but only three have been traced.'

'That's something to follow up I suppose but unlikely don't you think? There must be something we're missing. You're good at thinking laterally. We just need a lucky break.'

'What can we say to Mrs G about our doubts Tony?'

'Don't mention a word for the time being. She's suffered too much to deal with it, what with the selling of her home and the suicide note. Let's just be a little evasive but support her as best we can. There's no evidence of criminal activity so far, just an underhand bastard who didn't have the balls to own up to his own wife about the mess he's made. What a coward, eh?'

'I so agree. It's heartbreaking. We'll go your way unless any other evidence comes up. You're the boss!' replied Cathy, winking as she left the office. 'A drink later to take our mind off the case?' she asked as her passing shot.

He nodded. 'Usual place,' he said, but she was gone.

CHAPTER 9

I UNROLLED MY sleeping bag. It was late summer and so I didn't need much to keep warm. I'd long since learnt to ignore the rustle of field mice or even a rat or two sniffing around for crumbs. My rucksack was tightly closed so they could not steal much. What was it that the bible said about a farmer? When he reaps the harvest he must leave the edges of the field for the needy? Something like that anyway. If a mouse could benefit from my left-overs then I was glad. Maybe some of St Francis was rubbing off on me after all. The next day, I worked out by marks on the dust by the door, was Tuesday; my day for trudging across footpaths back into town to have my one hot meal of the week and a change of clothes. With that in mind I soon slipped into a dreamless slumber.

The following morning the sky was clear. After packing my bag I was careful to leave the little shed as I had found it, with the door tight shut - even if it wasn't locked. It was a perfect day for the three mile walk into Drumford and I couldn't help but sing to myself on the way. The small birds, sparrows I think, were twittering in the overgrown hedge by my side. I helped myself to some more blackberries which I ate straight away and washed them down with the last third of my bottle of water.

The route was familiar, first taking the lane to Canbury village. Suddenly I heard a loud vehicle behind me and so jumped on to the verge, just in time to avoid the school bus. The children waved from the back window as they disappeared from view. One particular girl caught my eye but I'm not quite sure if I recognised her or not. One little boy made a silly face with his fingers wagging in his ears. I laughed and he grinned. There was nothing malicious about it; only childhood humour shining through. I was touched that they noticed me. After all, it was the first 'human' interaction I'd had for a few days.

Just before the 20 mph speed restriction sign, to mark the village boundary, I took the path sharp right which edged the back of the school grounds. I recognised the girl again, peering at me through the railings of the playground and wondered who she was. The moment passed and soon I was taking the track through Canbury Woods and then crossing three open fields before I reached the river - only a stream really. It was fortunate that a path by the water took me all the way into the heart of Drumford town. I only had to take three steps to the pavement and turn left before I was standing in front of The Ark, an aptly named meeting place for the homeless and needy, adjacent to the Drumford Roman Catholic Church. Who'd have thought in the past that I would once be ranked among them?

'Hello Mrs G,' Laura O'Conner called out as I entered the gate. She was one of the Irish sisters, twins actually, who ran this centre like an iced Christmas cake; all smooth and sweet, whenever possible anyway. It was an apt description of Laura too, although she could be tough when required. Her sister's name was Orla. It was easy to tell the difference because, although both had gingery blonde hair, Laura's was cropped short around her oval face whereas Orla's locks were long and plaited. The overall effect was similar with their delicately freckled features shining through.

'What would you like today?' winked Laura. How about this sexy black number?' she asked as she held a sturdy black sweatshirt towards me. 'There's even some glamorous troos to match.' The twinkle in her eyes rested on the leggings in her other hand.

I smiled, my eyes drifting to the floor. It was touching the way they were both sensitive to my shyness. Given an hour or so I would open up a little, but I found company a trifle hard to handle these days, after my imposed solitude.

'The bath's free Mrs G. Why don't you take a soak before trying on your new outfit?'

'Thank you,' I whispered as I closed the door behind me, relieved to be on my own again.

Fifteen minutes later I emerged. I knew if I stayed a moment longer there would be a thump on the door and so I did not wish to outstay my welcome in my selfishness.

'There y'are then. Give us a twirl Mrs G,' Laura's unflinching enthusiasm to put me at my ease was infectious.

'Off you go to see that great big sister of mine and she'll give you something t' fill yer insides too.'

My eyes beamed my gratitude before I headed to the Nissen hut out in the back yard which had been recommissioned to be a canteen. In the summer months we even had an assortment of donated plastic garden furniture outside. The place had been a Territorial Army Camp and almost certainly part of an old barracks in the war until, that is, the unit outgrew its needs in the recent conflicts around the time of Afghanistan. With a bit of tweaking it was perfect for its current use; a refuge, meeting place and foodbank. Since the latest years of austerity and the refugee crisis it has been bursting at its fences. There were even cabins for the homeless to have a bed for the night and the Big Issue guy came regularly to tout for new sellers.

Laura was busy ordering her volunteers into action and didn't notice me at first. When she did she grinned. I used to serve her in the library. She was the brainy one of the sisters and I often felt humbled by the way she chose to work here after college rather than get a high powered job. Personally I thought she'd make a wonderful nurse. The twins were the only paid workers there but I knew for certain that they were paid not much more than the minimum wage. They'd been involved in charity work since they were young. I think it was in their blood and whilst at London Uni Laura had told me that she'd helped at Centre Point during her vacation. A noble cause. Some people are just like that. So selfless.

'Hey Mrs G,' she beamed. 'We have chicken stew or vegetable curry. I expect you'd like the vegetable curry.'

I nodded. She knew that I had been a vegetarian for the last couple of years. I talked to all the animals out in the fields, you see. There was no way I was going to eat them.

'Here you go then.'

'Thanks Laura.' I nodded before carrying a tray, including a steaming cuppa, carefully back out to an empty table in the sheltered courtyard, the sunshine flooding in. Sighing with contentment I tucked into my meal. After gulping a couple of mouthfuls I purposefully slowed down in order to savour each bite.

'Oh, this is so good,' my voice barely left my lips.

'Yes it is that,' replied a loner I recognised on the next table. He did not start up conversation but his remark was enough for us to continue our meal in companionable silence, white round table next to white round table. A kindred spirit I observed, as I glanced surreptitiously to see him tucking into his curry too. I'd never seen him eat meat either.

Old Ben finished well before me and burped. I knew that he'd been a farmer who had fallen on hard times and sadly had turned to drink. That is until the Sally Army had dried him out and given him a bit of self esteem. I also knew that he now helped to sort out food in the foodbank after his weekly visit here to have a bath and change. He'd tried The Big Issue for a while but found selling to people who had known and respected him too humiliating. I wondered why he didn't move to neighbouring Bedford but never had the courage to ask.

By the time I'd eaten my last morsel and come out of my reverie he'd moved on and I saw his back disappear to the foodbank in the next Nissen hut along. I savoured my cup of tea. Usually I was glad to leave the centre and return to my life of isolation, but today I held back for a while, wondering if I should offer to help out too; to give something back as it were. As soon as the thought had entered my head I found myself scurrying to the gates and was relieved to be back on the banks of the stream and heading towards open countryside once more.

My home had no boundaries, few demands and minimal time constraints. Reaching the woods I chose to rest on an old tree stump for a while, gazing back across the field towards Drumford. I'm not sure how long I remained there but the light was beginning to take on that yellowish misty hue. Throwing my rucksack on my back I strode purposefully on until I reached my refuge for the night; that old tumbledown shed.

The following morning was a perfect day to forage. The farmers do not leave the edges of the fields unharvested for the poor these days, although some do for the wildlife. Nevertheless, since I am a non practising Jewish girl I decided early in my itinerant days that I would claim my right to glean. Today was one of those days.

The field near my Oak Tree Meadow was all golden bristles where the combines had been harvesting a couple of weeks before. Being a tricky shape it must have been one of the last to be gathered in. I bent my back to peer down at the soil and a multitude of stray grains of oats were just lying there for my benefit. I rummaged for the paper bag I'd kept from my sandwiches. Soon it was half full of grain. I groaned as I straightened my back, thinking of the photos in history books of women gleaning in the fields, their skirts brushing the ground and their scarves loosely draped over their heads to protect themselves from the elements, whether it be rain or sunshine.

Folding the bag down a couple of times I slid it into the bottom compartment of my rucksack. Then I found a small plastic container for the few remaining blackberries, clinging on to the sun drenched side of the hedge. The morning passed quickly until I had found several ingredients of leaves; mainly dandelion and some clover flowers. Together with the grain and blackberries, I had collected only enough for the next couple of days.

Always leave some for the person or creature following, was my motto. Their need might be greater than mine.

CHAPTER 10

IT WAS A month later in the autumn of 2016 that I discovered The Grange. I was overwhelmed by its charm, but I was also extremely cold. Unsettled days, sometimes bright and calm but others stormy were reflected in my own restlessness. I was seeking alternative shelter because the nights were chilly and my shed could be extremely draughty. Barns were a possibility but harder to remain hidden. I had taken a path through a small spinney towards Westgate Farm. I'd never walked that way before but reasoned that there may be an out building I could purloin. Instead I stumbled upon this elegant neglected house and stood mesmerised for a while, admiring the carved stonework and the ivy wrapping itself around its Georgian windows. The place had an air of solitude, which was verging on abandonment and yet it was not unloved, almost as if it was waiting. I heard a noise and rushed into the shadows of a nearby barn. There I overheard a man shouting for a lady called Angelina to come to the phone.

I could just glimpse a kindly looking lady in her thirties with black hair tied back in a ribbon and an old fashioned apron covering her baggy dungarees, rushing out of a side door of the old house. She's probably the farmer's young wife, I thought. Her dark complexion spoke of southern Europe, maybe Italy, Greece or Croatia.

Once I was sure that I was unobserved I walked as silently as I could around the edge of the courtyard, not daring to walk brazenly across the middle. I tried the side door and to my surprise it opened and led directly into a scullery. It felt like a time warp, akin to a living museum like the one at Iron Bridge I'd visited long ago. The deep sinks, mangle and even a butter churn stood, as if cleaned and at the ready for the servants to return. Through a large oak door and up a huge stone step was the kitchen and although the black range was stone cold I could imagine the heat in days gone by and even put my hands out to warm them, feeling the heat of centuries seeping through my body. A couple of copper pots and pans still hung from the walls, green at the edges from years of disuse. The walk-in pantry, though bare, still held that musty smell of food lingering in the stonework. Apart from a fine layer of dust it was spotlessly clean, as if the owners had been away for a considerable length of time. I smiled. Gerald used to be so infuriated when I left our house scrubbed from top to bottom and all the laundry completed before we left on a journey. He just did not understand the satisfaction of returning to a clean and tidy home, so keen was he to escape.

At the back of the kitchen was a small battered green door leaving flakes of paint on the hard oak floor. To my delight this led to a small winding staircase up to the top floor of the house - under the eaves you'd call it - tiny rooms where the servants used to sleep. Peering in one of the empty rooms I could see, in my mind's eye, a tiny dresser and chair on which might have stood a photo of a sweetheart back home or the family left in the nearby town of Bedford. I imagined a servant girl leaving town to come into service here at maybe twelve years old; if she could afford a photograph that is. I wasn't sure. There would have been a bed of course - a mattress of straw or ticking, a simple wooden affair - small but adequate. I was brought half out of my reverie by a noise downstairs, and I could visualise the cook overseeing a young lad whose first job of the day was to stoke the fire. Maybe he was sweet on my young girl who occupied this room but I knew intuitively that my girl had her sights on the one she'd left behind.

I shook myself. What on earth was I dreaming about? Mind you, I would never be alone in life, I mused, as long as I had my imagination. A picture of a nun flashed before me. How strange I thought, but I let the vision go.

I listened carefully. The silence filled the room and seeped into every corner. I left my few belongings neatly in a corner and peered out of one of the tiny windows just in time to see Angelina - yes, that's a nice name - disappearing through a gap in the hedge, which most probably led to her garden. I walked downstairs with ease this time, unencumbered by my meagre belongings bumping into the stone walls as I navigated the tight spiral staircase. I paused and listened. Nothing. Then I gingerly opened the door into the kitchen and stepped down into the scullery. I tried the door. It was locked. After my initial panic I began to smile. After all, I had plenty of provisions and a grand shelter for the night.

I climbed back up to my room; well, it was my room now I thought, even if it was just for the night. Spreading my belongings out on the floor, they totally filled the space. There was my sleeping bag, which end to end touched facing walls. I took my outer coat off and wrapped it in a ball for a pillow. Then I opened the bag with my food, carefully placing them on a plastic carrier to make sure I shed no crumbs. I was still very particular about things like that. Determined not to panic I tried to work out how many days my meagre rations and water might last; a bit like being marooned on a desert island, I thought. I'd seen them do this in several films - stranded in a lifeboat or living in a war zone with shops barely open and food queues when they were.

No, I thought, I'm much better off than some, and Angelina is bound to return to continue whatever task she was doing when she was disturbed today. I wonder what her husband is like, I mused. I hoped he was kind and loving. Fleetingly I had glimpsed an expression of contentment as she had turned and strode away.

Three days I calculated and divided the food up accordingly, putting it in separate paper bags from the baker's. There were already lines marked down my water bottle. It had seen better days but I filled it when I could and always made sure I drank at least a third of a litre a day, more if I was near the public water fountain in Belmont Park, or at The Ark.

I yawned. Shadows crossed the floor as the old house, surrounded by mature trees was plunged into evening before its time. I tended to pace my days to the natural rhythms of daylight hours. The weather at that moment was crisp and clear with only a sharp frost now and then but, being October, the nights were drawing in. My watch had long since stopped. I only kept it as a memento of happier times. *Lady Pink Hat*, they called me in villages surrounding Drumford. I smiled as I hung my hat over the antique brass window catch, making sure the pink wasn't visible from outside.

I tried the other doors in the corridor. Three rooms were bare like the one I'd chosen, but the fourth was full of all sorts of things. There were boxes of brush and comb sets from days gone by, candle holders and even a gazunder; a welcome chamber pot. I was all set then for a few days self imposed siege.

Feeling the familiar hunger pangs which never really retreated, I savoured my supper of yesterday's bread and a sausage roll, which had been handed to me outside the baker's earlier that day. I made this more palatable with the salad seed mix, washed down with the remainder of my first third of water, and then congratulated myself on my good fortune.

After supper, feeling an urgency to explore before darkness finally consumed every inch of the place, I decided to risk going downstairs once more. Finding my way to the centre of the landing, I strolled down the sweeping staircase, swishing my hands from side to side as if I was a lady in my finery. Once I'd reached the hall at the bottom I paused to listen. Silence. I opened door after door but most of the rooms on this floor were empty, except a couple which were full of shrouded furniture.

When I reached the final door, furthest away from the stairs, to my delight it was a library, still packed from floor to ceiling with old books. I could see that some were ancient tomes placed on the highest shelves and reached by a sturdy wooden ladder. The room was situated on the corner of the building with alcoves facing west and south, catching maximum natural light, especially in the evenings. At the far end was a small door and when I peered behind it I was pleased to find another staircase going upwards. Turning back I stared around me. It was a librarian's wildest fantasy - or mine anyway.

Ah, I thought, this is what Angelina has been busy doing.

Starting with the books on the top shelf she had been cleaning them one by one and arranging them in boxes. Looking closer at the books, the older ones spoke of value. On one side of the room the wooden crates were labelled 'fiction' and on the other 'non-fiction'. Beside each box was a clip board with a list of titles, author, publisher and date of publication but in the final column was an estimated value. There was a lap top on a corner writing desk and a pair of white glove next to a lap top. It was obvious that Angelina had been too impatient to wait to find out the value of some of the rarest editions and had already looked them up on the Internet.

In one box alone there were first editions of *Lord of the Flies* by Golding, *The Catcher in the Rye* by Salinger, and even a copy of *The Sun also Rises,* a Hemingway of course. The listed estimated prices were £18,000, £19,000 and £75,000 respectively.

'Wow,' I whispered 'Who'd have thought it?'

Then there was an antiquarian *Pride and Prejudice* in an 1894 illustrated leather peacock edition listed at £3,500 and an 1880 red leather edition of *The Mayor of Casterbridge* for over £3,000.

Discovering this hidden library was surely a *six* for me. Reverently I put on a pair of gloves, cream with age, lying rolled on the bottom shelf and picked up a copy of *A Christmas Carol* from a high shelf and leafed through it. There were beautiful woodcut illustrations and a gilt wreath around the title on the cover. I placed it carefully back on the shelf. So absorbed was I in my reverie that I suddenly jumped when I heard a noise down the corridor. Quickly, putting the book back on the shelf, I rushed to the little door and, as quietly as I could, I climbed the stairs, pleased, though not surprised, to find myself back on the second floor, the gloves still on my hands.

I paused to listen. I could hear singing downstairs. Slowly and soundlessly I crept along the landing, stopping where the main staircase opened up. I listened again. Angelina was humming an unusual haunting tune. No idea what it was. Far beyond my time probably or from where she had grown up, but thankfully she was making enough noise to disguise my rush towards the back staircase and the relative safely of my little room.

CHAPTER 11

ANGELINA SANG HER favourite folk song from back home in Croatia as she found her way to the library in The Grange. It made her feet want to dance and her arms sway as she crossed the farmyard. The task ahead was one she had rashly promised her husband Jonathan that she would try to complete before the next winter. He hoped the books, no good to anyone stuck in the old building, might pay their daughters fees for private school and some more. To be truthful Angelina would prefer Greta to go to a local school until she was at least eleven but had dared not broach the subject as yet. She also didn't relish the task of spending her days with dusty old books. She'd rather tend the vegetable garden, bake or sew some more dresses for Greta, their eight year old daughter.

Inadvertently she sniffed as she opened the great oak library door. What was that odd smell? She looked behind the curtains and under the tables and chairs, then peered up the little staircase and listened. Nothing. Singing lifted her mood. It reminded Angelina of her own mother, who loved to sing lullabies when she was little. She shrugged her shoulders and, raising her voice louder still, she began the long task ahead. Next time she came maybe she would bring a radio and some spray freshener. Perhaps there was a dead mouse behind the skirting board. She shuddered, trying not to think of her own loneliness. Her daughter would be home soon and her day filled with light once more.

Half an hour passed really quickly until Angelina heard the sound of the coach pull up at the end of the farm track. She dashed downstairs and rushed along the track waving to Greta, meeting her half way. Her daughter gave her such a hug, both smiling and laughing.

'Do you mind if we get a cold drink and then go to the library upstairs in The Grange? I'd just like to do another hour before coming in to make supper.'

'Can I bring my colouring?'

'Of course you can. Bring the radio too if you like.'

They walked companionably back to their own farmhouse kitchen, had some orange juice and a biscuit and then retraced their steps.

After Greta felt she'd been patient for an hour or so she exclaimed 'I want to go and watch TV now.'

'I think you should say *I would like to* not *I want to*, to be polite.' Angelina tried to correct her daughter when she could, although it was hard sometimes, not being a native speaker. 'but I agree with you, it's time to go home.'

As they walked across the yard Greta ran in circles around her mother, full of energy after being cooped up for a while. Then she ran around The Grange as far as she could without getting caught in brambles and ivy. As she did so she glanced up and thought she caught a glimpse of a face in a window right at the top of the house. She blinked and the image had gone. Was she imagining things? More subdued this time, Greta turned and followed her mother into the farmhouse.

That night Angelina read Greta a bedtime story; her favourite book of the moment, Roald Dahl's *Matilda.* Greta could read it herself but she loved this special time with her mother reading to her. Today, though, Greta could not concentrate and kept interrupting.

'I saw a lady's face at the window at the side of the old house today.'

'You mean The Grange. I'm sure there are no ghosts Greta, otherwise I would have seen them.'

'But Mum, I recognised the lady. I'm not sure where from, but I'm sure I've seen her before.'

'What happened then? Tell me what you saw.'

'I just told you. I saw a face at the window and then it was gone.'

Angelina decided to try to make light of it because otherwise Greta would never sleep.

'I'm sure you were seeing things Greta, but I promise I'll look in the morning. Now, shall we read the next chapter?'

By the time Angelina had reached the last sentence Greta's eyes were closing. She kissed her daughter gently on the forehead and crept out of the room. Pausing at the top of the stairs she peered in the gloom towards The Grange. It looked as it always had since she had lived at Westgate Farm, vacant and unloved. She sighed, but remembering the strange smell she vowed to check in the morning.

CHAPTER 12

ONCE I WAS sure that Angelina and her daughter had left the building I looked out of the window under the eaves, just catching the sight of a young girl of about eight years staring back at me. She looked strangely familiar. I hid back in the shadows and when I next glanced out the little girl had gone. Creeping downstairs I tried the kitchen door but it was locked. Not disappointed in the least, that evening I began to carry out Angelina's great task, cleaning the books and carefully making a record of each one, organising the cataloguing system to be more logical.

I glanced up from my task peering out of the window, glimpsing the courtyard through the ivy. It was empty and the barn door, where I'd been hiding earlier, was now shut and padlocked. Dusk was creeping in, soaking up the colour and chasing away the shadows until the buildings had turned to dark shades of brown and the sky sweeps of grey, navy blue and indigo, with only hints of the dying light. Bats flickered past the window and disappeared under the eaves of the roof.

It was time to stop and I had to feel my way up the back staircase. On the landing the rising moon shone through a narrow window forming eerie shadows, lighting my way to the other staircase and back up to my little room.

Pausing for a moment I noticed that the corridor turned at the end, concealing the rest of the landing. Intrigued, I peered around the corner and found a single door which opened revealing another spiral staircase descending, with slit windows facing west. Through gaps in the treetops the final glow after sunset illuminated the pitted stone walls with a faint orangey red hue. There was a shoulder height dark oak wooden door at the bottom. The handle turned but the door only gave a few inches, so strong was the ivy growing on the other side. I waited a few minutes and then, realising that it was nearly pitch black and I'd have to find my way back up I gave a big heave, putting my whole weight on the door. It moved just enough to form a crack for me to pass through, but I decided to leave it until the morning to investigate further. Although relieved that I wasn't totally trapped in, I was momentarily amused by a fleeting idea of a headline in the local newspaper, 'Mysterious Dead Body Found in Abandoned Farmhouse.' I crept back up the stairs, feeling the wall with my left hand and gingerly resting each foot one step at a time before shifting my weight upwards. Soon I was back on the landing, the moon shining through the doorway guiding me to my little attic room.

It was too early to settle down for the night so I felt in my pocket for the smoothed edges of my dice. I was unconcerned about the rumbling sound rolling it made on the worn wooden floor. Landing on its side again between a *one* and a *zero*, I sighed, remembering.

My visit to the solicitors a few days after reading Gerald's suicide letter was almost certainly a *zero*, although it only confirmed the stark truth that the house had been remortgaged.

'Your husband seemed so excited about a business opportunity he'd found; a project for your retirement,' Mr Stevenson had explained. 'I believed every word and organised the legal documentation with the building society to sell the house.' He paused. 'I'm so sorry Mrs Gibbons. The property was always only in your husband's name since you earned so little.'

I was speechless, although nothing seemed to surprise me now. The ease with which Gerald had unravelled our lives so secretly astonished me at first, but now I was resigned to more bad news. Surely nothing more could hurt me. I couldn't even mourn Gerald's death because no corpse had been found. It would take seven years before I could declare him officially dead, Mr Stevenson explained, unless there was positive identification.

'What is this business?' I asked, suddenly realising that this could be the most promising lead to my wayward husband.

'I'm afraid he didn't divulge that information Mrs Gibbons. He was going to call back in a month's time to discuss the legal aspects of it. I have not heard from him since our last meeting. I promise that I will call you or the police if I hear anything, since fraud would almost certainly be involved following your letter from Mr Gibbons.'

I thanked Mr Stevenson for his time and a lukewarm hand shake passed between us. Somehow I don't recall finding my way home but as I opened the front door the phone rang. It was Jamal. He'd heard something of my plight from a man at the corner shop café in town where we sometimes met to have a catch up. He'd also spotted me later and called me from across the street, but I had not responded to his shout, so deep was I in my own reverie. Despite my protestations he said that he was coming around right away.

When he arrived we sat as we always did with cups of tea at the kitchen table. I told him everything, surprised as to how light headed I felt after sharing my grief.

'I'll help you Mrs G. You've done enough for us since we came to England. It's time I was there for you. When do you have to move out of here?'

I showed him Gerald's letter.

'Right,' he said. 'I'll take a week off work and come and give you a hand. I know my pal Brian will come too. He's unemployed at the moment so he's free.'

My musings were brought back to the present and I threw the dice one more time, just in case that elusive *six* appeared, but it was just a *two*. My mind drifted back to that fateful week of the 'big move out.'

Jamal was true to his word and he and his friend Brian cleared the house room by room. With a bit of wheeling and dealing they sold all of the contents - some things privately and some at the auction rooms in Bedford.

'You'll need cash Mrs G, not things,' Jamal explained when I tried to protest.

'Where will I go?' I said, the frown on my brow reflecting the forlorn state of my mind.

'You're coming to live with Ahmed and me in our flat,' Jamal replied, as if I'd missed the most obvious.

'But..' I started to protest, then realised I had no chance of resisting by Jamal's warning glance. Strangely enough, from that moment on I started to relax and though I had little part in the destruction of all that I'd known for the past thirty five years, in a sense it felt an odd release, as if I was shedding a huge burden.

I made those dreaded phone calls to my sister-in-law Charlotte, my friend Karen and my brother Jeff. I described my dire situation, Gerald's suicide note and my next step, somehow persuading them that there was nothing they could do. I promised to be in touch after I'd moved out. After that I just made tea and sandwiches and gazed on, not even caring to gather a few precious or memorable trinkets. They meant nothing to me now.

Within a week most of the house was cleared and sold except the minimum for survival, if and when I wished to set up home again in the future. Jamal had arranged it all. I was so grateful to him and fortunate to have his support and guidance. He was thinking for me. Just as well since my mind was scrambled eggs.

'Brian's a little late this morning because he's borrowing his Dad's white van. A friend of ours owns a storage company and he's agreed to take this stuff at only a fiver a month, far below the going rate. I'll pay it for the time being. If you pack your last few bits and pieces into the suitcase I've left in the spare bedroom, then we'll move you out today.'

Jamal must have seen my startled expression so he continued softly, as if soothing a child who'd fallen over. 'It's for the best Mrs G. There's no point in clinging on. Moving out day is on Monday anyway, so we might as well get you packed up and into our flat today.'

I sighed. 'I expect you're right. I'm so gr...'

'There's no need to thank me Mrs G. It's what any family would do for their treasured auntie.'

I felt a momentary glow inside which relieved the bleakness.

'You're more like a mother to me Mrs G, you always have been.'

Jamal turned before I could see his watery eyes; mine were filling up too. I felt fortunate. Can you believe it? In that very moment, surrounded by a predicament not of my own making I felt blessed. How strange was that?

It was early afternoon and I recall vividly standing in our empty bedroom over-looking the park. I said a silent goodbye to the home I'd shared with Gerald since we married in 1979 and without turning back I walked down the stairs and out of the house to the beginning of my new life. Whatever the future held for me my numbness was slightly softened by the feeling that I was loved and cared for.

Back at The Grange the warm memory of Jamal brought a smile to my face. I threw the dice again. A *six* at last. I fell asleep contentedly dreaming of the library downstairs and a task I relished. Was this my destiny?

CHAPTER 13

I AWOKE WITH the glimmer of first light, guessing it to be about 5 am when birds were already dancing between hedges. I looked out and three swallows, very late stragglers from the flock, were gathering on the roof of the barn, making ready for their winter migration. While I rolled up my sleeping bag ready for a quick get-away I prayed that they would make their long journey safely, then I enjoyed enough of my rations to keep my stomach from rumbling too much.

Reasoning that sunrise would be at least an hour off and that I was unlikely to be disturbed, I decided to explore the house. No ghosts had spooked me in the night, in fact I'd had the best night's sleep in a couple of years. I know it felt ridiculous but I experienced the strange sensation of 'coming home'.

Down in the library I stood for a while surveying the books. Without thinking I put on the gloves in my pocket and rearranged the crates into book shop type categories, with rare, antiquarian, signed copies and first editions all having their own place. They were soon labelled and I set to work. Book after book I took down, cleaned, recorded and placed in the most appropriate box, only omitting to check their value. I looked up and sunlight was reflecting a myriad of colours on the tree tops. I paused a moment, barely breathing.

Climbing back to my room in the eaves, I gathered my few possessions up in the rucksack and slipped down the newly discovered back staircase. With a last push on the door with my shoulder I could bend down and squeeze through the ivy, holding the gazunder in front of me. Leaving my rucksack hidden I crept out into the wooded area, retrieving a trowel I kept in a plastic bag deep in one of my coat pockets. I scraped a hole just large enough to empty the contents of the gazunder into and then gave it a covering with earth, twigs and leaves before hiding the pot behind a pollarded tree. My ears pricked to the sound of a stream close by and within minutes I was rinsing my hands in the icy cold water. As I straightened my back I could hear cows in a distant field. I made sure that I replaced the ivy so that the door was obscured once more before putting my rucksack on my back. In the early morning light I crunched on fallen leaves along the footpath in the spinney, before climbing over the style and reaching a short stretch of open farmland. Although tempted, I did not glance over my shoulder until I had reached the relative safety of Canbury Lane and very soon I was back in Oak Tree Meadow, or that's what I called my favourite clearing. An intake of breath exhaled my tension as I glanced around me.

My eyes spied some cob nuts in the hedgerows and I must have whiled away an hour or so collecting them. It was perfect fodder since they were light, would keep a while and I could not guarantee that any would be left next time I came by. I decided to have a well deserved rest after that and looking up at the sky I thought, by the sun, that it must be nearly midday. How time had flown. My watch battery had long since spent but I wore the time piece for the sake of nostalgia. It had been a gift from Gerald in the early years of our marriage. I sat in peaceful reflection watching birds enjoying the oats I'd left behind the day before and some blue tits twittering around the few remaining ripe blackberries. I smiled then whispered to my feathered friends, telling them the tale of my exploits. On days like that

I often nibbled at bits and pieces and so I took a handful of nuts, speaking absentmindedly between mouthfuls.

For the next couple of weeks I ambled about the countryside, enjoying an unexpected Indian summer, taking refuge in my little shed at dusk. I was afraid to go back to The Grange too soon but I often thought about it. Following the good spell there was a week of continuous rain at the end of October and so I sought shelter and company at the centre in town. At times like those it became a habit to help out in the cafe area, clearing tables and practising making conversation with the clients, although most were as reticent as I to open up. However grateful, I hated the dormitory and longed to be back in the open air. It was over three weeks before I dared to return to my new sanctuary.

CHAPTER 14

ON THE SAME morning that Dorothy had left The Grange, pleased to have gained her freedom so easily, Angelina returned to the old house. Before using the key she checked the door handle just in case and it was firmly locked. Sighing, she slipped the key in and once opened she was greeted by that pungent smell again. A frenzied search revealed nothing untoward; no dead mice or anything else which would have accounted for the weird odour. After spraying the kitchen liberally, she walked up the staircase to the library and was concerned that the smell there was even stronger. Imagine her surprise when she found that some of her job of cataloguing had been done for her and all the books were piled in such an organised manner, in a way that she would never have dreamed of doing herself. All the fiction crates were labelled alphabetically by author's surname and the older books were in boxes with labels like Antiquarian or First Editions. The spreadsheets with each crate had been updated to the new system and the pile of her amateur versions was on the seat of the chair by the desk.

A *library fairy*, she thought to herself with a glimmer of a smile. Retreating to the staircase, using the aerosol liberally in her wake, she climbed the stairs, her nerve ends tingling. Trying one of the rooms in the eaves where the smell seemed the greatest there was no actual evidence of life although the dusty floor had smears as if something or someone had dragged a blanket across it.

Intrigued now, rather than scared, she walked to the end of the hall and down the back stairwell where Greta had assured her she'd seen a face. Sure enough, when she pushed the door at the bottom it gave ever so slightly, even though she could see tangled ivy across the entrance. Sleeping Beauty came to mind. As far as she knew there was no key to this door in the farmhouse and so she had a dilemma as to what she should do about it. *The library fairy* obviously wished her no harm but what was her story and should she tell her husband Jonathan.

She closed the door, spraying liberally as she retraced her steps through the house. Back in the library she was pleased that the room smelt sweet again, as did the kitchen, which she was careful to lock behind her, tossing the spent aerosol into the dustbin as she passed by. She would not be able to do anymore sorting herself for a few days now since she worked part time at Canbury Veterinary Surgery as a receptionist for three days per week. It was a payment-in-kind arrangement with Jonathan for veterinary bills, which was mutually beneficial. It just meant though, that she had as little ready cash available as her husband, which was frustrating at times, and she resorted to paying by card when she could.

That evening Greta was full of her tales once more. Over tea she said, 'Mum, you know that face I saw yesterday.'

Angelina looked around, relieved that Jonathan was out milking.'

'You mean the face you *think* you saw.'

Ignoring the fact that her mum didn't appear to believe her, Greta ploughed on, 'Well, I saw her again and I know who she is.'

''Who is she then?' asked Angelina, interested, albeit a little wary.

'She's *Lady Pink Hat*, you know, the old lady who's a tramp and walks along the lanes. I often wave to her from the school bus and she sometimes waves back.' Greta paused, her expression puzzled. 'Why do you think she does it?'

Angelina was a bit distracted by this solution to the mysterious intruder. 'What do you mean?'

'Why do you think she walks the lanes and looks as if she sleeps out in the open?' Greta asked.

'Well, Greta. Sometimes people fall on hard times, I mean, they are unlucky. Things go wrong in their lives and they lose their home and sometimes their family too.'

'That's so sad Mum. Don't you think we should help her?'

'Your Dad supports homeless charities Greta and we give donations of food to the Drumford Foodbank.'

'Is that where people like *Lady Pink Hat* go to get food?'

'Yes, I'm sure they do.'

'Well, can *we* do anything else to help *Lady Pink Hat*, then?'

Not wanting Greta to get involved, but wishing to encourage her daughter to be generous to the needy nevertheless, Angelina paused before giving her response.

'I'm not sure what more we *can* do for *Lady Pink Hat*, Greta. We may never see her again. But what *you* can do is to choose a couple of groceries for the Drumford Foodbank trolley each time we go to the supermarket.'

'OK Mum I'd like to do that. Will you read the final chapters of my story now?'

And so Angelina settled down to read to her daughter, although her mind was racing elsewhere. Once she was sure Greta was fast asleep she crept up the attic steps and pulled out an old trunk which had come from Jonathan mother's bungalow before she passed away with cancer. Choosing several items of clean but musty clothing she held them in her arms in front of her as she renegotiated the steep steps, dropping them in the spare room next to Greta's.

Back in the kitchen, as she was waiting for the kettle to boil, she found some packets of biscuits and some old water bottles which she filled from the tap. Grabbing a couple of carrier bags she returned to the spare room and crammed all her findings into them before hiding both under the spare bed. She was not sure what she had set in motion. Did her sense of altruism justify the secrecy? Did her intention to help the poor woman absolve her for telling a lie by omission? Angelina wasn't sure.

The following morning, before going to work, she popped over to The Grange. She left the carrier bags in the attic room which had showed signs of life and then she retreated downstairs, locking the kitchen door before going straight to their car.

Angelina was excited when she returned that afternoon and could not contain her impatience to check The Grange. Her disappointment when she found that all was just as she had left it was huge, although she was pleased that Greta seemed to have forgotten about their unexpected visitor and was full of talk of costumes for World Book Day instead. For the next two nights Angelina was busy sewing a Queen of Hearts costume until late into the night, ready for the Friday.

The weekend and the following couple of weeks came and went, full of family events, and so it was not until three weeks later that Angelina walked over to The Grange once more. There was no sign of *Lady Pink Hat* but there *was* evidence of the industrious *library fairy,* who had catalogued two new shelves of books and dusted several more. Angelina smiled that her visitor had also taken the hint and used the new aerosol spray behind her. The farmer's wife found it hard to contain her excitement as she retrieved the now empty water bottles, refilled them and returned them to the attic room, along with a few more packets of dry food which she placed in a sealed Tupperware box. This time she left an old dustpan and brush too. Only one set of clothes had been taken so there were plenty spare as yet, but she did leave a large bowl of water, a flannel, soap and an old towel.

This arrangement went on in the same pattern for most of November. Angelina resisted the temptation to try to make face to face contact with her unexpected guest but she was thrilled that her task of sorting out the library was racing along.

The next time she was in Drumford she popped into the library for Greta to choose some new books. As she sat drinking a cup of coffee she noticed a headline about the increasing number of homeless people in the area. She happened to mention it to the girl in the cafe as she paid for a cake for Greta and her own drink, and was surprised by the young girl's response.

'Our Dot from the library is homeless now. She's seen in the countryside around here. It's scandalous what her husband did.'

'What do you mean?'

'Well, Dorothy worked here in the library for years. Used to run the place. Such a lovely lady. She ended up losing everything and took to the streets. So sad! The children call her *Lady Pink Hat!*'

Angelina frowned and smiled her thanks. She didn't know what to say. At least her mysterious *library fairy* was a real librarian so there was nothing to fear and Angelina wondered, not for the first time, about the nature of coincidences.

CHAPTER 15

IT WAS NOT until one crisp morning early in November that I headed back towards The Grange, excited to return. I entered unobtrusively through the ivy covered rear door, pulling the overgrowth back down as I closed the door behind me. I stopped to listen. All was quiet. Smiling I climbed the back spiral staircase to the room in the eaves. Imagine my surprise when I found a bag with clean, albeit second-hand sweatshirts and slacks. They certainly didn't belong to Angelina, who was slender and tall, whereas I, although less portly than my last days before the Big Life Change, am short - only five foot three. Although slimmer than I had been at home, I was still carrying some of the normal middle age spread of a woman of a certain age.

On a small alcove in the wall was a tightly knotted carrier bag in which I found biscuits, nuts and dried fruit and a couple of large bottles of water. Perfect. I felt an immediate affinity to Angelina who I started to think of as my patron. I would do my best to slip in and out unnoticed in thanks for her generosity.

After a small snack I slipped down the second staircase to the library, reluctant to use the sweeping grand oak stairs in the heart of the house. The library was much as I had found it the last time, only there was now an extra pair of white gloves and an air freshener waiting for me on the window ledge. Almost on autopilot I reached up and began my task, soon settling in my own rhythm, oblivious to the fact that a couple of hours passed. As I added yet another book to a boxes at my feet I stretched, a twinge in my back alerting me that it was time to have a break and so I retraced the steps to my room in the eaves for refreshments.

Afterwards I couldn't resist looking out of the window and caught a glimpse of Angelina feeding the chickens in the yard. What a lovely vision of rural life, I thought. I was just daydreaming when I saw her husband approaching and so quickly I pulled back into the shadows and sat on the floor away from view. I took a moment or two to shake out my sleeping bag ready for later before heading back down to resume my job, eager to earn my board and lodgings.

I was mesmerised, fascinated by tomes dating back to the eighteenth century. Many must be extremely valuable I surmised, yet again touched by the trust Angelina had placed in me. I looked at the lap top but, tempted though I was, I left it untouched and the estimated value column blank. Reaching up to the top shelf of the next section I was surprised to pull down *The Brief History of The Grange*. Although eager to delve into its pages I noted its position on the shelf, gave it a dust and then left the book aside on a mahogany writing desk in the centre of the room. While I worked it drew my attention and I kept glancing over towards it; the buff cover with gold inlay title beckoning me.

Dusk would descend in about an hour so I retreated upstairs to sip some water before taking the back staircase to hide in the spinney to do my ablutions. My elder brother had taught me well when we'd wild camped as teenagers and I am forever indebted to him for this and other survival skills. It was even more surprising that I had remembered them. Rinsing my hands in the small stream, which was icing over in places where overhanging rocks formed sheltered pools, I returned to my little room. I rarely used the wooden lidded ceramic gazunder, only in emergencies. It was heavy to carry down the spiral staircase and I dreaded having an accident and dropping it on the way.

On my following visit I was surprised and touched by the thoughtfulness of my benefactor to find a bowl of water, soap and a towel, next to which was a small torch. Returning to the library I sat for a few moments, my shoulders relaxing as I let out an audible sigh of pure contentment. My grin spread as I could resist the temptation no longer and was soon absorbed in the historical account of my temporary home. My concentration was so deep that I hadn't realised that I was squinting in the twilight. Just as I was about to close the book my eyes alighted on the report of the disappearance of a young nun. She had run away leaving a suicide note but no body was ever found. I shivered, aware of the parallel to my husband's disappearance. I sat back squinting at the page. It was no good. I would have to leave it for another day. I dared not remove the volume from the library and so I placed it on its correct shelf and headed for the stairs. It was only when I'd shut the door behind me that I risked the torch to enable me to climb safely to my attic room.

As I prepared to settle down for the night my mind was buzzing with theories. Did the nun really commit suicide? It had been two years since Gerald's disappearance. Had he really killed himself? I wasn't sure that he would have had the courage. Did the nun run away with a lover? Come to think of it had Gerald met someone else too? I realised that we had grown apart so much over the years that I wasn't sure I knew him anymore. Isn't that tragic, I thought. Was the nun murdered? I'm sure Gerald wasn't murdered. It was all too calculated; the disappearance of the money, the holiday to remember him by and the suicide note. All too planned. I was sure that I would find the answers one day but didn't know where to start and to a certain extent I knew that I had to leave it to the experts. What had that kindly policewoman said last time we met? She had certainly been embarrassed by my change in fortune.

I strained to remember. It was two years ago, six months after Gerald's disappearance and about the time of me becoming homeless of my own choice. My mind drifted as I nibbled biscuits and drank some water. Absentmindedly I threw the dice. A *two* again and my memory settled on my last moments in the normal world.

After I had closed my home for the last time and moved into Jamal and Ahmed's flat, Jamal kindly sleeping on the sofa allowing me to use his room, I settled into a blur of activities, with solicitor's meetings, interviews with the police, the bank and social services, trying to untangle the threads of life as I knew it. Then, suddenly the meetings stopped. The kindly policewoman visited me in the boy's flat one afternoon.

'Mrs G,' Cathy Peterson began, hesitating before continuing. 'We seem to have drawn a blank. Every lead we have been given has led to a dead end and the Chief Inspector is withdrawing us from the case unless new evidence comes to light. We usually deal with more serious crimes you see.'

'I understand,' I found myself saying in a daze, although I didn't really. How could someone as large as life one day, and Gerald was certainly large with his six foot two stature, just disappear?

'I'm sorry Mrs G. I tried to protest but there was nothing I could do, what with the cut backs and stretched resources with terrorist threats and everything.'

'Let's have a cup of tea,' I said, 'and talk about something else for a while,' my only method of escapism.

'I must go I'm afraid, but do get in touch if you think of anything else.'

'I will,' I said as I closed the door after her.

After that I found some sort of routine. I'd cook a meal for the 'boys' every day and make them copious cups of tea and coffee. This meant that I had to shop but, not being able to face our friendly corner shop keeper, I walked half a mile further to our nearest supermarket for the sake of anonymity. This was not always a successful avoidance tactic since it was a town where I was recognised by many, but it lessened the pain and the need for conversation.

Life continued to a degree.

CHAPTER 16

DURING THE FOLLOWING weeks at Jamal and Ahmed's flat I remember feeling utterly lost at times, devoid of purpose. I dared not even contemplate what I should do for the rest of my life. I just busied myself cleaning and cooking, trying not to dwell on my misfortune.

A few days after DC Peterson's visit I was due to visit Karen, my wheelchair bound friend in Bedford. I'd done so once a fortnight for as long as I could remember. It usually gave me respite but this time I found it more of a trial than the relaxing afternoon I needed.

'Why are they dropping the case?' Karen asked. She had a soft complexion surrounded by naturally curly short dark hair in a fifties style, but this time her usually cheerful features were replaced by a frown.

'They have no new evidence and they haven't found a body.'

'But there must be more they can do.'

'Well, the bank account mystery is still being looked into by a different department but the local people don't hold much hope for retracing Gerald's steps. He didn't use any of his cards or accounts, which I know about, after the airport.'

'But he can't have just vanished. Surely there must be a trace of him somewhere.'

'Oh, Karen. They just have more pressing work to do. The Red Cross seem to have more resources when dealing with missing persons cases like this.'

'That's ridiculous! Why do they leave it to a charity to work it out? You've paid your taxes as much as anyone else has.' Then Karen's face coloured with embarrassment. 'Well, you have done all your life until this happened.'

'You can't blame them Karen. Think of that little girl's murder in Drumford. It's far more urgent than Gerald's disappearance and if my husband really did commit suicide, then all they are doing is trying to retrace his last steps.'

Karen looked at me, her expression quizzical as her eyes bore into mine. 'Do you really think he's dead Dot? Is that what your heart says?'

I paused, breathing deeply before answering. 'It's been six months Karen. I've been through every emotion under the sun – anger, hurt, resentment, despair, fear for the future and even humour at times.'

'Humour!' Karen spluttered. 'How can you laugh at what Gerald did?'

'But that's the only truth I know Karen. He was meticulous to cover all his tracks so painstakingly. I almost admire him and it makes me laugh. I think that I never really knew him you see, so I'm laughing at myself too. Self preservation. Utter despair would destroy me.'

Karen tutted, shaking her head as she poured another cup of tea for us both. She lived in a self contained bungalow in Bedford, not far from the town centre. It had been altered totally to fit Karen's needs to be as independent as possible. She could even go out and shop on her own. The difference between her life and mine was marked.

'At least I've still got a roof over my head. That's something to be thankful for. Jamal and Ahmed have been brilliant. I'm pleased that Ahmed's settled down now.'

'What's he doing with himself now?'

'He's away for two weeks on some training course. I have a feeling that he would like to become an Imam or something. I'm not sure. He doesn't talk much but he is polite and helpful.'

Karen just nodded.

'It works out well really. My benefits pay for the food and I make sure there's a hot meal waiting for them when they get back from work.'

'For how long though?'

'Oh, I don't know. I just can't think of it. Just day to day existence.'

Little did I know that everything was soon going to change yet again.

I hugged Karen before catching the bus back to Drumford, only to find Jamal waiting for me, running his hands distractedly through his short black hair.

I clicked pause for a moment in my memories as if unwilling to recall what happened next. I sighed as I threw my dice once more - a *one* - another black moment in my life.

'Come in Auntie and sit down. I'm afraid something's happened.'

'What's up Jamal? I can see it in your eyes that it's bad news so tell me what's wrong.'

I was still hovering at the door. Jamal reached to take my coat off me and hung it in the hall before beckoning me to the sofa. In a daze I sat down and watched Jamal pour the tea. Why do we always solve our ills with tea, I found myself thinking as I lifted the cup to my lips, the soothing hot liquid slipping down my throat. I waited.

'It's Ahmed.'

'Is he hurt?' the colour draining from my face. 'Where is he? We should go to him.'

'I don't know how to say this Auntie but the Imam from Drumford Mosque has just rung. He's so sorry to tell us that thinks Ahmed has travelled to Syria to fight with Isis with Abdul, that close friend of his.'

'Oh no!' I cried. 'I thought he was doing so well in his work at the Mosque - for the needy, he always said.'

Jamal looked close to tears. 'I know Auntie. He hasn't breathed a word about it to me. I was sure the Imam was keeping an eye on him.'

'Didn't you have any idea at all?'

'Not at all Auntie. I promise you. If only he had been able to confide in me I could have tried to dissuade him, but I feel so helpless. There was nothing I could do.'

'I know Ahmed has been a little distant of late, but I put it down to growing up. I did not dream... no, there's no way this had even crossed my mind.' I paused, my fingers massaging my temples to ward off an impending headache. 'How could I have missed the signs to such tragic consequences? I was so sure that he was working on an aid project to the Middle East.'

'Don't blame yourself Auntie. You've done so much for my brother ... for both of us. It could never be your fault. A bad man worked among them. Changed them. Led them to do this terrible thing.'

There was a knock at the door. Jamal went to open it and through the misty haze of my muddled mind I could hear familiar and almost comforting voices in the hall.

DC Cathy Peterson and DS Tony Brown came into the already cramped living room cum kitchen area, a far cry from the beautiful house where they had visited me before.

'I'm so sorry Mrs G but we need to ask you both some questions and with your permission to search Ahmed's room.'

I gestured for them to sit down but DS Tony Brown ushered Jamal into the hall and up the narrow staircase.

They must have retreated to Jamal's room out of earshot, the place where I had been sleeping. There was no time, though, to worry about what Jamal was saying.

'I'm sorry to be visiting under such difficult circumstances again Mrs G but please can you tell me what you know?'

'I don't know anything Constable. Jamal has only just told me that Ahmed has disappeared. He went on holiday with a friend to Shropshire a couple of weeks ago. 'Outdoor activities,' is what he described the trip as.'

'Did he say anything else?'

'As far as I understood they were planning an aid trip to the Middle East. That's all I know. He hasn't talked much about it.'

'What's the name of his friend Mrs G and have you an address of where he was staying?'

'His friend's name is Abdul Hussain. Nice quiet lad. Seemed a good influence on Ahmed and they worked together at the mosque for under privileged in the community and Syrian Aid. Ahmed went to stay with his family a few days before the trip but he didn't leave an address.'

The policewoman raised her eyebrows.

'I should have checked, I know, but he's nearly twenty two years old. I don't feel it is my place anymore to keep tabs on the boys. I'm sure the Imam at the mosque knows. Ahmed was due back home tomorrow.'

'How did you know that something was wrong Mrs G?'

'Jamal has only just told me that the Imam rang to say that he thinks Ahmed has gone off to Syria to fight for Isis. The Imam was so sorry to tell us. He's such a nice man. I have so much respect for him.'

'Yes, we've already spoken with the Imam. He is doing all he can with his own contacts to trace Ahmed and bring him back, if that's at all possible. He had no idea what was happening.'

'I have every confidence in him officer. He seemed genuinely kind and caring towards the boys.'

'Have *you* been aware of any signs in the past few months Mrs G? Has Ahmed said anything to make you suspicious that he might be planning this?'

'Not at all Constable. He's a quiet lad, sometimes grumpy. A young man of little words. He seemed to enjoy his work at the Mosque and I thought he was happy. He was quite animated when he was looking forward to going away, but he's only taken enough clothes for a couple of weeks. I'm sure of that.'

'What about when he said goodbye? Was there anything different?'

'Not at all. He just said, Goodbye Auntie and thank you for everything.'

I reddened at this point, realising that it *had* been an odd thing to say and sounded quite final. I hadn't noticed it at the time.

'The Imam also told us that the project had been infiltrated by some seedy individuals but that he is now overseeing the official project personally.'

I nodded.

'He's promised to work closely with us to eradicate those evil people. A bit late for saving Ahmed though ...'

I sighed.

'Thank you for now Mrs Gibbons. May I begin to search his room and we'll have to take away any devices he's left – PC's, mobiles, anything like that? Is that OK?'

I nodded again and as I heard her footsteps on the stairs I held my head in my hands. I was incredulous. Up until that moment I had felt beyond doubt that Gerald would never commit suicide, almost as certainly as I was that Ahmed wouldn't do such a thing. He was such a timid boy. I couldn't in a million years imagine him fighting. I shuddered. A thought repeated in my head. Do we ever truly *know* anyone?

In his bedroom Jamal was having a tougher time with DS Brown.

'I don't believe that you had no idea that your brother was contemplating this Jamal. He must have said or done something to make you suspicious.'

'There was nothing officer, I assure you. My brother has always been a bit different – removed from reality in some ways. He never wanted to get an ordinary job but I was so pleased when he began working at the Mosque.'

'Do you know why he chose that work Jamal?'

'My brother always wanted to help people but I know he felt strongly that British society didn't care for the needy enough. Injustice I think you'd call it.'

'Can you explain?'

'Well, every good Muslim gives a proportion of their earnings to the poor. We also still have a huge responsibility for our elders to. You'd rarely see loved ones sent away to a home, unless there was some great illness. It's not done in our culture. Ahmed felt very strongly about this.'

'Altruism is all very honourable, but don't you think Ahmed owed a great deal to British society for taking him in and giving him a new life.'

'Altruism?'

'I'm sorry ~ self less, willing to do things for others.'

'Yes, Ahmed is just like that. I know that he did appreciate everything in his own way. He certainly cared for Mrs G and was grateful for all she did for us. He rarely showed his thanks though. That wasn't Ahmed's way.'

'So when did you know he was contemplating travelling to join Isis?'

'I didn't know officer. That's the honest truth. I knew he was going on this holiday – a fitness thing he said. Ahmed has always enjoyed physical activities. He's a keen runner and has joined a gym.'

'What gym?'

'He goes to 'Go Go' in Drumford, up the High Street, a couple of times a week.'

DS Brown jotted this down for later. 'Go on. So when did you know he was going away?'

'I knew nothing, officer. That's the honest truth!' Jamal grew red in the face, his frustration at not being believed beginning to simmer. He took a deep breath. 'The first thing I knew was when the Imam telephoned me this morning with his fears for Ahmed's safety and his assurance that they were doing all they could to get him back.'

DS Brown nodded and closed his notebook. 'May we search your room too, Jamal?'

'Go ahead officer. Mrs G sleeps in here at the moment but I've got absolutely nothing to hide.'

With that DS Brown headed next door to join his colleague and Jamal retreated downstairs to the living room to be with me. He sat in silence opposite, his eyes glazed staring out of the window. Then he turned back to me.

'What is going to happen to us Mrs G? If Ahmed doesn't return I can't pay the rent for the flat.' His voice trailed off to a whisper. 'How could he do this to us?'

I had no words of comfort. I could sense a hole in his heart where his brother had been and love replaced by fear and doubt.

After a few minutes another couple of policemen let themselves into the flat; the front door had been left ajar. I had been aware of them standing outside and some communication had taken place in muffled words on mobiles, impossible to decipher. They nodded as they passed us, since the front door led straight into the open plan living area of a lounge-kitchen. They headed upstairs to collect computer equipment, a few plastic bags of Ahmed's possessions and piles of paper. They had been up and down three times before Jamal leapt to his feet.

'That's mine, you have no right to take my PC too,' Jamal protested, struggling with the policeman.'

I jumped to my feet. 'Let him go Jamal, or you'll get into trouble too.' I'd never seen him so anxious and angry.

'But I saved up for months for it. It's mine. How dare they! I've got nothing to do with this. Tell them Mrs G.'

I felt helpless - a bit like the moment when a child implores his mother to mend his favourite toy but it's impossible. Nothing can explain hurt away and for the first time her child sees through the mother's Superwoman disguise. A poignant moment and I felt the pain in Jamal's eyes acutely.

DS Brown had rushed downstairs and entered the fray. 'I'm afraid you'll have to accompany us the police station Jamal. Please come quietly.'

'No, I shouted. Why on earth do you have to take him away too?' I said, my hands reaching out to Jamal and my eyes imploring the officer to leave him alone.

DS Cathy Peterson came down and stood by my side. 'Jamal's just being taken in for further questioning. He'll be home again soon.' Her eyes shone with sympathy.

Within five minutes all was quiet. The police had left and I was alone.

Stunned was a mild way to describe the state of my mind. This time it went into shut down, blanking out reality. Definitely a *one* in my life. No doubt about it. I curled up on the sofa, for a while comforted by the smell of Jamal. In desperation, to feel closer still, I climbed the stairs and fell into Ahmed's bed.

CHAPTER 17

FOR THE NEXT day at The Grange I tried to put thoughts of the past behind me. I spent the time in the library, sorting, boxing, reading and recording on the sheets. I'd seen Angelina go out by car and although I was always on the alert as to any sounds inside the house I had come to ignore the farmyard sounds seeping into me from the outside. It was a wet and windy day so I was revelling in my temporary shelter and the task before me only added to my joy.

That evening, as I lay in my sleeping bag, I mused that I should not outstay my welcome and my optimism lifted by an unexpected sunset of deep red. I tossed the dice absentmindedly but unfortunately it lodged on the edge of my sleeping bag. Another *zero*. My mind drifted back to Jamal and Ahmed's flat. It seemed so long ago and yet it never ceased to inspire me as to the infinite ways the human brain adapted to a new reality, however unfamiliar it seemed at the time.

I must have slept for a couple of hours in Ahmed's bed, Jamal's smell still lingering on the sheets, but when I woke I was on autopilot. I borrowed one of Ahmed's rucksacks that he had used for travelling on aid missions; a large tough waterproof thing I had bought for his birthday a couple of years back. I packed a few changes of clothes, essential toiletries, a spare pair of shoes and a couple of personal mementos and at the last minute I grabbed the sleeping bag. It was actually Jamal's but I doubted that he would begrudge me it. It had its own waterproof cover which attached itself to the rucksack. I put on my stoutest walking shoes and my thickest maroon outdoor coat. At the last moment I grabbed my pink floppy felt hat from the broom cupboard. It was adorned with a couple of moth holes, but I was extremely fond of it. Gerald hated it and called me The Bag Lady. Why, I was never sure.

Leaving my door key on the kitchen worktop, but not even a note, I walked down the path without a backward glance. Initially heading for Belmont Park, I ambled through the gardens until I reached the avenue of larch trees near my old house. I could just see a lady with a push chair locking the front door and realised with a sudden flash of inspiration that we really own nothing in this life. Everything has its time for us – even husbands I thought without a hint of sarcasm – well almost.

Turning my back on my known world I took the foot bridge over The River Ree and stumbled out into the open countryside. For the first time since Gerald's disappearance tears flowed unhindered down my cheeks soaking my coat. It was as if all the pent up emotions and numbness were draining away. I sobbed, gulping the warm air, oblivious to the warm summer sunshine or the natural world I passed by. I have no idea where I slept that first night, or even for the following week. Some days it rained incessantly, my mind clouding over as a reflection of my watery eyes. For several hours each day I experienced acute pain, piercing sensations I'd felt many times after Gerald's disappearance, akin to severe heartburn. Inconsolable I just walked on and slept.

I must have bought provisions during that period but I have no recollection of such mundane things. Grief and loss engulfed me, my mind blotting out my consciousness. As mists filled the mornings, and at times the whole day, it was as if a veil had descended, screening the life I once knew. I think I must have huddled behind hedgerows at night, wrapping my sleeping bag around me like a shroud. I don't really recall. Maybe one day I might. Who knows?

It was on one sunny morning a couple of weeks later that a coach sped by bringing me out of my trance. I recognised the lane as Canbury Lane and just caught a glimpse of the children's faces as it veered around a sharp bend. I found myself praying for their safety and strangely enough that was the moment when the acute agony eased, like a soothing balm on an insect bite – the sting was still there but it had lost the sharp edges of its venom.

I had arrived on the outskirts of the village of Canbury and without thinking I paused to sit on a gnarled tree stump, which had been crafted into a rough seat. I noticed, as if for the first time in my life, mothers and children milling on the green in front of me, children restless, their parents nattering. The distance was too great to hear what they were saying. All at once the cluster broke up and, like rays of a star they dispersed in all directions. I say all. There were only four routes from The Village Green. Within moments cars passed me by too; mainly large four wheel drive people carriers with children in the back squabbling, their mother's eyes glazing over as they tried hard to concentrate at the wheel, their vehicles looming above the tarmac in their superiority. Suddenly all was quiet again and only one mother and her daughter were left walking towards me, but soon they too had dispersed down a driveway before peace resumed.

I frowned at the memory, grasping the present momentarily and centring on my now familiar surroundings at The Grange. I could feel my heart rate lower and breathed deeply, listening to the familiar sounds of the cows being led to the nearby barn for milking. The normality of their unwavering routine soothed me and I nearly fell off to sleep.

Just before it was too dark to see I dragged myself from my hypnagogic state, fumbled for my dice and threw a *two*, transported back in time yet again to my moment of awakening:

Sitting on that log bench, which had seen many generations of villagers go about their daily business, an acute sense of self finally returned. I had been in denial, that's for sure. Looking down my shoes came into focus. They needed a polish but they were strong. The rucksack, slung down on the grass beside me, reminded me of Ahmed and Jamal and I began to well up again. Through a watery haze I stared at my hands in a way I'd never done before. Elegant fingers with nails a bit too long now, a few brown patches and wrinkles as a sign of my age or endless washing up before, at the age of fifty, Gerald had treated me to a dishwasher. It was this mundane thought that brought me to the healthy realisation that I was feeling a bit peckish. I hadn't eaten for a while and a survival instinct set in. Money would be short soon, I thought, and I had to be careful; change my eating habits drastically.

Back on my feet I lifted the rucksack on to my back. The weight of all that I possessed lay heavily on my shoulders. Walking towards the village of Canbury I glanced up, catching a glimpse of the young girl at her window. She smiled, probably at my pink hat. Calling in at the village store on The Green where, ever practical I bought a small sliced loaf of bread and some cheese; both were drastically reduced because today was their sell by date – and a large bottle of water. I had no awareness that, in a couple of months, I would be too shabby to be allowed inside this little shop, but those losses were part of my unknown future. For now I was focussed on surviving the next few steps. Now each moment in my life counted, even though the past appeared worthless.

I walked further along the lane and soon passed the village boundary. After about two miles I spied a little clearing, climbed over the stile and walked up the grassy slope. Pausing at its centre I gazed up at the trees, whose leaves must have stretched over the area long before I was born, and silent tears fell softly down my cheek. As I stood in this sunny spot, where dappled light shone brightly through the canopy, I took a deep breath and reached for a dry handkerchief. Ever a stickler for real cotton, the one I drew out of my pocket was my mother's and this gave a certain timeless comfort. My tears ceased.

Since the weather was pleasant and dry, I did not hesitate to find a corner in the shade and stretch out my sleeping bag. Taking off my coat for the first time in two weeks I was relieved to let the suffocating warmth and heaviness of it fall on to the grass. I sat in silence for many minutes. Gradually I realised that it was not silent at all and sounds around me began to seep into my consciousness. The leaves rustled overhead; an aeroplane hummed far up in the skies; birds were singing, initially with urgent warnings as to my presence. They too seemed to relax and sing with quieter voices, as if saying, 'she's alright. We'll come to no harm.' Then I heard the beautiful haunting voice of a blackbird on a branch not far above my head. Although life as I knew it had ceased, it was as if I was suddenly blessed with a natural ability to meditate in the here and now, a life which had narrowed to the few possessions I carried. There was a void beyond today of which I had no conception, and yet in the last few moments I had been handed a gift; the ability to find a sense of calm in the present and also a glimmer of courage to take tentative steps forward.

As if on a picnic in the countryside I retrieved the paper bag from my rucksack and nibbled slowly through a third of my rations. Without any pre-planning I was already in survival mode. A psychiatrist would have heralded it as good; a sign of strength of character. To me it was instinctive. I drank a third of my water too, then took another deep breath.

After my meagre supper I took a stroll around my domain, finding myself chatting to the birds in the hedgerows. A squirrel rushed passed me and up the sprawling oak tree, under whose canopy I had sheltered from the rays of the early evening sunlight.

It may be hard to imagine but I had nothing in my mind as I settled out in the open in my sleeping bag that night, which I used more for its comforting closeness than the need of warmth. I did not wonder how Jamal was getting on or whether he'd been released. I did not think of Ahmed or try to guess where he might be, or even if he was safe. I think thoughts like that would have destroyed me totally. I certainly did not think of Gerald of whom I'd heard nothing since his suicide letter. I dropped off to sleep listening to my feathered friends settling for the night and the breeze through the trees. I was aware of the colours of an orange sunset through the beech tree and the moon appearing on the horizon between the boughs of the oak before ascending a branch at a time. I was finally surrounded by a multitude of twinkling stars, spied though the gaps between the leaves. In fact, I barely thought at all as a peace flooded through me which I can only describe as spiritual. I was comfortable. I had food and warmth. I breathed in the scent of the meadow. Tomorrow was another day.

The next morning was as sunny as the last. God knows how my mood would have suffered if it had been raining, me drenched to the bone. That had happened before *my awakening* when I had been oblivious to it, and certainly many times since, after I had gained the strength of mind to cope. What is it that the Bible says about only being tested to the limit of our endurance and no more? I was on that limit in those first few months but with each day, although I was totally unaware of the change in me, I grew stronger. That little clearing, which became my first home since I had walked out on a 'normal' existence, was to become a favourite haven for me. Undisturbed, unworldly but with a connection to nature that I'd never experienced in all the years of my life.

With absolutely no idea where I was going next I walked on and with each step there was a sense of healing and of letting go. Since then I have *lived each day as it came.* A cliché I know but nonetheless true. In the warmer, dryer months I have wandered the countryside learning the network of footpaths and tiny lanes by heart, never venturing more than ten miles from familiar places. Once a week I have made a habit of taking the walk back to Drumford. It was a fellow itinerant traveller who had passed me by on one extremely wet and windy day who happened to mention The Ark; a hostel and soup kitchen organised by the local Roman Catholic Church, but run mostly by volunteers and funded through charity and the church. In truth I had been aware of it; since I had donated food there many times over the years, but never for one moment had I thought that one day I would be one of its recipients. Recently I had avoided company where I could. The spoken word seemed superfluous to my life. I used my voice sparingly and then barely at all. It was at The Ark, though, that my frosty protective coating began to dissolve a little.

The two Irish sisters who ran it soon put me at my ease with their gentle humour and abundant kindness. It was a relief to enjoy one hot meal, a bath and change of clothes. They offered a swap; a full set of 'new to me' glad rags in exchange for mine. I had the occasional pleasure of being given back my own clothes but that was another lesson learnt, to let go of possessiveness. I owned nothing in this life. Even life itself was a gift which I did not wish to abuse, but nevertheless I had no desire at that time to return to the 'real world' whatever that might be.

I stopped worrying. It was an unconscious act which I wish I'd learnt long ago. The biblical phrase, 'consider the lilies of the field, how they grow. They don't toil, neither do they spin'.... came to mind and then disappeared on the breeze.

At first I had been able to use the bank machine, occasionally withdrawing a little cash. That was until they froze the account and I had to pay them a visit.

'We had all of these letters and statements returned to us with, 'unknown at this address – return to sender' on them. Without an address we are unable to keep your account open. You never respond to our emails either.'

I struggled to find words to say to this young girl who frowned at me from behind the screen and looked about fourteen years old. I did not wonder what had happened to Jamal's flat or even how he was. At that time my brain was still in *shut down* as to the past, my old life a reflection of my account. I walked out and didn't go back until recently. For a while I just drifted wherever the mood took me. I suppose they would call it Mindfulness today according to leaflets in the library, but I had been fortunate to learn those skills for free.

It was now dark in my room in the eaves. I switched on my torch, unable to settle as yet, and threw a *five,* smiling in the gloom as I recalled a surprising but fortuitous incident.

On one extremely wet day, when the coat I had borrowed from the centre in exchange for my old maroon one, was letting in water at the seams, I had one of those warming unexpected encounters which made you realise the goodness of human nature. I was drenched as if I had stood under a waterfall. Stubbornly I trudged on, not willing to trade my freedom for the advantage of dry clothes. It was one of those days when I wanted everyone to feel sympathy for my plight and I didn't even wave to the children as their bus passed. Just as I thought life could not get any worse a car drove too close and, although I leapt on to the grassy verge between myself and the impenetrable hedgerow, the car soaked me further as it sped through a large puddle. I was wet from head to foot.

Angry at my lot and indulging in self pity I was about to swear at my assailant as he sped off unawares, or so I thought. Instead, to my surprise, the car came to a halt a hundred yards up the road and a man leapt out, one who I would come to know well in the future. He opened the back passenger door and grabbed a waterproof coat, the likes of which farmers use every day, with a large hood which swamped but nonetheless comforted me. I didn't have a chance to thank this Good Samaritan because he thrust the article into my hands and fled back to the protection of his car.

I stripped off the coat I was wearing and threw this one around me, soon snuggled from the wind and rain. Yes, I was damp inside but, like a wet suit, the air between the layers kept me warm enough to shed my pride, turn and trudge back to Drumford. That coat, which must have been expensive in its day and bought at one of those country gentlemen's stores, was with me through to next spring. Selfishly, I suppose now, I asked Orla, one of the twins who ran The Ark, if she would dry it out and return it to me personally. It was a gift which taught me a valuable lesson and I didn't want to share it. My old maroon woollen coat had by now seen better days and, however fond I was of it, I could not mourn its demise. I could only wear one coat at a time and this one covered most weathers that English winters, and even summers, were likely to throw at me.

Last winter, when the weather was really bad I took the offered shelter in the The Ark. Laura, one of the sisters, even persuaded me to become a Big Issue seller for a while when I was so grateful for my treasured new coat. I went to the nearby town of Bedford for anonymity's sake and Laura encouraged me to put the money I earned into a savings account called The Credit Union which was administered at The Ark. They allowed me to put the centre as my address; probably not strictly speaking legal, but I left my account book with them and only drew out those savings to pay the centre the meagre charge for their services. They were all so respectful.

Travelling to Bedford on the bus once a week for nearly a year selling the magazine outside what was once British Home Stores became my routine. Occasionally, in the early weeks, I visited Karen, always attempting to avoid any controversial subjects. We often just reminisced about our younger days, which suited me just fine, but then she started to pry. She became suspicious about my clothes and saw me once in Bedford selling The Big Issue and so that was that.

Most of the time, though, I preferred to be on the move; roaming between villages. I never begged but there was always one kind soul or another who offered me food or drink; sometimes even a cup of tea. The bakers in Drumford always looked out for me at the end of my Wednesday trip before heading back to my solitude. A young lass, who could only have been about eighteen, and almost certainly knew me from my library days, would pop out of the shop and hand me a carrier bag of goodies and a most welcome cup of steaming soup. I was not allowed in the shop, of course. She would wish me luck before rushing back to her work. The funny thing was that I felt I had all the luck in the world. Whenever I was in need, someone would come to my rescue. It was a sobering but in some ways a beautiful existence.

Occasionally, when I allowed myself to think, which was rare apart from my recent roll-of-the-dice memories, I wondered if the waste and extravagance of the West had been the catalyst which lured my Ahmed, but these observations obviously overlooked the lies of Isis; the danger and the vicious nature of those who fought; their abominable treatment of women and the recent terror incidents. I shuddered. No, it was awful to think of such things.

I've caught sight of Jamal on a couple of occasions. He tried to call out and reach me once but I skipped up an alleyway and escaped over into the park before he could catch up with me. I'm not ready to face my past yet. I have only just learnt to live in the present without fear. Maybe it's wrong of me. One day I will be strong enough to be concerned as to how he's getting on and ask for news. but not yet. If I'd wanted to cut myself off totally I would have walked to an entirely different part of the country, where I wasn't known. But I didn't. I've not visited Karen since, either. I wish I could bring myself to do that, but I can't; too many questions devoid of answers.

I like to think myself as following in the footsteps of St Francis or many a hermit who has taken refuge from civilisation and found nature calling them, but as yet I've not found that holy place in which to meditate on my soul.

So, now that I could be facing my second winter homeless, is it wrong to dream that I've found not only shelter but a purpose in my life, having drifted for eighteen months? I couldn't bear that hostel again for long periods of time but neither could I face the endless interviews with social services to see if I'm entitled to any benefits. I suppose I should be. I'm sixty next spring when I can access my small public sector pension. It's another seven years until I reach pensionable age for my state pension I think, unless they've changed the rules since I dropped out of society. Maybe it's as high as 70 years now. I've no idea. I'm a WAPSI, so they tell me, or is it a WASPI? Women Against State Pension Inequality. Yes, that's me. Not that you'd know it.

Back in my attic room it was dark and a noise broke into my reverie. It sounded like a girl on a swing, back and forth, back and forth and then there was moaning. Maybe it was just an owl. At first I felt a foreboding which chilled my heart. I shivered as the sound began to rock me to sleep. Without hesitation I curled up in my sleeping bag and slept soundly. In my dream my dice was on a continuous loop, rolling and stopping, rolling and stopping, never once landing on that elusive *six*.

The following morning to my astonishment, my dice had rolled out of my coat pocket and on to the floor. A *six!* Maybe it was the sign I needed, when hope turned into joy as I began to relax, revelling in a life with books once more and my comparative stability.

CHAPTER 18

THE NUN'S STORY was spinning around in my mind whilst working and walking into town over the next couple of months. I talked to Laura from The Ark about the possibility of writing down the tale and she offered me as much scrap paper as I wanted. She also slipped a couple of pens into my pocket one day when I'd expressed my wish to do some creative writing.

'Excellent therapy,' she said as she winked at me. 'Now Dot, there's a Creative Writing Class on a Tuesday if you'd like to change your visits to us to a day earlier.'

'Oh thank you Laura, I might just do that.'

The following week, I sat nervously awaiting my first class. The tutor, whose name was Jill, asked us to describe a day in our life and write it down and as homework she asked us to jot down ideas for stories and then just to let the words flow.

For me the subject matter was easy. Over the next couple of months before Christmas I took a wad of paper each week and each night, by torchlight, I began to handwrite the nun's story which was floating in my head. Here is the beginning for you. I'm not sure where it's going as yet.

The Nun's Tale Part 1

Millie at The Grange

1760

It was just a feeling; an instinct almost. You could not call it sixth sense. As Millie Talbot was perched astride her three legged stool one day she sensed eyes boring into her back. She peered over her shoulder, but not fast enough. There was no-one there, only the great open barn door and chickens scrabbling in the dusty yard. She turned back to her cow; a lazy friendly beast who waited with patience as Millie's hands hovered momentarily beside the full udder, breaking the flow of milk into the churn below. Millie sighed and then joined in with the singing, her companions barely noticing her pause or change of expression.

'Did you see Mother Superior's face, Millie, when she caught Evie staring out of the winder at prayers yesterday?' her fellow aspirant nun whispered. 'Do you know what's got into the girl?'

'I know what's got into her,' another girl smirked, whispering to her friend as they worked on the opposite side of the barn. Those two had only recently joined Canbury Convent from the nearby village of Canbury and they giggled as Millie frowned. She worried about her sister Evie, who had said little to her in recent weeks. It was if her mind was on other things but Millie was too naive to guess what it might be.

The four girls had been given the task of milking the cows at West Gate Farm each evening. This was adjacent to The

Grange, the large house in which they were housed and instructed by the nuns, while they sought guidance as to whether the path of a nun was their calling. Each wore grey tabards which skimmed the floor, over a simple long sleeved white dress. A grey scarf hung loosely over their heads, which they pinned to their hair to save it slipping down as they worked.

Every day was the same for Millie. She felt a presence, but when she turned nobody was there. Nevertheless Millie found herself looking forward to this time of the day and the intriguing feelings stirred an excitement which was novel to her. She never spoke to the other girls of it; or to her younger sister Evie for that matter. Evie had been allocated morning and evening tasks in the kitchens.

The Convent itself was behind a ten foot stone wall, a short walk through the woods from The Grange and West Gate Farm. The aspirant nuns had no idea that there was an underground passageway between the two buildings. It was behind a locked door in the cellar which was a forbidden area for the girls. They had sometimes wondered how the nuns, who kept a close eye on them and taught them, appeared silently at just the wrong moments, catching them laughing raucously at each other's jokes, or sneaking back into The Grange after hours. It was a balancing act between servitude and a longing to be carefree and out in the world. Little did they know that freedom, which sounded so enticing as they bent in hours of prayer, often led to far more heart ache. In their confined but sheltered life they actually wanted for nothing.

It was in August that Millie's future was to be decided. If she was deemed suitable, following her time as an aspirant at The Grange, then she and others like her would be given a service to celebrate their commitment. This also acted as a final goodbye to their relationship with family, friends and the life they knew. After this they would transfer residence to inside the convent walls and their training as novice nuns would begin in earnest.

For now though, seven times each day the aspirant nuns were escorted along the path and through the woodland. There they entered a small door set in a larger solid oak gate which rose to the height of the wall and spanned twice as much. The gateman opened the tiny hatch next to the door and, once he had ascertained their identity, he unlocked it for them to enter. They followed the Liturgy of Hours said in Latin; Lauds ~ their morning prayer, followed by Terce, Sext, None, Vespers, and finally Compline just before bedtime. They were not required at this stage to attend Matins which was held just before dawn. Between these liturgies the aspirants were required to carry out various duties at The Grange and at the farm to ensure the day ran smoothly. The limited time in between was filled with contemplative prayer in their rooms, bible study with or without a Sister from the Convent, or instruction and guidance sessions. It was a routine Millie found quite comforting but Evie battled with it continuously and twice she had been reprimanded by the Mother Superior for being found in areas out of bounds.

After evening milking one day, Millie was walking down the shaded passage at the side of the house to the back entrance of The Grange. She felt a tap on her shoulder, as if someone in the spinney had thrown a small pebble at her. She glanced around and her eyes searched across the undergrowth but there was no sign of anyone. Racing the last few steps and into safety, she leaned against the door a moment or two to regain her breath.

The back entrance led to a narrow passageway and a spiral staircase up to the eaves where the girls slept. On another occasion she stopped in her tracks as she thought she heard giggling in the bracken, but peering through the undergrowth revealed nothing except the occasional bird scratching, or leaves rustling in the slight breeze. A squirrel broke its cover startling her as it bound across the path and raced up the nearby trunk of an old oak, looking down at her between dappled leaves. Maybe he had been retrieving nuts hidden last autumn, or he had forgotten where to look for them and had been rummaging for clues, a particular scent or a minute landmark disturbed by the busy life on the forest floor. The noises might have been a blackbird singing a strange imitation song; as is their wont. All these things Millie reflected on as she climbed the staircase, dismissing yet another mystery.

The girls were not permitted to mix with the farm workers and there was a wall in the barn to divide the milking area with the stables, so that there was no occasion where they should have had the opportunity to meet. Unfortunately those restrictions led to intrigue, enhancing the appeal of such encounters. The pathway down the side of the milking barn was strictly out of bounds and the girls were told that the gate was always locked, but it was a short-cut and so they often climbed over the gate, excited by the thought of bending the rules.

The sense of being watched never left Millie. She was a sensible girl and though she could not admit that her presence at The Grange was her true calling, she accepted her fate with good grace. After all, their recently widowed mother had five daughters to care for. The Reverend Philips had seeded this idea into Millie's mama's mind as a perfect solution for her two youngest, so that she could focus on supporting and finding decent marriages for her other daughters, not rich ones you understand, but hard working men who would keep a roof over their heads and, God willing, food on their plates.

It was two weeks later, when Millie's inquisitive nature had reached its heights, that she caught sight of a young man beckoning her towards the dark alley. Even though she dismissed the gesture and pointedly walked in the other direction keeping in the light of day, she was smiling to herself, flattered by the admiration. It gave a much needed spark to an otherwise monotonous day, so no harm was done.

These near encounters continued for much of the late spring and occasionally she would also hear a repeat of strange noises in the woods. Her time at The Grange was nearing its end. If her fate was confirmed then soon she would retreat into the confines of the convent and her life as she knew it would be dead to her. The 'almost' encounters were thus even more alluring, as forbidden fruit always is.

By the end of May Millie was aware of the audacity of her admirer who had become bolder each day – sometimes several times a day. She had even seen his face a few times, a handsome lad a couple of years her senior; tall with cheeky smiling eyes. She kept all these thoughts to dream about in the little room she shared with Evie, but she was reluctant to confide in her little sister.

The inevitable came to pass. She was late in one night, it being her turn to feed the chickens in the yard, before retiring for quiet contemplation in their room. Millie did not resist when a hand came behind her and covered her mouth. She just sank back into those firm arms as if it was the most natural experience in the world.

Realising that he had found a willing ally Jack took his hand away, slowly at first in case the young girl, who had been tantalizing him for so long, screamed. They stood there for a few moments, both stunned, the awareness of each other *intense. Choosing her moment, but not wanting to jeopardise her future, Millie turned in Jack's arms, stretched up and kissed him full on the lips. Jack was too surprised to reciprocate because Millie slipped from his grasp and vanished into The Grange before he could act. He went home grinning with the mischief of the night.*

Each day in the following week Millie felt eyes bore into her from the shadows but Jack did not approach her again until her rota had brought her back to feeding the poultry and she was alone. This time their embrace was more passionate and on subsequent occasions Millie succumbed to his charms and submitted herself to him, believing wholeheartedly that they were meant to be together. How many a girl had fallen prey to that very lie to justify their acts over the centuries? Millie had fallen in love. They held many trysts in the next couple of months, each more daring than the last and Millie was now unable to resist his advances. The predictable happened and Millie became pregnant.

Telling no-one of her plight, not even Evie, Millie ran away in the dead of one night in early August – a matter of weeks before her position as an aspirant nun was to be reviewed. That future was not to be hers; in fact it was far from her mind as she rushed to an unknown destiny.

Feeling sure that Jack would follow her, Millie kept her distance from The Grange, but close enough for Jack to find her. Surely he would come and make everything right, she thought. She headed west of Canbury, working alongside the poor - gleaning the grain left over by the farmers. At night she found all manner of places to sleep but on fine summer's nights she slept rough. She had found a special place on the outskirts of the village, hidden from the lane by a tall hedgerow, a tiny meadow surrounded by saplings in leaf including an oak and a horse chestnut.

The Mother Superior sent out a search party for Millie and she was spotted one day and dragged unceremoniously back to The Convent. Once enclosed by gated walls, she seemed far removed from her more casual former life at The Grange. Millie was made a prisoner, unable to see or speak to anyone and food was passed through a hatch to her tiny cell. All she was expected to do was pray for forgiveness and implore to her God to find some way in which she could pay penance. Each day she was taken to the Mother Superior and thrashed for her sins until she became too great with child to ignore.

Millie was distraught, but believing her punishment was the will of God she tried to forget Jack. It was only the child growing inside her that gave Millie a reason to live. That precious promise gave her a glimmer of hope for which she thanked her God for every day, praying that the child could be kept safe and well. One day, without pre-warning Millie was collected from the cell, a hessian cloth over her head hiding her shame, and she was bundled into a waiting buggy. She could feel the vibrations as the cart jolted over every stone on the track and she wondered where she was being taken; almost, but not quite, past caring. Her baby stirred.

'You are ready to come, my sweet,' she whispered, under her confinement. 'Wait a little while yet, I pray. It's not safe here.'

Believing that Millie's presence would taint the lives of the other novice nuns she was dispatched to Drumford Workhouse, none too soon, because her baby was delivered that very night. The infant was taken away from her at birth but Millie was forbidden to return to her old life. A well meaning benefactor arranged for Millie to become a maid in Belmont House. On her day off each week she would scour the streets of Drumford just hoping to catch a glimpse of her child, the tiny boy she had crooned over for precious moments on the day he was born, thanks to a kindly young nurse.

Millie tried asking at The Workhouse but was turned away three times until on one occasion a lady dressed in deep blue satin finery spotted Millie loitering outside. She waved for her coachman to wait before turning to Millie and asking,

'Are you the girl who keeps asking of the whereabouts of her baby?'

'Yes I am,' Millie replied as boldly as she could muster.

'Come with me and I'll show you something that will reassure you.'

At first Millie hesitated but the lady had such a kindly non-judgemental face that she climbed into the carriage sitting facing her.

They were heading towards the village of Canbury.

'Firstly, you want to know who I am. I am Lady Canbury, the benefactor who paid for your care, but I also oversaw the adoption of your baby, as I do with all young girls in your unfortunate situation who arrive at Drumford Workhouse. There are a few young couples with good homes in the region who cannot bear children for all manner of reasons. I take it on myself to carry out the task of matching unwanted babies to their new parents, but I also visit regularly to ensure that the infant is well cared for. Now, if you tell me your story truthfully, then we'll see what we can do to put your mind at rest.'

Millie told her full story, sparing nothing, including her maltreatment at the hands of the Mother Superior. Lady Canbury just nodded with what appeared to be sympathy, putting Millie at her ease. By the time her story was spent they had reached the village.

'Now, I am to visit your little baby this afternoon as it happens, to check that all is as it should be. I know the couple *well. Their family has worked on our estate for generations. I will take you with me as long as you agree to the following conditions.*

Millie nodded.

*'Firstly, you do not try to hold the little boy or make any sign that he is yours while we are with the couple. Secondly you do not speak at all. I will introduce you as my assistant. Just smile please. Thirdly, after we leave, you must promise me that you will never contact, pester, visit or even try to see the child again because he is not **your** child anymore. Do you agree and do you understand why I'm doing this?'*

'Yes Madam. I agree.'

Just in case Millie was in any doubt Lady Canbury reiterated, 'I am taking you to reassure you that the child is happy and generously looked after, but after that you must leave him and the family alone. Do I make myself clear?'

'Yes, I understand Madam.'

And so Millie visited her little baby and however difficult it was for her to walk away, she did so for the sake of her child, knowing full well that he had a far better life now than she could ever give him as a single maid. As she saw him in the lady's arms her heart strings were pulled taught to breaking point, but she also understood that the little mite had no recognition of her as he cooed contentedly in this stranger's arms.'

On the way back to Drumford they barely spoke but as they reached the gates of Belmont House Lady Canbury turned to her.

'My dear, you have seen what you needed to see. You are one of the fortunate ones. At least you have the chance to begin a new life and not to look back. I can't pretend that you won't pine for your child for many months, even years to come, but the pain will be easier to bear knowing that he is content.'

'You have been so kind Lady Canbury, but may I ask what my child's name is now, do you think?'

'His name is Thomas Croft. The Crofts have officially adopted him and given him their name now. He is their child. You do understand that Millie, don't you?' Lady Canbury looked upon Millie with a stern but kindly expression.

Millie nodded, staring out at the passing scenery as they sped back to Drumford where Millie thanked Lady Canbury and she was gone. In the months to come she tried not to dwell on her misfortunes, but to remember that she had a roof over her head, a job of work she quite enjoyed and that she'd escaped the life of a nun.

On her days off she just strolled to town and sometimes treated herself to a cup of tea with the little money she saved from her wages. One day, on her return, the master's son found her strolling down by the lake, a place which was out of bounds to the servants.

'What will you give me to keep silent in this affair,' he grinned at her, slipping down from his horse and tying the reins to a tree trunk, while Millie attempted to run back to the house.

'Not so fast you,' Master Belmont called as he grabbed her arm and pulled her behind a large oak tree.

Unbeknown to both of them, the stable-hand Jack had been watching Millie from afar for a couple of weeks now and had been gathering up courage to speak to her. He leapt to her side, punching the Master's son on the shoulder so that, to their surprise, he fell backwards and bumped his head on a tree stump as he landed in the fallen leaves.

Jack wasted no time. He bent down to check whether Master Belmont was breathing or not. He was not sure at first but then he felt a faint pulse. That was enough to stir him into action. Quickly Jack pulled Millie, almost dragging her *towards the spinney. Once in the relative seclusion of the woods they ran a few hundred yards to a small gate, which he helped her to climb over, leading them to a path running out of Drumford beside the River Ree. Millie and Jack were on the run.*

One night, a few days later, I was browsing through one of the diaries of the Convent, a large leather bound tome with scrawled handwriting which was difficult to decipher in parts. I was about to close it for the night when my eyes were drawn to the last couple of sentences, written almost as an afterthought at the bottom of a page.

"Evie Talbot an aspirant nun and the young sister of Millie Talbot, who has recently disappeared from Belmont House, hung herself in the attic of The Grange last Thursday. The inquest was today and we were told that she was with child."

My fingers felt icy as I flicked through the next few pages, frantic to glean any more about the demise of Evie Talbot, sister of Millie. There was nothing. No description of a funeral or hint as to what Evie's story might be. Neither girl was mentioned again in the remainder of the journal, as if they had left behind them blank pages to be forgotten. As I settled for the night I wondered about Evie. A vivid picture came to my mind of a young girl swinging in the attic above my head. I shivered and then a strange thing happened, as if there was a presence in the room and a breath of cool air wafted through.

As I drifted off to sleep that night I could hear the creaking of the swing, to and fro, to and fro, until the final moan and all was still. There was nothing for it but to redraft the story with new information. It was as if Evie was conducting me, leading me to where I needed to go next. I had no fear of her. She was my friend.

The following afternoon I crept out of The Grange. I had seen both Angelina and her husband driving off in their Land Rover and now recognised the farmer as the man who had kindly stopped to give me his coat.

Gingerly I walked to the stream and followed the barely visible path, which might have been no more than an animal track, towards the edge of the woods. To my astonishment and pleasure I found signs of old ruins, which were almost certainly the remains of the Convent. There were only fragments of wall here and there but enough for me to be convinced of its whereabouts. To say that I was thrilled was an understatement.

Bending down I laid my hands on the rugged edges of the stones, willing them to share their story. I remained there until the cold was seeping through my hands to my arms and my back began to ache. Satisfied I returned to the library in The Grange to continue my task, knowing that soon I must be gone.

CHAPTER 19

IT WAS A week before Christmas. I knew it was time to pack up my things and head for The Ark to find a bed for the festivities. I had no plans to return to The Grange until after New Year. The pile of hand written sheets under some large books in a dark corner of the library was growing. I was excited as to what adventures my pair would encounter as they ran from the law, and imagined them so in love that they did not care. They had other ideas of course!

It was my second Ark Christmas and I must admit that I found my first one last year a jolly affair, not the depressing realisation of my circumstances that it might have been. Last year I naturally blended in with the helpers, rather than the clients, and this year I imagined would be no exception.

I was just about to leave when I spotted a shadow out in the farmyard which quickly disappeared from view, slipping between The Grange and the barn. The shadow looked strangely familiar. Without a doubt it was Jamal.

Afraid that he would be spotted, I crept down and out of my secret doorway and felt my way in the early morning gloom along the side of the building. I almost bumped into him.

'Shhhh,' I whispered. 'Follow me,' I beckoned.

Once inside the relative safely of my little room he sat down on my sleeping bag as I indicated.

'Oh Auntie, I can't tell you how I tracked you down here, but it's such a relief to find you at last.'

Under normal circumstances I would put the kettle on but instead I offered Jamal some of my meagre remains of water.

'Oh, no no, thank you,' he said as he reached in his pocket and pulled out a small carton of milk and two plastic cups which we shared.

'Jamal, before we each begin our stories I want you to know that I am heading back to Drumford today and need to go as soon as I can. Will you walk with me and then we can talk as we walk.'

'OK, Auntie. Sounds good to me.'

Always the gentleman, he picked up my rucksack. I took my carrier bag and followed him down and out into the spinney. We kept quiet until we were back on Canbury Lane. Turning to look at each other we smiled, too shy to share a more overt sign of affection. Instead Jamal took my hand in his and looked me in the face.

'How are you Auntie? I've been so worried about you since your disappearance.'

'There's little to tell you Jamal except to apologise. I couldn't take anymore, so I escaped from all I knew and became homeless. It's not as hard as you think; quite liberating really. That is until the winter months but I've been so fortunate to find The Grange.'

We started to walk side by side. A school bus passed us and Greta waved to us. Without hesitation I waved back. Jamal's eyebrows shot up questioningly.

'Oh, that's a long story.'

'Does the farmer know you're in the old house Mrs G?'

'Yes, well, the farmer's wife certainly does. She leaves out clean clothes and food for me.'

'Why would she do that?' Jamal frowned again.

'I'm sorting out their long lost library. It's a dream job for me and I'm quite content.'

'I can see you'd be in your element but I imagine the farmer wouldn't be too happy.'

'Indeed. Thankfully he doesn't know and long may it stay that way. Anyway how about you? What happened after I left? Did the police release you the next day and has Ahmed really left for Syria?'

'I was so upset. They questioned me off and on until early the following morning when the Imam must have phoned the police station and convinced the police that I had nothing to do with it.'

'Oh, that's a relief.' I was pleased that the Imam had been true to his word and looked out for Jamal when he was in need. 'And your brother?'

'The Imam told the police officer that Ahmed was in Syria, but was not certain whether he was fighting for Isis or not.'

'The confusion with the charity work he was doing I should think. And when did they let you out?'

'About 6 O'clock. I went straight to Drumford Mosque. The Imam sat me down and we said some prayers until I was calm. He suggested that I rest before going down to London to see if they could tell me anymore.'

'Did you go back to the flat?'

'Yes.' Jamal paused frowning, but avoided eye contact with me as was his custom. 'Finding you gone was terrible, though I couldn't blame you. I decided to make my goal in life to find you all; my brother first, then you and then Mr G. I went to the London mosque in Southall the next day but they couldn't, or wouldn't tell me anything. No-one would talk to me.'

'That must have been awful for you.'

'It got worse Mrs G. I didn't know what to do so I returned to Drumford, only to find that the warehouse had put me out of a job too. I hadn't contacted them in three days you see. I was so confused and they'd heard rumours that I was in trouble with the police.'

'Oh Jamal. I'm so sorry that I wasn't there for you. I just couldn't ..'

'I know Auntie. Your troubles were as great as mine.'

'So how did you manage?'

'Well, I couldn't afford the rent on my own and so Brian offered me a place at his. I decided that I needed money and so I..' and he paused here, his face reddening with embarrassment.

'You can tell me anything Jamal,' I said gently. 'Nothing more can hurt me.'

'Well, I sold all of our things and then I sold all your belongings in store, to save the storage fees too.'

'Oh, that's fine Jamal. They mean nothing to me now. Please tell me everything?'

'Well, after I had closed up the flat for the last time I sat in a nearby cafe wondering what to do first. I had three missing persons in my life and didn't know where to begin. I decided to use the money to go in search of you all, but how? Oddly enough, when I ambled up to the High Street that day, I thought I spotted your back turning down into Belmont Park. When I got to the gate though, you'd disappeared.'

We had reached Canbury village and Jamal popped into the village shop to buy some sandwiches for us, two take-away cups of tea and a bar of chocolate to share. A treat for me! We sat on the bench on the village green for our refreshments; Jamal huddled deep in his scarf and bobble hat, feeling the chill of the winter morning, his breath making mist in front of our eyes.

When we had finished eating in companionable silence I asked, 'So what did you do next?'

'I had to make a plan. My first priority had to be Ahmed. If there was anything I could do to stop him I would have done it. I went back to Drumford Mosque and talked around. One young man, and I won't name him, spoke to me one day and asked me to meet him by the children's playground in the corner of Drumford Park later that afternoon. Not wanting to waste the day I went into the library and the unemployment office, to see if anyone had heard what had happened to but also if there were any suitable jobs. Nothing.'

Jamal looked up at me and, reassured by the compassion in my eyes, he continued, 'At 2 pm I was in the park, just outside the gated area so that it would not be suspicious. This young man met me; we shook hands and then we walked through the winter gardens, where we could talk more privately.'

Jamal paused, collecting his thoughts and then looked at me in a daze. I smiled.

'Where was I Auntie?'

'You were telling me about the man in the park.'

'Oh yes, he asked me to promise not to tell the Imam or anyone at The Mosque about our conversation, otherwise he would be thrown out.'

I frowned.

'He needed to be accepted at the Mosque, you see. I promised and then he told me I mustn't speak to anyone in authority about him either.'

'That might have been harder. Go on,' I said, thinking of the police.

'He said that he didn't want me to think bad of him because he was working undercover, helping the Terrorist Crime Squad. I suddenly understood and was no longer frightened that he was going to try to radicalise me too.'

'That makes sense Jamal. Did he have news of Ahmed though?'

'Yes he did. Ahmed *has* joined ISIS and *has* gone back to Syria, Auntie. I couldn't hide that I was afraid, but I knew here,' and Jamal paused placing his hand on his left rib cage, 'that it was true. He hasn't gone to be a suicide bomber either, thank goodness. He's gone to fight, so the man said.'

I sighed. 'So, as far as we know he's still alive.' I was hanging *on to a silk thread* of hope.

'Yes Auntie. As far as they know. A very brave, but foolhardy man. Misguided big time! - were the man's exact words.'

I hated to see Jamal so fraught, pain etched deep within those brown eyes. I covered his hands with my own. It seemed a natural gesture of sympathy, love even.

'Couldn't they stop him?' Though I knew before I'd finished forming the question that it was futile.

'Ahmed *was on their radar,* were his words. I'm not sure I understood but I knew what he meant anyway. They would have tried to stop him but he hid what he was doing with his charity work,'

I felt that glimmer of what I knew to be helpless hope nibble at my consciousness. 'And could he have gone to take aid or something? Could he really be innocent Jamal?'

'It would be lovely if that was true Auntie, but no; they know he's gone to do no good this time Auntie. They hide bad with good, these people. Very clever.'

Jamal's crestfallen face haunted me still in its memory. 'Did he tell you anymore?'

'Yes, that their intelligence showed that my brother *has* left the country. He explained that usually recruits leave quickly, flying to Turkey. Ahmed had just disappeared before they knew he'd left England.'

I paused. 'Oh Jamal, saying I'm so sad to you is hardly enough comfort. Is there anything else we can do?'

'I told the man I was afraid for my brother and asked if there was anything I could do. I told him that Ahmed had not got in touch with me at all and I was so worried. He was all I had.' Jamal coloured again at this point.

'Don't worry Jamal, Ahmed is your only living relative. I understand.'

'Oh, I didn't mean to offend Auntie.'

'You didn't Jamal,' and I squeezed his hand. He smiled a tentative smile, not quite reaching his eyes, but catching my glance momentarily. 'Was there anything else?'

'I told the man I was so disappointed in my brother, and shocked that he would be so gullible. Is that the right word?"

It was my turn to smile affirmation, pleased that, even under this stress, Jamal was trying out new vocabulary. 'Go on.'

'We parted company, not wanting to be seen together. He asked me to contact him if Ahmed got in touch, or if I heard anything, and he gave me his contact details. I was to put it on my phone, disguised in another name, and then destroy the card, then use What's App to get in touch with him.'

'And you Jamal. What did you do?'

'He disappeared into the bushes and I strolled towards the lake to sit amongst the ruins of Belmont House. It was peaceful. I knew that it was one of your favourite spots Mrs G, and you took us there many times.'

I smiled. 'Yes I love it to this day.'

'It's become my safe place too; a link to times when life was simpler when we lived with you Mrs G.'

'Oh Jamal, I'm so sorry I left you without a word.'

'Oh no Auntie, you don't need to explain. You had recently lost your husband too, but I now knew how you felt. I'm not sure whether knowing where Ahmed has gone to is better than Mr G's total disappearance. I really don't know. Both are painful.'

We walked on, quietly digesting all that we had shared, enjoying the view over the fields towards Drumford and catching sight of the river glinting in the December sunshine.

When we had reached the river I asked, 'And so you stayed at Brian's?'

'Yes, he kindly let me sleep on his floor. In fact I gave Brian some of your furniture and I used his bedsit as a base when I could.'

'It sounds as if you've got a longer story to tell me. Would you mind if we called into The Ark to make sure I have a bed for the next few nights. We could even have a hot meal there, if you're not too proud.'

'Oh Auntie; if it's good enough for you then I'm happy. Let's go.'

CHAPTER 20

WE WALKED MY usual trail along the river and up to the entrance of The Ark. There was no-one brave enough to eat in the courtyard that day.

'Hello Laura,' I said as we reached the main desk, behind which was the clothes room.

'What can we do for you today?' she said.

I could see her wondering about my clothes, which of course were quite clean. I knew she was itching to question me about them but a bit embarrassed to ask in front of my guest.

'Have you a place for me for the festivities Laura?'

'Oh, let's have a look at the bookings. She winked at Jamal. 'Is it for the two of you?'

'Oh no,' exclaimed Jamal his face becoming a darker shade of brown, 'I have a place to stay. Just for Mrs G thanks.'

'This is Jamal, Laura. He was my foster son for two special years. He's just found me again.'

I could see that Laura's eyes were welling up through her smile. I knew she was fond of me. 'Oh that's lovely! Hello Jamal. Pleased to meet you! I hope you are dining with us today to keep Dot here company, now that you're back together again.'

'Yes, I'd like to do that.' Jamal smiled back at Laura.

'I'll have my usual after lunch if that's OK Laura.'

Knowing that I was talking about having a bath she grinned, 'No problem Dot. Come back whenever you're ready.'

I led Jamal through to the dining area where I introduced him to Orla. I noticed that there was a spark between the pair straight away, but kept the thought to myself. We found a table on our own and settled to eat sausages, mine were vegetarian, and mash with lashings of tomato sauce. Gerald would never allow the stuff in our house and so I always felt a bit devilish squirting it on the side of my plate. We exchanged polite conversation until Jamal fetched two cups of steaming coffee. His shoulders relaxed as he began to share the remainder of his tale.

'After I knew that there was little I could do to save Ahmed I went back to Brian's flat. His father was there. He runs a breaker's yard and he needed people from time to time to make deliveries and collections around the country.'

'I am pleased for you Jamal.'

'It's casual work mind, but I was happy to have anything I could get. I had permission to work but as yet I did not have permanent residency here and so claiming benefits was out of the question. I didn't like to anyway. This country has blessed me with a new start. I wanted to give something back and not take.'

Jamal sipped his coffee and I smiled reassuringly. I was aware that he must be feeling a certain amount of guilt for his brother's actions – totally unjustified but it was human nature.

'For the next couple of months the work was fairly steady Auntie. I had little rent to pay and so began to save up a bit. I popped into town occasionally and went to places I knew you used to go to on a regular basis – the park, the little cafe on the corner and of course the library. I asked the librarian at the desk if she'd heard anything of you. I think she felt quite sorry for me and I could tell she was fond of you Dot.'

'But how did you find me Jamal.'

'Well, one day, when I was choosing a couple of books to read, she called me over.'

'The young librarian said she didn't know if it was any help but in the previous week a group of local school children came on a trip from Canbury School. She overheard one of them talk about Lady Pink Hat. Well, her *ears pricked up*, is that what you say?' Jamal's head tilted to one side and smiled.

'Yes, it's a lovely expression. It reminds me of foxes. Anyway, go on.'

'She said she remembered that you had a favourite pink floppy hat; quite distinctive, I think were her words. Well, of course I knew it was you so I was very excited.'

'There is a school bus which passes me walking near Canbury sometimes I think the children gave me that name. I quite like it really. A bit eccentric but harmless.'

'eh?'

'Oh Jamal, I'll explain another time. Do go on.'

'One day she overheard a little girl, Greta I think the librarian lady called her, telling her friend about seeing Lady Pink Hat at her parents' farm, in an old house near their farmhouse.'

'Ah, The Grange,' I said knowingly.

'Yes, but then apparently the girl pretended to be a ghost going whoooo! She chased her friend around the book racks until her teacher put a halt to it.' I chuckled at the thought and Jamal continued, 'That's all she said but it got me thinking. There couldn't be many farms near Canbury, especially ones with an old house in the yard.'

I smiled at Jamal, guessing the end of his story, but eager to hear it nevertheless.

'As you can imagine I thanked the librarian and promised that I would let her know if I found you. I sneaked around three farmyards until I saw the one that you were staying in. I had a feeling that I was getting closer to you and was just creeping around the side of the old house when I bumped into you.'

'And here we are!' and we chinked coffee cups, a habit that had made us laugh in happier times. After we had drunk down the remaining dregs of our coffee I was a bit embarrassed to say that I had to go and have a bath. Fortunately Jamal sensed my discomfort and was aware that it was time to make his leave.

'I'll let you settle in now, but since I've found you, can we meet up over the holiday period? I have no work on for the next week.'

'It would be lovely to have a cuppa and a chat but,' I paused, coughing to hide my embarrassment.

'Don't worry Mrs G. I have enough money. How about at the corner cafe around 11 am say?

'That's perfect,' I said smiling.

As we stood to say goodbye Jamal took my hands between his. I had forgotten how tall he was as he peered down on me.

'Now, don't you go running off again. I couldn't bear to lose you two times.'

'Twice,' I corrected him and we laughed. 'I promise Jamal, but take good care of yourself too,' I said as he let go of my hands. 'And thank you so much,' I added as he began to walk away.

I luxuriated in the warm water of my bath, followed by a rub down with a rough but spotlessly clean towel. Laura had given me a colourful change of clothes for the festive season too, and I felt truly blessed.

That evening we had our last creative writing session of the year. Jill returned chapters I had given her to read and stories from the other members and then she gave us one to one feedback while we wrote festive poetry. She was openly excited about my project but gave the advice, 'Write about what you know Dot and places you've been. Don't try to be too ambitious.'

CHAPTER 21

JAMAL WAS THERE to meet me outside the cafe the next morning. I had found sleeping in the dormitory amongst people with variable levels of hygiene a bit of a trial and had slept little. I never do the first night though, but I tried to put this from my mind, dwelling on the positives. He ushered me inside.

Once we had ordered coffee Jamal asked, 'Well, how was your night Auntie?'

'Oh Jamal, I must be grateful that I have a roof over my head and a meal paid for. Once I couldn't even say that. Not long after I became homeless I sold The Big Issue in Bedford one day a week for nearly a year and tried to save every penny so that I could pay the £1 they ask for a meal and a cuppa at The Ark. I can also give a tiny contribution for my bed each night too. I'm much better off than some, I can tell you.'

'I'm sure you are Auntie. I'm glad to have this opportunity to talk to you because I need your help.'

'I can't give ...'

'Oh no, I don't need any money Auntie, and the coffee here is on me by the way. No it's not that.' Jamal paused.

'Go on.'

'Now that I've found you and I also know where Ahmed is,' Jamal frowned. 'There's not a lot I can do to help him at the moment. No, what I'd really like to do next, if you are willing to help me, is to try and look for Mr G.' He paused, diverting his eyes from my face. 'Or at least to find the truth about what actually happened to him,' he added in a barely audible whisper.

I was shocked to be honest. I'd managed these past months to avoid thinking about my former life. I'd blanked it off. Instead I enjoyed pausing to watch a hare scamper across a field of stubble, a hawk gliding over the hedgerows ready to swoop for its prey, or spotting a tiny vole sniffing for its hole in the undergrowth. These things took up one hundred percent of my concentration. Latterly, of course, my mind had been filled with books and my Nun's Tale. There had been no time to dwell. No time to think about my wayward husband. It was as if I'd started afresh, but here was Jamal confronting me with threads of my former life which seemed to be wrapping themselves around me afresh. However I was also touched by his concern. What could I say to this young man, hardly more than a boy, who had suffered so much?

'It's nice of you to think of it but I don't know where we'd start Jamal. I'm not sure if I even *want* to know the truth.'

'But wouldn't it put your mind at rest. I'm still frantically worried about Ahmed, but there's nothing I can do about it. It's so good to be with you again Mrs G. I was lost when you disappeared.'

'I'm glad you found me too,' I smiled at him, attempting to relieve myself of the burden of guilt. 'I thought about Mr G many times when I was in your flat. I felt anger, hurt, sadness and at other times I was totally bewildered.'

I looked at Jamal's puzzled expression which I interpreted in an instant. 'It means I really could not understand what had happened to me. I was confused – stunned might be a word you would use more.' I could feel my eyes misting over. 'More recently it's just been easier to forget. Can you understand that?'

'Not really Mrs G. I'd travel the world over in search of Ahmed if I knew I had a hope of bringing him back.'

'What do you suggest we do then?' I said with hesitation, realising that what Jamal needed was a project to focus on. What harm could it do?

'Well, I've been asking around. Did you know that The Red Cross tries to trace missing persons?'

'I think the police went down that route. If they'd found anything then they didn't tell me.'

'There are two things I'd like us to try. Firstly I'd like us both to go to The Red Cross after the New Year, Auntie. Until then I'd like you to tell me a bit about your life with Mr G. Tell me about places you went to together that meant something to you. I've been reading about missing people. With young people they tend to head to the big cities, thinking they'll find excitement and work maybe – an easy place to find some nook to hide in.'

I smiled at this turn of phrase Jamal must have picked up recently.

'I've read the word *nook* in a book Auntie. It is right isn't it?'

I nodded, 'perfect Jamal, please go on.'

'Anyway, I've also read that older people, on the whole, tend to revisit haunts of the past; places where they have been happy or maybe go in search of their roots. When we meet for coffee each morning I'll make a note of anywhere you can think of and do my best to follow up those leads, especially if my job takes me in that direction. What do you say?'

I thought for a while. What did I have to lose? 'OK,' I answered, 'shall we begin tomorrow and I'll have a think about it overnight.'

'That sounds like a plan Mrs G. Tomorrow it is then. It's Christmas Eve isn't it? Are you going to the service at Drumford Parish Church?'

'I wasn't thinking to, but since you mention it, I'll go if you'll come with me.'

'Of course I will Auntie. I hope you sleep better tonight.'

We parted company outside the cafe, his hand just grasping mine momentarily before he left, as if he had to reassure himself that I was real.

When I disappeared it never dawned on me that Jamal would take it so hard and I felt the great impact of remorse.

CHAPTER 22

WE MET AT the cafe at 11 am on the 24th. I'd been dwelling on Jamal's questions all through the previous evening and then dropped off into a heavy dreamless sleep. There were so many memories to share with him that I could hardly contain myself as we waited for our coffees. He sat with a notebook in front of him, poised ready to write.

'Well,' I said. 'We were married in Drumford Church but went away to Brighton for a couple of nights for our honeymoon.'

'Do you remember where you stayed?'

'The Bell View Guest House, a couple of streets from the sea front. It wasn't posh or anything but it was really special to us.'

'Did you live in Drumford all of your married life?'

'Oh yes, we never moved.'

'So where else did you visit?

'We were a bit boring. Until a few years back we had a campervan and frequently travelled down to Cornwall – The Lizard. We stayed at a site near Coverack every other year.'

'And?'

'Well, on alternate years we headed north. Cumbria and Northumberland were our favourites, never in one place although we became very fond of a pub in a village near Penrith. We'd often stop there a night before setting off either east or west. The Queen's Head I think it was called, in a village beginning with 'T'. They were very friendly people, until the last time we stayed there and the owners said that they were selling up and moving over to Spain. The next time we visited it was all boarded up. A shame really. Such a lovely place.'

'Can you remember the name of the village?'

'Not off the top of my head. Let me think for a moment.'

Jamal remained quiet watching me closely as my eyes narrowed and pursed my lips.

Suddenly it came to me and my face relaxed. 'Tirry or Tirral or something like that. Yes, that's it. Tirril near Ulswater. Beautiful spot. We are talking about ten years ago now, although Gerald was up there on business once and did remark recently that it was still empty.'

'Would you be able to find it on a map?'

'I should think so. We could pop to the library but I think it closed at noon today; it being Christmas Eve.'

OK, and did you go abroad on holiday at all?'

'Only four times recently. One holiday in Scotland.' I laughed, 'I mustn't call Scotland abroad yet must I, but it was our first holiday out of England. Next we went to France, then another holiday in Greece and the last in New York; after which he performed his disappearing act at the airport.'

'Let's forget New York for now. Tell me about your holiday in Scotland.'

'We travelled up the east coast through Northumberland. We were so lucky with the weather and visited Holy Island on the way. In fact it was a tale of three Holy isles because next we camped near to Edinburgh and had a boat trip along the Forth to Inchcolm Abbey which they call the Iona of the east. Gerald loved seeing the Forth Rail Bridge in all its glory from the boat. It was a magical day with seals basking on the buoys and we even spotted a pod of dolphins in the distance.'

'That sounds lovely. I'm not all that sure what dolphins are but I'll Google it later. Go on. You said three Holy islands?'

'Yes, that's right. After that we drove over the old Forth Road Bridge. I hear there's a new one now but we haven't returned since then. We camped outside Perth near Scone Palace. We were heading north west and our next stop was Oban, the gateway to the isles.'

'Hang on a minute Mrs G. I can't keep up with you.'

'Let's have a look.' I peered over his notes. 'Yes you've got it right. Edinbur, Purth, then Oban and Mull. You need a *gh* on the end of Edinburgh and an *e* in Perth. You're doing really well Jamal. It's not easy.'

'Is that right?' Jamal turned the paper to me. I nodded and smiled. 'I like you telling it like a story but I'm not very good at picking out the places Mrs G.'

'OK. After camping overnight we took the ferry to Mull; a beautiful journey which took about an hour. It was another hour to drive across the island to Fionnphort, a little hamlet on the west coast where the ferry leaves for Iona. Don't worry about the hamlet but you need *I o n a.* Yes that's good.' I paused a moment then continued, 'Anyway, the campsite there was different from any in my previous experience; so wild and beautiful, with the island of Iona tantalizingly close across the water. Everyone was so friendly. We made this our base for a few days, exploring on foot and taking the ferry to Iona on a couple of occasions. I must say, of all of the places Gerald and I visited, this was our most memorable, apart from New York of course.'

'I think maybe a careful look at a map would help me, Mrs G?'

'Yes I agree Jamal. Well, on the way back south we stopped overnight near Peebles and visited New Lanark Mills, an amazing restored eighteenth century purpose built village, much like Cadbury's or Bournville, only so beautiful, set down a river gorge. I must admit we were quite taken by its history, both of us. They really looked after their workers when it was built – food, health, welfare, spiritual guidance and accommodation. It was innovative in its day, that's for sure.'

I don't think I need the detail but is this right, *New Lanark Mills?*'

'Yes, nearly. There's an *r* in Lanark though.'

Jamal frowned a little as I reached over to point to the missing letter. I smiled encouragement.

'After that we stopped once more on the edge of the Lake District and had a meal in The Queen's Head; the pub I've mentioned before. I've no idea why, but it became a favourite haunt of ours.'

'Phew! It all sounds really nice but you said you visited Greece and France too. They're big places I believe. Do you remember any details about your trips?'

'Oh Jamal. In France we took our campervan and toured the Loire Valley and the Dordogne. Our Greek holiday was on the island of Corfu but I have no idea of the names of the places. If I think about it over the next few days then maybe more will come back to me. Here let's write those down for you.'

'That's great Mrs G. Lots for me to work on. When we go to the library after Christmas we could look for a map of *Corfu* on the Internet. Let's leave it for now. What time is the service?'

'At 6 o'clock tonight. There'll be a carol service with all the children around the crib. If you're sure you want to come I'll meet you at the gate at 5.45 pm. Is that OK?'

'That's fine Mrs G. I'll see you later then.'

The remainder of my Christmas went in a whirl. Jamal not only came to church with me, which gave me such pleasure, but he also came to help at the Christmas Dinner at The Ark on Christmas Day. I could tell that the attraction between Jamal and Orla was growing and for me it was the best gift I could have been given. I did wonder, as I glanced up and spotted them holding hands at one point, while all of us gave a rendition of *We Wish You a Merry Christmas,* how it might work out. Orla, as far as I knew was Roman Catholic. I wondered what difficulties they might encounter as I fell asleep that night. As I dropped off I experienced an inner glow, a feeling of being loved and wanted and I remembered something the Imam said to me once. "If only we could concentrate on our likenesses rather than our differences, then the world would be a far better place. After all, the roots of all our religions have the same origins."

On Boxing Day Jamal was invited to join Brian's family for lunch, but he popped in to say hello in the evening for half an hour. I think it might have been on the pretence to speak with Orla, but anyway he explained to me that the two of them had decided to take the train from Bedford to Brighton the next day. While they were gone I had a quiet but busy day reading and writing my story, which Orla had locked away for me in a cupboard.

On the 28th we had arranged to have coffee together, all three of us.

'We found the Bell View Guest House, Auntie. The lady who ran it, Mrs Mc Donald, a lovely Scottish lady, said that she'd done so for forty years. Unsurprisingly, she didn't remember you and Mr G though, but she did show us the bridal suite where you must have stayed. Orla was that embarrassed,' Jamal laughed.

Orla giggled, digging Jamal in the ribs, 'Enough of that Jamal! 'Then we went on the pier Mrs G and had fish and chips, like you suggested. Great they were.'

'We were always looking out for Mr G though,' Jamal continued. 'We even went into the police station and gave them a photo to copy.' He looked a bit sheepish here. 'I rescued it from a pile you'd put aside to throw out. It was a long shot but maybe they'll come up with something. What have you been doing today Mrs G?'

'I've been writing. I found this diary in one of the books at The Grange and it's inspired me to do some creative writing.'

'Can I have a read?'

'No, not yet Jamal. One day perhaps. I don't want to talk about it to anyone except to my tutor for now.'

'Good for you Mrs G. I'll look forward to reading it as well. What will you do next Jamal,' Orla glanced at him as she spoke.

'Shall we go to the library tomorrow Mrs G?' said Jamal.

'Yes, that's fine. I expect you are back to work Orla.'

'I'm afraid so and I must go back to The Ark now in fact.'

'I'll walk you there,' Jamal smiled at Orla, her cheeks glowing in response, then getting up he broke the spell and turned to me. '11 am as usual then Mrs G?'

'That'll be lovely and,' I got to my feet and rested my hands on each of their arms, 'thank you so much the pair of you.'

'No need,' smiled Jamal, then my eyes followed them walking along the street hand in hand until they were out of sight. Even then Jamal turned and waved before disappearing.

I enjoyed a stroll in the park and day dreamed as I walked. I reflected on how my circumstances had changed. I was still homeless, yes, but I now had a purpose. Jamal too. My expectations for him coming up with anything were slim but looking for Gerald gave him something to focus on and mask his own loss for a while. I also thought of that Bridal Suite and my nervousness as a new bride. I had been high on optimism for our future life together and held hopes of conceiving that elusive family.

In the period of time between Christmas and New Year, that unobtainable exclusive club for families, I bided my time and found quiet corners in The Ark in order to write. Not always easy but on the whole folks left me alone and I could tune out of the everyday sounds as I concentrated. I absorbed my whole self into the life of my characters, with them as my companions. My discussions with Jamal had miraculously focussed my attention on the journey Millie and Jack were to undertake too, although they still gave me many surprises on the way.

The Nun's Tale Part 2

Millie and Jack on the Canals

As they stood on the hillside over-looking Drumford, Millie vowed that she would return one day and find her son and that She would never forget him. Jack forbade her from talking about it and became angry at the slightest mention. Relations between them were strained.

They had little money when they escaped Belmont Park but Jack knew that they had to get right away and at speed. Which way to go? He decided that north would be best, to unknown places. Once out of Bedfordshire they felt safe from the parish constables who might have known them, or familiar faces who would have betrayed them for a reward. Had the gentleman died and would he be facing murder charges? There was no way of knowing the truth, but the uncertainty and threat of possible hanging gnawed into him and kept them both moving, ever watchful of strangers asking questions.

Relying on Millie's meagre savings to get by, they didn't stop walking until they reached Northampton. It was the end of August and harvest time. There were plenty of farms who were grateful for casual labour, no questions asked. They lighted upon a farm in Kingsthorpe through which a tributary of the River Nene flowed. In shared lodgings with two other families Millie was put to use cleaning and baking for the men who worked in the fields. Each day she was aware of the poor at the edge of the fields and gave thanks that she had been spared that life. Surely her life, now Jack was with her, would improve.

Ever restless and fearful, a couple of weeks in one place was enough before moving on, ever northwards. Once the harvest was over at one farm they would slip away before the celebrations took place, uncertain as to whether they were being followed. In fact, on one occasion Jack heard rumours that two riders had arrived in the town looking for a runaway couple. They had been working out in a field on the outskirts of West Bridgford near Nottingham when one of the men, who was working in the farthest field, saw two riders in the distance. He mentioned it that evening as they ate supper.

Jack and Millie didn't stay long enough to glean any details, but fled that very evening. As they ate their meagre meal Jack signalled to Millie to come with him back to the outhouses where they were staying.

'We must gather our things together immediately Millie, and head north, avoiding Nottingham if we can.' She didn't need to ask why.

They were just crossing the Trent as the sun was setting, sending colours of stunning magnitude in the harvest dust, when their first fortunate coincidence struck. A barge, which had discharged its cargo of wood in the city and taken on full barrels, was having difficulties. The lad, who should be leading the horse was so nervous that he had spooked the animal by stumbling over a tree stump. The horse had reared in the confusion and stamped on the boy's leg.

'Ohhhh,' screamed the boy, writhing in agony on the bank. Millie rushed to his side and took his hand. Her gentleness hushed him.

'Just you lay back and I'll see what I can do,' she smiled. Millie tended the lad, taking her scarf and wrapping it tightly around the lad's leg to stop the bleeding.

Without hesitation Jack, who had spent a lifetime with horses at Grange Farm, ran down from the bridge and grabbed the reins, talking soothingly as he gained control of the beast.

Soon trust had developed between Jack and the horse and he tied him securely to a mooring. Once Jack felt reassured that the animal would remain calm he turned his attention to the irate bargeman whose barge was almost at right angles to the bank, a danger to him, his vessel and other river users on this busy stretch of waterway.

'Hey you,' the bargeman yelled, 'tie that rope and grab hold of this one.'

With no time to carry out the first instruction Jack stretched to catch the second rope, the first slipping from his grasp in the confusion.

'You idiot,' shouted the frustrated bargeman, helplessly standing on the edge of his barge as it drifted away from the bank.

'I'm doing my best,' shouted Jack as he pulled the barge towards him and secured it firmly, while the bargeman nimbly ran to the far end of his barge and retrieved the other rope from the water.

'... and this one,' he barked as the rope flew through the air towards Jack, who guided the barge parallel to the bank and secured the rope to another mooring just as the bargeman leapt off, his wife following close behind.

'You stupid boy!' his wife yelled as she reached Millie. 'What are we going to do now? Suppose you can't walk at all.'

Millie continued to tend to the wounds, ignoring the woman's attitude. 'Have you a piece of wood I can use as a splint?' she asked sweetly, hoping her kindly attitude might soften the woman's demeanour.

'Oh yes, I'll fetch some,' the woman replied, grunting with disgust and huffing and puffing as she climbed back on to the barge to retrieve one of the larger pieces of kindling wood. By the time she'd returned, her husband and Jack were deep in conversation. The lad was sitting up, and although his face was ashen with pain, he was leaning back against Millie's breasts and was enjoying the mixed messages of comfort.

'So you'd be willing to lead the barge all the way to Hull then, while my son recovers?'

'It would do us a favour to be honest with you. We are heading north and the roads will be barely passable as autumn turns to winter.'

'You'd want no pay like. Just food and a place to lay yer head for the night.'

'Yes, that's right.'

'Yer know that it's pretty cramped down there under the tarpaulin?'

'Oh yes. That's no matter.'

The man looked puzzled for a while but finally agreed, although Jack could see that he was wondering what the catch was.

Millie and the reluctant wife carried the lad on to the barge and Millie made him as comfortable as possible on a straw sack. The women jostled in the sparse space which they were to share while Jack and the bargeman set to work.

Soon Jack had found a good pace and only needed to be shown how the locks worked once to be able to master their complexity. He enjoyed walking in the fresh air and whistled the afternoon away.

That night as they shared supper, a hearty vegetable broth, Jack was curious about their cargo, 'So you're taking the barrels of beer to Hull then. Is that a port?'

'Yes, lad. It's a big port on the east coast. It's where we're from.'

'Where will the beer go to next?'

'Russia, I expect. We unload the beer and then load wood from Russia for the return journey.'

'Is that for furniture making then?'

'No lad. Burton on Trent, which was the town we've just come from, makes the best beer and it needs to be matured in wooden barrels. The wood is to make the barrels. Good exchange I'd say, wouldn't you? Me name's Alf by the way and the wife's Joan.'

'Jack and she's Millie; so grateful to you to take us on,' said Jack nodding his head towards Millie before they settled in the cramped space for the night.

At dusk two nights later Jack was just tying Major, the horse, to graze on grass near the tow path when he spied two riders approaching, talking to another bargeman half a mile back after the last bend in the canal. Jack hid behind bushes nearby as nonchalantly as he could as if to relieve himself and waited. Soon enough the horses approached and he listened intently.

'Good evening to you,' one of the gentlemen directed his attention to Alf.

'Good evenin,' Alf replied, tapping his cap out of respect.

'Have you seen a young couple hereabouts, around twenty years old I would say? The lass's name's Millie.'

From Jack's vantage point he could see Alf's expression which had remained totally neutral. The barge man took in a breath. 'Well.' Then he paused for effect. 'I've not seen many folks along this tow path. What do they look like, can you tell me that?'

Jack willed Millie not to show her face above the tarpaulin and almost gasped when a head appeared, but it was Alf's wife. 'And why pray might you be lookin' for them, may I ask?'

The gent looked from one to the other, a fierce looking woman and the more kindly looking man. 'Tallish lad with black curly hair and a younger long fair haired lass; pretty girl by all accounts,' he said. 'The girl absconded from her work down at Belmont House in Drumford near Bedford and the lad is wanted for questioning by our constable for assault.'

'Why you looking all t'way up here then? Bedford's miles away down south isn't is?'

'Madam,' the first gentleman continued trying to be patient. 'We have followed their tracks north and a couple matching their description were seen fleeing a farm not far south of Nottingham a couple of days ago. Have either of you seen them or we must be on our way?'

At that point the other rider turned his horse, obviously exasperated by the lack of response and infuriated by the questions from these lesser folks. Jack almost gasped when he realised that it was Master Belmont in person, the one he had knocked to the ground. Millie, on the other hand, recognised his voice and shrank even further under cover, putting her finger to her lips to silence the young lad Billie, who was inclined to speak.

'No, we've seen no one of that description hereabouts. There was a fair haired lad walking up yonder a couple of hours ago but he was on his own.' He gave a subtle but clear warning glance to his wife to keep quiet for once.

'Well, if you see a couple matching our description please let the river authorities know and they'll get word to us somehow. Good night to you.' And they turned their horses back along the tow path towards the last village of Kelham, where they would probably find accommodation for the night.

When the gentlemen were out of sight Alf sighed. 'You can both come out now but before we go any further you can tell us your story. The truth mind and we'll decide what to do wi' you.' He looked sternly at their scared faces and then softened. 'But we'll eat first missus.' He turned to his wife who busied herself with getting the meal served.

They ate a wholesome broth, Millie almost too nervous to eat for fear of being turned in. Once complete they huddled around the stove for warmth because it was a particularly cold September night.

'Well?' said Alf, looking pointedly at them both. 'We knew there was sommat wrong with the pair of you.'

Jack started, 'Millie here was in service at Belmont Manor. We'd met at The Grange, a place just outside Drumford, because she was training to be a nun.' He blushed at this point, taking a breath. 'Well, let's say that it didn't work out that way and I became very fond of her.'

The wife grinned at Millie, whose cheeks went a bright crimson, visible in the fading light. 'Not so holier than thou lass,' she smirked.

'Be quiet, Joan,' hushed Alf looking to Jack to continue.

'Anyway, Millie here found work at Belmont House and on my days off I went to see if I could catch a glimpse of her. One day she'd wandered down to the lake where she wasn't supposed to go and the master, one of the gents you saw just now; the quiet one; he tried to force Millie,' he paused here at a loss for words, 'you know, he tried to rape her. Well, I couldn't stand by and let him and so I came out from my hiding place and pushed him. Unfortunately he fell back, his head landing on a tree stump with quite a crack and...'

'You fled, not knowing if he was dead or alive,' said Alf.

'We checked to see if he was breathing, but we weren't too sure,' said Jack, bowing his head in shame, as did Millie.

It was Joan who took over now and asked Alf to come off the boat to discuss their situation. Millie and Jack could hear them whispering but could not make out what they were *saying, just the odd word. When they returned it was Alf who spoke.*

'Right the pair o' you. We're law abiding folks and what you did was wrong, but we can't condone what the so called gent tried to do to Millie here either and no harm's done as far as we can see, except to his pride. It would be a great injustice if either of you were hanged for the offence. The law is always weighed against us poorer folks anyway.' He paused looking at them both and then continued. 'We've agreed to help you both since you in turn are helping us out of our predicament. We knew there was sommat odd about you though, but we won't turn you in as long as you do as we ask.' Alf turned to his wife who continued, 'Alf will shave those locks off your head lad and lend you one of his caps. I'll cut your hair too Millie and we'll dye it with tea. A waste of good tea leaves but needs must. We'll make up the strong tea solution now and pour it carefully over your head, rubbing it in and wrapping it with one of my dark brown scarves to do its work overnight.'

Once Jack's hair was shaved off Alf said, 'We must get a few hours shut eye but in the early hours we should move on to try to give ourselves a bit of distance from this area. Fortunately nobody knows us around here because we are from Hull, but the other barge folks do and you can't be too careful.'

By six the following morning they had travelled another twenty miles further up the river and risked having a rest before moving on and working another twelve hour day. They did not stop until the sun was dipping over the fields once more. They'd reached Gainsborough.

'We've enough space between us and our pursuers to breathe a little, but you must remember that their speed could be twice as fast as us. Be vigilant at all times. You're not safe

yet.' It was the longest speech Alf had made and Millie was touched by the care she could discern in his voice.

As it happened they did not see the horsemen again and began to relax as their journey continued all the way to the River Humber and Hull, Alf and Joan's destination. During the days Millie sensed that even Joan's severe countenance had softened towards them as Millie busied herself with tending to Billie and darning. Once they reached the Humber there was no time to think as they navigated into the main river and headed for the port.

The following night, after Alf and Jack had unloaded the cargo of barrels, they ate together one last time.

'So you won't be returning with us to Burton then I shouldn't think?' Alf asked, knowing what their response would be.

'I think we'll continue to head north Alf. Will you manage without us since Billie's not yet recovered enough to take over?'

'That's alright lad. We come from near here. My cousin's son will do it willingly. He's been pestering me to take him on this past year so now's his chance to prove himself. We'll leave our Billie with me sister. Now, I know of someone who might take you across to Leeds which is west of here. My brother's going that way if that's any help. Where are you headin?'

'Dunno really. As far north as possible I'd say. Is Leeds north then?'

'Leeds is west of here but it will give you lots of options. I've heard there's jobs at the docks but I think you'd best be far away from Hull too. There's Liverpool which is west of here but maybe it's a bit south of us too.'

'I don't know where we're heading but all I know is that we'll continue north if we can, but thanks anyway.'

'Well, once at Leeds you can get the stage coach from Keighley but it'll cost yer. Here's five shillings for yer trouble but we've got one more bit of advice for you both.'

'Oh, what's that,' Jack said a little more suspiciously than he'd meant to.

Millie shot him a look. 'We're so grateful for all your help Alf. You too Joan.'

'A pleasure,' said Alf who was quite fond of the pair now. 'Now, before we introduce you to this brother of mine we think you need te change yer names. It's still too dangerous, even though you're disguised a bit now.'

'I don't know why we didn't think of that before,' said Jack. 'We'll be Maud and Archie from now on. What do you think?'

'Sounds perfect,' Alf replied.

'How about us having a drink together to celebrate and I will introduce you to me brother Peter. He's off to Leeds tomorrow so it will suit you well. He often travels on his own so he could do with a bit of company.'

Archie and Alf headed to an alehouse in the back streets of Hull harbour leaving the ladies behind on the barge.

'They'll as like as not come back drunk Maud. That's not such a bad name and at least it begins with the same letter. My sister's name is Maud.'

'I don't think I've ever seen ...' and Maud hesitated, 'Archie drunk.'

'Oh, my Alf is always a bit frisky so I warn you. This is the only time we have the luxury of a bit of space if he's a mind to. He's always pleased with hisself when he's shed a load.' At which point Joan roared with laughter at her own joke.

Not understanding why her companion was full of mirth Maud said, 'I'm sure Archie won't do that. He wouldn't touch me.'

Joan gave Maud a sideways look, shrugged her shoulders but said nothing. 'Best to give your hair another dose of tea before you leave us while we're waiting then.'

Alf and Archie did come back more than a little inebriated and Maud encouraged Archie to come to the end of the barge nearest to Billie. At first he was amorous, adopting tactics he'd used to lure Millie back at The Grange, but she'd have none of his advances and in the end he fell into a drink induced stupor.

The following morning all was forgotten and Archie helped Alf manoeuvre the barge and load his new cargo before they bade Alf and Joan farewell and walked half a mile along the river bank to meet up with Peter who was loading large bales. Archie helped him to stack the last of them. They talked very little as Archie and Peter prepared his barge,

The Merry Girl, to leave, but once underway Archie asked, 'So what are we carrying in those bales Peter?'

'Flax for the mills near Leeds.'

'What's that for then?'

'It's to weave into linen. The flax comes all the way from eastern Baltic countries across the North Sea.'

'Have you travelled over the sea then?'

'Oh no. The Merry Girl isn't sea worthy. You need quite a different vessel for that; a larger one for a start, and much wider. We're heading out west now, first on the Humber and then we pick up the Aire and Calder Canal.'

There was no more time to talk since Peter needed to navigate the busy stretch of water up the Humber away from the port of Hull and so Archie took charge of Bright, his nag. Archie naturally adopted the responsibility of dealing with the lock gates while Peter steered. He often travelled in tandem with another couple and their barge, spreading the work load between them, but his best friend Graeme had hurt *his back lifting awkwardly and was confined to his parents' cottage for a few weeks, so this arrangement was ideal. Maud, meanwhile, took the time to organise the crazy mess of a living space Peter seemed to be used to. Once it was done she began to prepare a potato soup.*

The three settled into the rhythm of life on board and after a few hours the pair stopped looking over their shoulder for men on horseback. They travelled a twelve hour day, Archie marvelling at the peacefulness around them as he strolled between the locks leading the docile Bright. At three miles per hour it was going to take them two days to reach Leeds.

On the second day Peter began to ask questions but Archie was reticent to disclose too much. The less people knew about their past the better.

'So where're ye off to then?'

'We're heading north but we're not sure where. We need to find work on the way if we can.'

'You could always work at' mills, even if it's just through the winter months, or if you're determined to head further there's always oats to be harvested at this time of year. You'd have to go back east for cabbages and Brussels sprouts though.' Peter scratched his head.

'You think we could get work with the oat harvest then?'

'Possibly, if you're in luck. It's mainly sheep and cattle grazing about here. Most people work at' mills or in the mines. Here are a few coppers for your trouble and an old leather water bottle of mine. I think you'll need both on yer travels.'

'Thanks for that and for your advice Peter. It's been good travelling with you.'

'You sure yer not comin back wi' me?'

'Thanks all the same Peter, we'd have liked to give you company for your return trip but the weather's going to turn soon so we'd best be on our way tomorrow.'

Archie and Peter moored The Merry Girl just along from Water Hall Mills. They settled down for their last night together and by morning a delicate mist had settled over the still water in the glow of sunrise. Maud was first to stir and she stood breathing in the fresh cool air. She gasped at the imposing three storey red brick building ahead of them reflected in the still waters; two swans added to the completeness of this idyllic picture. Maud would remember this moment and was reluctant to leave the relative safely of Peter's barge.

The men appeared a few moments later, glad to take their fill of porridge, which Maud had simmered overnight on the dying embers of the stove. Next Archie helped Peter manoeuvre The Merry Girl to the mill and they were pleased to be first to unload his cargo of flax. Once this task was complete Archie's last responsibility was to return the barge to its moorings of the night before, on the other side of the canal, before it was time for the two of them to take their leave.

'It's eleven miles from Leeds to the nearest turnpike in Bradford and then nearly ten miles to Keighley. You'd probably best to keep your money and walk it though. It's not so far.'

They bade Peter farewell and set off at a good pace. The air was crisp but thankfully it was dry and they reached the outskirts of Bradford just as it was getting dark. Luck would have it that they spied a tiny shepherd hut in the hills fairly close to the road, but far enough away from the farm for them not to be noticed in the gloom. They traipsed up the field and peered in. Fortunately it was empty and so they settled down for the night, eating the last of the bread Peter had given them.

It was still dark when Archie woke Maud. 'We must be away now before anyone's about. Come on.'

With Maud hurrying behind, Archie strode along the road towards the town. It was market day and Maud was able to use some money sparingly for some provisions; apples, a hunk of bread and some cheese would last them a few days.

Archie was restless, wishing to distance them from civilisation and so they headed on towards Keighley where Archie looked out for shelter for the night, Maud dragging a few yards behind him, her eyes drooping. This time they were not so fortunate and huddled together in an area of scrubland. After only a couple of hours the cold had reached deep within them and so they continued in the waxing moon light until they had skirted the town.

By dawn both struggled, foot sore and exhausted. Finding the shelter and anonymity of a woodland on the outskirts of Skipton they gathered a bed of leaves in the hollow of an ancient tree trunk and Archie lay a fan of broken branches over them. Maud was already asleep although her eyelids were flickering in a dreamlike state. He could see her features in the dappled moonlight. Momentarily he thought of Maud's sister Evie and his face softened, only to be replaced by a frown as Maud opened her eyes.

'Go back to sleep,' he said, choking back his emotion before pulling Maud close, predominantly to share her warmth. For a while Maud lay there, unsure as to the source of the sheer pain she'd witnessed in Archie's eyes, before she fell back into a deep sleep.

The pair slept on late and when they awoke they shared some of their food. Neither showed enthusiasm for another walk ahead. As they were heading back to the road the sound of dogs barking reached their ears; the frenzied kerfuffle was all too familiar, reminding them of their life at The Grange where the sight of The Hunt was a regular event.

Both quickened their pace but the noise was gaining on them. Archie glanced up at a large oak tree ahead and grabbed the lower branch, swinging himself up to safety. He pulled Maud up beside him just in time. They were trespassing he knew, but what he did not know was that the woodland was owned by Skipton Castle.

A hound paused at the tree, suspiciously excited by their scent. Luck would have it that a fox sprang out of his hiding not far away and chased off towards the east, the hound and his fellow dogs in hot pursuit. A couple of riders paused nearby. Maud gasped making the horse snicker as she recognised one of the men. After a moment, which felt like a lifetime, he too thrashed his horse with his whip and rode off after the hounds.

Quiet descended with only the sound of the gentle rustle of leaves in the trees; their refuge. Maud breathed out. She was shaking. Archie too fought off the fear of capture and thoughts of the consequences. The gallows sprang to mind. He shivered too. They waited several minutes, their breaths steadying in unison.

Archie dropped to the ground first, holding his arms out to protect Maud's fall, but unfortunately she fell awkwardly and twisted her ankle. Demoralised and confused they sat resting against the wide girth of the tree. How could they have come so far and yet not travelled any closer to safety? Archie passed the remainder of their water bottle to Maud whose teeth were chattering. They shared the water between them before Archie crept as stealthily as he could to the edge of the forest and the road. He was distraught and not for the first time wondered what had possessed him to follow Maud from

The Grange; although in his heart he knew the reason full well. He'd had no alternative but to escape his past but he longed for the twinkle of a willing girl. Now though, he was tempted to leave Maud there in the woods. After all, she'd only hinder his progress and had rebuffed his advances. How dare she! Their money was safe in his pocket. He gave it a chink to make sure. He peered through the mist along the road, its whiteness clouding his indecision.

Just as he was about to make his escape he heard the sound of horses' hooves and so he retreated into the shadow of the bushes. The whoosh of a cart was now unmistakable and he was just about to appear and flag it down when a shuffle behind him signalled Maud, who had dragged herself after him, her left foot trailing somewhat in her wake. The farmer, sensing their predicament but also a way of making a few pennies stopped.

'Where you headin?'

Remembering the sign back along the road from yesterday Archie said, 'Kendal, eventually.'

'Well,' the farmer paused. 'I can take you both to Ingleton for two pence. Take it or leave it. I'm gonna visit relatives there, but its payment up front mind.'

Archie nodded. 'Thank you.'

'Hop in the back of the cart then and mind me veg won't you. No! Don't sit on them. Push them aside. That's right. Let yer wife in first. Give her a hand man.'

The farmer's exasperated tone motivated Archie to be more considerate.

'Oh, there you go Mrs,' he said, lifting Maud like a sack of potatoes into the cart, following close behind her. He turned to see the farmer's outstretched hand and pulled out two coppers, careful to hide the rest of his money from leering

eyes. Then they were away before he had a chance to sit down and he nearly tumbled off.

The farmer hooted with mirth as Archie, red faced, squeezed into the tiny space between Maud and a pile of carrots. The journey was uncomfortably bumpy and not much faster than walking pace, had Maud been able to. Maud, on the other hand, was so grateful she gave Archie a shy smile.

Archie was pleased that the farmer wanted no introductions or to hold conversation. The wind had whipped the mist away but the clouds were heavy with rain. The occasional shower soaked through their coats and reminded them that winter wouldn't be far behind. Maud shivered, her ankle throbbing. She was so relieved to be resting it.

Before they arrived Archie enquired,

'Is there any work about?'

The farmer looked thoughtful.

'Your best bet is to make your way to Kendal and help with the oat harvest that's just starting. Apart for a few veg for ourselves and our kin, it's mainly livestock around these parts. Or there's always the coalfield at Ingleton or the mill of course.'

Not liking the thought of mining and being more used to farming Archie asked, 'How far away is Kendal from here?'

'A little less than twenty mile I'd say.'

'Any ideas as to the best way to get there with the wife ...' and Archie nodded in Maud's direction.

'Plenty of coal carts going that way. Filthy mind, but I expect you'd have no trouble if you're prepared to pay your way. I'll see what I can do.'

'Thanks.'

The farmer stopped in the village of Ingleton and there were two coal carts pulled up at the local hostelry.

'Wait here,' he said as he headed for the door.

Ten minutes later, just as Archie was getting restless, the farmer came out with a coalman.

'Two pence and I'll take you all the way to a farm I know near Kendal where you should be able to find work.'

'Agreed,' replied Archie, No questions asked, was added in silent eye contact. He helped Maud to transfer into the coal cart, trying, without much success, to find a patch of sacking to sit on that wasn't too blackened.

They thanked the farmer and were on their way. Their fortune at gaining transport was marred by the change in weather as the rain, at first light showers, became torrential. The driver of the cart had to stop more than once for Archie to encourage the horses to pull them out of deep squelchy pits in the road. Many a time Archie swore under his breath that he would have been better off walking on his own and wondered if their chances of escape were greater if they had parted.

It was almost dark when they arrived at the farm where the coal was duly delivered and the coalman's passengers dispatched into the clucking care of the farmer's wife, Edith.

'Yes, we do need labourers as it happens. There's lots of sickness around here and all healthy hands are needed to do their part. I'll put you in a dry barn but don't worry; the sick ones have been sent back to be tended in the village. We can't take any chances of losing any more workers.'

As they followed her across the yard and into the barn she sighed, 'you poor things! I'll find you some clean dry clothes and there's soup warming in the pot over there. Help yersels.'

Maud dished out two platefuls of soup before sinking on to a pile of straw, water dripping from her eyelashes into the steaming broth, her body tingling as the stress of the journey caught up with her. The warmth of the soup began to thaw *her as it slipped down. She glanced around the barn, a shy smile catching the eyes of three women and their families, with whom they would be sharing this accommodation.*

There was a flurry at the door as Edith returned and lay down some clothes for them, 'Tomorrow's Sunday,' she said. 'That'll give the crops a chance to dry out after this storm and then work'll start early for you on Monday. You're used to farm ways then?'

They nodded, trying to smile.

'There's where you'll sleep,' she gestured towards a vacant area of bales covered in sacking. Maud made to get to her feet but Edith noticed her face contort with pain.

'You've hurt your ankle?' she asked peering down at Maud's swollen foot. 'I'll give you some'at to bind that with. Are ye any good at helping me with the bairns and in the kitchen?'

'Yes, I'm experienced with children and cooking.' Maud was just about to say about her work in Belmont House when Archie shot a warning look across to her in the gloom. This didn't go totally unnoticed with their hostess but she chose to ignore it since she was desperate for workers.

'You can drape your soaking clothes over the rafters for the night and hang them out to dry in the morning after prayers. You're lucky. Going to church has been banned due to the sickness in the village so you'll have to say your prayers as you rest, ready for the hard work mind. We don't abide slackers.'

Maud smiled her gratitude and limped towards the area where they were to sleep, a sack was hanging to hide her modesty as she changed. Once more comfortable they helped themselves to another bowl of broth and some oat cakes and then Maud wrapped some cloth strips tightly around her foot. After that they settled down for the night and soon Maud was fast asleep and dreaming of her boy. She was running; running ever faster but glancing over her shoulder as Drumford disappeared from view altogether.

Yet again their time near Kendal was short, ever watchful of the horizon and fearful of strangers asking questions.

'We should be married,' Archie said quietly once they were alone.

'Oh I'd like that so much,' Maud beamed, thinking that her troubles would finally be over. 'But how is that possible?'

'I've heard of this place just over the border into Scotland called Gretna Green where we would be allowed to be married. You are only nineteen but there we can find some people to be our witnesses and it can be arranged. We'll have to change our surnames too though.

'What shall we call ourselves Jack?'

'Don't call me that!' whispered Archie, frowning. 'I've thought of all of that. I will be Archie Dowling and you will be Maud Fry. What do you think about being Mrs Dowling?'

'Oh, that would be perfect- Archie,' Maud added giving Archie a warm smile with a hint of shyness which was so becoming and made Archie long for her all the more and forget his recent doubts.

Early the following morning, before the cock crowed, they crept away from the farm, Maud's ankle now fully healed. Once at Oddendale, on the main turnpike road from Lancaster, they managed to secure another lift on a coal cart which took them to the outskirts of Penrith, dropping off coal deliveries as they went.

That evening they reached the small village of Tirril and stopped at an inn called The Queen's Head. Archie paid nine pence for board and lodgings for the night and they were shown to a dusty box room upstairs at the back of the public house, hardly more than a cupboard. Nevertheless there was a bowl of water on a small table by the door, fresh ticking and a chamber pot in the corner; sheer luxury after the straw sacking at the farm.

A tap on the door signalled the arrival of a meagre meal of ale, bread and cheese. When they settled down for the night Archie made advances towards Maud, since this was the first time they had slept alone since their escape.

Maud pushed him away. 'Not until after the wedding. We'll do things properly this time Archie and be respectable.'

Archie turned away gruffly and was snoring almost as soon as he hit the hay. Maud sat on the edge of the bedding looking at him and for the first time wondered yet again what had happened to her sister Evie. She tried to imagine her next of kin in a tiny room at the Convent. Would Evie go on to take orders? Maud wondered. As she curled up next to Archie she smiled. Yes, Evie would make a good nun; far better than herself. With that she blushed as she settled down to sleep, thinking of all that had brought her so much shame. Her last thought was thankfulness that her father had not been alive to witness it.

The following morning, before they left the boarding house, Archie reminded Maud that their old names should never be mentioned again. Full on a large helping of porridge and tea they began to trudge the twenty odd miles towards Carlisle. The weather was fair and Maud was in good spirits.

In Carlisle they risked staying in the town, feeling bolder as the distance between them and their pursuers had increased. The following morning Archie bought a cheap second-hand ring. He also took Maud to the pawn shop and they exchanged their coats at knock down prices, knowing that they could return them the following day if they wished.

On Thursday 4th October 1780 they walked the ten miles in the autumn sunshine to Gretna Green, dressed in their *new-to-them coats, with the ring safely in Archie's pocket. Having tried to tame her unruly auburn hair with her fingers, Maud used a clean scarf, found in the pocket of the coat, to make herself presentable. Even Archie saw the change in her and was proud to be by her side. At Gretna they found two willing witnesses on the streets; tourists who were just visiting from York out of curiosity, and Maud became Mrs Dowling. She only just remembered to sign her new name, hesitating as she wrote the M. Archie had never been taught the rudiments of writing and so he just placed a cross next to his name which the registrar had scribed so carefully.*

That night they found lodgings in Gretna as man and wife and Maud gave herself willingly and lovingly to her new husband. As she snuggled into his arms, Archie half asleep, she thought again of Evie.

'Did you know Evie, my little sister at the Grange?' she whispered.

Archie bristled.

'How was she when you left?' Maud voice was barely audible when she continued. There was a silent pause before Archie said, 'how should I know?' before storming out of the room, returning drunk and falling fast asleep, his back to her.

A parasite of a doubt crept unbidden into Maud's consciousness. She scratched, her mind turning to the possibility that there were fleas or bedbugs in the room, then she slipped into a fitful sleep, the peace she had felt on their wedding day all but shattered.

The next morning Archie's good spirits seemed to have returned and Maud thought she must have imagined it. Maybe he had been tired; she made excuses in her head and smiled up at him.

'What shall we do next, my husband?' she smiled invitingly.

He needed no more encouragement and soon he was taking her, with such a force that it took her breath away.

Afterwards they dressed in silence, an air of embarrassment lingering in the tense atmosphere.

'We could head south back to Carlisle to return these coats and stay in England or we could head north and maybe find work in Scotland. I was told there is a neep (swede) harvest not too far from here.'

Maud kept quiet, aware that Archie was really thinking aloud and so after a moment he continued, 'but I've heard that plenty of work can be found in the docklands too. Liverpool's south but there was mention of Glasgow last night. All I do know is that we've nigh on run out of money, so what do you think?'

Maud's surprise that she had been consulted was tinged with irritation that Archie had squandered some of their funds on drink the night before. Maud paused in thought.

'I think that staying over the border might be safer for us,' even though she had no concept of the distances involved to Glasgow.

'Don't ever mention our past life again,' Archie said, his voice full of spite. 'We are travelling north in search of work and that is that,' he said with a finality that drew to a close all thoughts of home and her child – their child – into the far recesses of her mind. Yet the boy was far from forgotten.

CHAPTER 23

JAMAL WAS GIVEN an unexpected job on the two days before New Year which coincidentally took him down to Devon in his van. He had been given an allowance for overnight accommodation for truckers in Exeter and so he decided to make a detour all the way down to Cornwall. To my surprise he took Orla with him. As to the nature of their relationship I didn't ask.

I was to see them both again at the New Year's Eve alcohol free party at The Ark. That's a party without alcohol and not free alcohol! There were a few faces missing that night and I guessed the temptation to drink themselves into a stupor was too great for some and they had chosen to sleep rough. For others a week at the hostel, however convivial the hospitality, had perhaps been too much for these loners. As someone who has learnt to enjoy my own company I could fully understand this, although I was aware of my good fortune. I had my own imagination to escape into, whenever I chose. Not many people could say that.

Jamal and Orla came into the dining area, where the tables had been cleared to the side for a home-made buffet, lovingly prepared and donated by the Women's Institute of the local St Joseph's Roman Catholic Church. Their manner was different. Eyes shining, they were holding hands quite openly. When Jamal saw me he grinned and they made their way towards me. I looked up, my eyebrows lifting as I tilted my head towards the couple.

'No news I'm afraid, Auntie. We went to all the areas on the Lizard you mentioned, even to a small mobile homes park which was being sold privately, and the landlord in the local pub said that there was a man of our description living there. We even spoke to the man but it wasn't Mr G. It being winter time the local people were enthusiastic to talk to us and share local gossip.'

'Never mind,' I said, perhaps a bit too brightly. 'You had a good time otherwise?'

'A lovely time Mrs G,' said Orla, 'apart from the disappointment about the person we thought might be your husband. We were so excited that we'd found him. It was quite a let-down.'

'Never mind,' I said repeating myself, 'Enjoy the evening instead.'

Jamal and Orla worked side by side at the counter pouring soft drinks and then teas and coffees. We drank elderflower champagne to welcome in the New Year, being brewed and donated appropriately by one of the elders of the church.

We stood side by side clinking plastic glasses.

'Cheers to a good 2017,' I said.

'And a happy one too,' added Orla, with Jamal just beaming at both of us.

I must admit to it being the best New Year since the boys were with us, although I remembered their nervousness when they heard fireworks outside at midnight for the first time. Too many bad memories of home. There was nothing like that in Jamal's smile tonight though, as we watched the fireworks over London on a TV screen in the corner of the room. That young man had certainly grown up.

I noticed his face clouding over momentarily, 'to absent family and friends,' he added, and we all hugged each other, Jamal and me for the first time ever. I could not help but think that it was all Orla's doing. The bubble burst in completeness as Laura bustled over and gave her sister a hug.

'A very happy New Year to you all,' she said as she drifted off to speak to every person in turn, always making sure that no-one felt left out. What gems these sisters are, I thought.

CHAPTER 24

I FELT A mixture of emotions when packing my bags on New Year's Day. I longed to get away from the dormitory and on my own but, now that Jamal and I were in touch, I craved to be nearby too. As I walked along the banks of the river I reasoned that it gave Jamal and Orla some space to sort out their own relationship.

I was also a little nervous about returning to The Grange. What if the farmer had found out about me? Would Angelina get into trouble? Did Greta tell her mother that she'd seen me from the coach on her last day of term walking with a young Asian man?

Fretting was unusual for me these days. Only a week back in the *real world* and I was thinking in my old ways again and forgetting my carefree existence. I longed to feel that abundance of peace I only experienced in solitude. However, I was glad to be making new positive memories of my time with Jamal, and Orla too; my personal paradox.

As I turned my back on Drumford my sense of calm returned. It was a bright crisp morning and the birds were twittering in the bushes. A late owl flew silently overhead and into Canbury Woods. I paused as a fox crossed my path, stopping to glance back at me, piercing me with his yellow eyes before disappearing into the undergrowth in search of rabbits no doubt. I sighed. This was my new life now and in some ways I couldn't imagine it any other way. People might be sad for me. I wanted to say, don't be. I'm one of the fortunate ones.

I hadn't noticed that I'd walked past the village green or even my special clearing, so deep was I in my reverie.

Soon I was lifting the ivy and creeping up the steps to 'my' room. All was as I had left it except that there was a small Tupperware container, inside of which I found to my delight two mince pies, some home-made Christmas cake, a fresh packet of cheese biscuits, some chocolate fingers and next to it a litre bottle of water. How sweet. Little was Angelina to know that I'd feasted well over the season. I wondered where she thought I had been and guiltily thought that she might imagine me huddled under a cardboard box somewhere. Nevertheless I was truly grateful and hoped my work in the library would come some way in showing my gratitude.

I drank some water and slowly savoured one of the pies, careful to catch the flakes of pastry in my spare jumper, to shake out next time I went downstairs. The last thing I wanted to do was to encourage vermin. Then I headed down to the library, going over to my pile of papers in order to put the chapters I had revised and my new chapters on top. I glanced around. Nothing seemed to have changed since my last visit so I set to work, not noticing the hours go by until suddenly I realised that the light was dimming. With the short days I could barely see to tidy everything away before heading back up to the eaves. There I refreshed myself, splashing cold water on my face and then wrote for another couple of hours in the moonlight and then by torchlight before performing my ablutions and settling down for the night.

Even though I warned him not to, Jamal returned to The Grange a few days later to say that he'd made an appointment for us both to see The Red Cross the following day, which he knew was my weekly visit to Drumford. From then on we met regularly in Drumford catching up on his news. The Red Cross had followed several leads the police had given them but so far without any trace, however they were grateful to take Jamal's number as a contact. Jamal had visited several places I'd mentioned where Gerald and I had holidayed in the past, but with no success either. My husband had completely disappeared.

'Where did Mr G grow up and did he talk of anywhere special that I should try?' Jamal asked me.

I mentioned a few more towns and Jamal jotted them on his ever lengthening list. Some had notes by them. Others were crossed out completely.

'How is your writing going Mrs G?'

Reluctantly I led him downstairs and showed him the growing pile of chapters.

'Would you like me to take it away and begin to word process it for you?' he said. 'That will make it easier to amend when you're proof reading the story.'

I could tell that he was itching to get his hands on the manuscript and I smiled.

'I don't think it's your sort of book Jamal.'

'Not to worry Mrs G. I'd like to type it for you anyway. I have lots of time in the evenings and my laptop is one thing the police did return to me.'

'Have you had any news from Ahmed at all?' I asked, remembering the eventful day of Jamal's brother's disappearance. I felt a shard of guilt that I hadn't enquired about him recently.

'No. Not a thing. But what's the English expression. No news is good news.'

'That's true.' I hugged him goodbye, an experience new to us but nevertheless comforting. Our experiences had made us closer than ever.

There was one day in February he came to The Grange because he was so excited.

'Mrs G, I have some news. I have not seen Mr G but I do know where he has been since he left Drumford. He didn't commit suicide, that's for sure.'

'What do you mean?' I said, feeling the chill of my husband's betrayal intermingled with a glimmer of hope – hope for what, I was uncertain about? Did I really want Gerald found? Could I envisage him back in my life? I shuddered; a *walking over my own grave* moment. I pushed that thought deep down inside of me to dwell on later when I was alone.

'Sit down and tell me all about it,' I said, visibly bracing myself, my shoulders lifting in defiance or protection. I'm not sure which.

'I was delivering in Carlisle and so made a detour on my way home to Tirril where there was that lovely pub, the one you found empty on your last visit. Well, the pub *was* boarded up but a man was just finishing the task and getting into his van. I introduced myself. His name was Dave. I asked him what had happened. Dave explained that a guy from down south had leased it for two years but found it hard to make a go of it. He'd left the previous week asking Dave to board it up and give the keys to the agent when he'd finished. I asked what the man's name was and he said Mr Peter Thomson but when I showed him the photo he said, yes, that's the guy!'

I sat back down on the sleeping bag next to Jamal.

'Are you all right Mrs G? Your face has gone very pale.'

Jamal got up and handed me some water.

'I don't know what to say Jamal. You've succeeded when the authorities have failed, but what do we do now?'

'I've thought of that. We need to go back to The Red Cross with the information. Surely with this lead they will be able to track him down, but at least it proves that he is still alive.'

I was quiet for a moment. 'What will happen next Jamal, you know, if they find him?'

Jamal looked at me quizzically. 'What do you want to happen Mrs G?'

'I just don't know Jamal, and that's the truth.'

When he left me ten minutes later I went down into the library where I felt most at home. I sat at the writing desk staring into the dark veins of the rose wood, my fingers tracing each tributary to the rich marquetry border; the palm of my hand resting on the smooth bevelled edge. I looked up as the sun shone momentarily through the stained glass, highlighting tiny particles of dust I must have disturbed on entering the room. I probably sat there for longer than an hour because, when I finally looked up Greta was staring at me from the doorway. How long had she been standing there? I had no idea.

The next thing I knew was that her mother was calling her from the yard. She whisked past me like a shadow and up the staircase. I could hear her footsteps racing along the landing above and then the patter of tiny feet down my secret staircase. Well, it was a secret no more. I glanced out of the window. Two torches were flashing, a small one coming from behind The Grange.

'What were you thinking of going out in the dark like that, Greta?' Angelina asked, her voice muffled by the single pane of coloured glass.

'I was looking for my pet hamster. I'd been playing with him in the garden this afternoon and he ran away.'

'Oh Greta,' I heard her mother say and they hugged, turning to walk back into the farmhouse together.

Out of the mouths of babes I thought as I mused on how easy it was, from a very early age, to learn to tell small white lies.

Although my mind was occupied with thoughts of Gerald, Jamal and Greta, I took the path of escapism; writing my story. That night, with Jill's last advice reverberating in my head to remember to use all my senses, I continued:

The Nun's Tale Part 3

The Long Cold Journey Northwards

Maud and Archie were desperate for work and so, late the following morning, they walked in the direction Archie had been advised.

Archie, aware that Maud's mood had simmered to a heavy sadness, tried at reconciliation for the fragile happiness felt during their wedding day.

'Life will get better, Maud. I promise you it will,' he said.

Maud shrugged her shoulders in resignation and remembered the pain of her father's death. 'I've come through worse Archie. We'll be alright as long as we're together,' she said. Did Archie flinch imperceptibly at her remark? She wasn't sure. She put it from her mind as they walked side by side.

'Where are we going to?'

'I've heard that there's need for workers in Nithsdale. It's about ten miles northwest of here. We should do it in half a day.'

Maud still felt dispirited. It was already afternoon and the days were shortening.

They set off in silence. Soon they were walking in a bleak landscape shrouded in mist. Maud did not ask Archie how he knew where to go. They just walked on. That night they huddled beneath the trees in a small apple orchard, eating the best of the fallen apples to relieve hunger pangs; the sweet smell of fermenting apples filling the air. The following day it was raining but they trudged on. To their left the moorland and craggy hills appeared and disappeared as the clouds billowed and then lifted for a while, giving a haunting quality. Maud thought about Evie but didn't dare mention her name again.

They finally arrived in Dalswinton and luck was on their side because a couple of itinerant workers had left the farm the previous week to return to family further south, and so the farmer was keen to hire folks.

Archie and Maud were given shelter in one of the workers' terraced cottages alongside three other families. The locals took up the majority of these terraces but the end terrace was for the outlins, the other outsiders as well as themselves. Maud and Archie found it impossible to understand the broad accents of the Dumfries folks at first. In their own cottage there were two couples from down south; one from the Liverpool area and another, Emma and John with their small baby were from Lancashire. The fourth family, parents and two wee boys, were from the island of Bute, which the Bedfordshire couple had never heard of. Archie introduced themselves as having travelled from Cambridgeshire and Maud soon made friends with Emma, delighted to help out with baby Jack, the coincidence of name was not lost on Maud as a reminder of all that she had left behind.

There was one fireplace for heating and cooking upstairs and downstairs and two families lived on each floor. Emma, Jack and John shared with Maud and Archie upstairs. The only creature comforts were a stack of three cooking pots, a pile of straw filled ticking which they distributed around the room at night time, woollen blankets and tallow candles which they were given in lieu of wages from their landlord, as was the pile of peat sheltering beside their front porch.

The following morning they were up at first light to eat the porridge left warming on the dying embers overnight. Tea brewed as the fire stirred to life, its warm peaty smell a comfort which Maud experienced for the first time.

'It's back breaking work but you'll soon get used to it,' Emma said as she poured out the steaming porridge. Maud held baby Jack, already bonding with the child. She reluctantly put the baby down to eat.

Within minutes Emma was hurrying them outside, strapping the baby on her back.

'Best not to be late,' she explained. 'You don't wanna lose yer job before you've started.' Then she winked at Maud as they joined the others walking out towards the fields. Once working Maud soon found a rhythm, pulling, shaking off the soil and then throwing the neeps into large baskets. The day was bright and clear and occasionally Maud stretched to enjoy the sun's warmth, knowing that it might be the last, since the end of October was approaching fast. They spoke little during the day but often singing could be heard wafting over the field.

The workers hands were raw to almost bleeding by the end of each day; soaking them in the icy bucket of water was a pain pleasure experience. After which Archie and Maud followed Emma's lead and slapped lard on, binding them with strips of cloth for protection. Some of the women had sheepskin gloves but they could not afford such a luxury.

'You'll get used to it,' Emma assured Maud and she was right. After a week or so the bleeding stopped and Maud's hands hardened to the daily onslaught.

Nights were cold though. They huddled around the peaty fireplace which they took turns to scrub each morning before work, while the other piled up the bedding and swept the floor. The women did not grumble; glad to have a roof over their heads. Talk at night was sometimes stilted as Maud and Archie made up a fictitious life. Maud and Emma prepared the food and once a week the men downed jars of ale bought by their landlord on payday. There was little to show for their labours by the end of each week. As privacy was non-existent, there was little physical contact between the couples, unless, that is, John and Archie were drunk, at which times they were rough in taking what they felt was their due.

At the end of November, on All Hallows Eve, they carved faces in the neeps for the children and the farmer provided a barn for a ceilidh. It was a joyous affair and Maud laughed and drank alongside her husband, truly relaxing for the first time since leaving Drumford. They tried to dance but Archie's state of inebriation led to a few collisions until he fell over completely, at which point he stumbled up and almost dragged Maud back to their cottage and raped her before falling asleep. Sore and distraught Maud was wide awake through the night, only to fall asleep just before the cock crowed, her tears spent.

It was December and the harvest was all but gathered in. At night they were aware of the disadvantages of the end terrace because those sleeping against the outside wall were frozen by morning. Being the last to arrive, this misfortune fell on Archie who, at times, pushed Maud in his place when he could bear it no more. On one occasion Maud awoke shivering so much that she could hardly move her fingers.

'Be careful putting them too near the fire. You'll catch frostbite or chilblains in the least if you warm them too quickly.' Emma took Maud's hands then her arms and began to rub them, gradually bringing the circulation back, the lard rubbing into the skin.

'There ye'are,' she said. 'Must get on with the breakfast, otherwise we'll be late.'

The women ate companionably, warmed by the comfort of a homely chat over tea, before completing their chores.

'What'll you do next Maud?'

'Oh, I dunno,' replied Maud. 'Archie's talking about going to Glasgow.'

'To the docks?'

'Yes I think so. That family from the island out west said that there should be work. It's a bit of a scrum to get it apparently but what choice do we have in winter.'

'You could go back down south to Liverpool, rather than heading further north.'

Maud coloured. She couldn't say why she was relieved to be over the border into Scotland. 'Is that what you're doing?'

'We're gonna head back down to Kendal. I miss me family. Try and get work in the paper mill mebbe. There were just too many of us with bairns in the house. We had to move on. Me father didn't say so, but we knew it couldn't go on. Then we spent some time on me brother's barge but there wasn't enough room with the bairn too. Me Dad was a barge man you see.'

'So what's changed then?'

'Well, I've had word that gran has passed away so they'll mebbe squeeze us in for the rest of the winter if we can pay our way. We just have to get work where we can. Devil of a time to be out on the streets though.'

'Why did you come so far north?'

'We followed the work. As simple as that. Followed the harvest.'

'We did much the same as you. Wheat harvest, then oats then here for the neeps.'

'Oh we did the apple harvest too, the early potato harvest first and then just kept moving on. Listened out for opportunities. I have a cousin who came here a few seasons ago. That's how it happens. By word of mouth usually. We'd *go to the Liverpool docks sooner than Glasgow. Why don't you join us? Travel together.'*

'I think Archie's set his heart on going north.'

'More's the pity. I'll miss yer.'

'You too.'

The evening before they were to be evicted Maud was almost certain that she was with child.'

'Oh that's good news, Maud, but not too good for travelling at this time of year,' Emma said as the friends hugged before each picked up their belongings to head out of the village of Dalswinton.

'At least we'll be doing the first leg of the journey together to Dumfries. Archie says that he's saved enough for us to catch transport from there. Let's hope the weather holds.'

'Let's hope so but don't count on it.'

It looked ominously black.

They marched purposefully off, aiming to get to Dumfries by mid afternoon by which time it was getting dark and flurries of snow were drifting in their faces. The friends shared a room with two other families before a tearful farewell the next morning. Archie had already gone out, so Maud was left alone to wait. She hadn't told him her news as yet for fear of angering him.

CHAPTER 25

I DON'T KNOW whether we'd become complacent. Hindsight is wonderful isn't it? We *had* planned to meet in Drumford, but Jamal was too excited and wanted to update me with further news of Gerald so he had made his way to the farm once more. I hadn't been able to warn him that the farmhouse had a new occupant – an Alsatian – a brute of a thing with a ferocious growl when strangers, even the postman came into the yard. Thankfully the dog appeared to be a big softie with Greta though. I'd heard Angelina grumbling that she had to pick up the mail from the post office in the shop in Canbury now.

Anyway, one afternoon I heard incessant barking and there was a disturbance outside in the farm yard. I kept very still but peered out of the leaded window. Jamal and the farmer were arguing, the farmer had his arm and was pulling him away from The Grange and I could see that his farm hand was on his mobile phone. I held my breath. What would Jamal say? Would he have to mention my presence? Jamal by now had been forced to sit on the steps of the farmhouse while he was being quizzed. I could see that they were barring his way so that he couldn't make a run for it. I felt powerless to help him. Should I reveal my whereabouts and explain who Jamal was? I did not want to get Angelina into any trouble either.

While I was mulling over my options several minutes must have passed and I was horrified when the noise of a police siren was heard coming closer along the lane. Next, I could just make out through the misted glass the sight of Jamal being bundled into a police van. I was devastated. The young person I had endeavoured to protect was now in trouble on my account. My body tensed as my anxiety spread. There was nothing I could do for the present though, and I guessed that he would be taken to Drumford's Temporary Police Station, so all I could do was to follow him there.

I watched the farmer feed and pet his dog before taking it with him in the tractor. Taking my cue I huddled into the farmer's coat, my slight exhale of breath at the irony that its wearer had in fact become his lodger. Then I collected my belongings together in my rucksack and slipped out of my not so secret door, pushing the undergrowth carefully over it as I left. Pausing for a moment I listened before creeping through the undergrowth, along the path and out on to the relative anonymity of the lane.

My walk the three miles to Drumford was not the carefree stroll I was used to. My mind whirled as it tried to assimilate what I'd seen and decide what I should do. After all, I was the one who had been trespassing too, and so Jamal's appearance was bound to reveal my own activities. With a heavy heart I realised that I was homeless once more. Keeping silent was not an option; Jamal's welfare was my priority.

Walking up to the counter in the makeshift police station in the centre of town a young policeman asked,

'Can I help you?'

'Yes, officer I think you can. Earlier today a young man, Jamal Hussain was taken in a police-van from Westgate Farm. I know Jamal and would like to vouch for him.'

'What's your name please?'

'Mrs Dorothy Gibbons.'

'And who might you be in relation to this young man?' the policeman asked with an inflection of suspicion in his voice.

'Until recently I was Jamal's foster carer. He was an asylum seeker but he was living with me for a couple of years. I'm probably the closest person he has to a relation. He has no family you see.' I don't know why I did not mention his brother because the police were very aware of Ahmed's case.

'Please can you fill in your details on this form while I see if there's someone who can speak to you?'

I stared at the form before me. Name – well that's OK. Address. Tears welled up in my eyes. I was just staring vacantly into space when I was relieved to see DC Cathy Peterson walking towards me.

'How are you Mrs Gibbons? Come this way and we can have a chat.'

I saw Cathy Peterson glancing at my rucksack and worn out shoes, her sigh matching her frown of understanding, or was it with a touch of guilt. I followed her into a tiny, windowless interview room which although clean smelt of stale sweat.

'I'd like to talk about you Mrs Gibbons and how you're coping, but first we must discuss Jamal Hussain. Is that OK with you?'

I nodded. What else could I say?

'So,' she continued, 'Please can you remind me of your relationship with Jamal?'

I outlined my time with Jamal and his personal situation, as far as I knew it, up until the moment when I left the flat, never looking back.

'Oh, Mrs Gibbons. I think they'd call what you experienced a breakdown. You'd had more than your brain could cope with and so you wanted out.'

'But what about Jamal? What are you going to do with him?'

'Slow down a minute Mrs G. First we need to know why he was at the farmhouse as far as you know. He was trespassing for a start but we don't know what his intentions were – was he looking to commit a crime?'

'Oh dear. I have so much to explain haven't I?'

'And before you even begin to explain, here are some more questions, but can we get you a cup of tea and a sandwich first?'

My grateful eyes answered, yes please, and Cathy nodded to the young police lady at the door who slipped out.

Turning back to me Cathy frowned, a warning that, although she was caring, she was still a police constable.

'Now where was I? How did you know that Jamal has been arrested? He refuses to speak to us. He hasn't said a word since we brought him in, even though it's clear from talking to him previously that he speaks perfectly good English. We asked him if he'd like to call anyone but he just shook his head.'

I paused a minute. 'It would be easier to explain how it came about starting from when I left Jamal and Ahmed's flat. Would that be OK?'

'Go ahead,' Cathy answered, 'but try to be as brief as possible and keep to the facts if you can.'

I sat and described my life on the streets, finding shelter where I could, avoiding Jamal when I saw him and then discovering The Grange, or did it discover me? I thought. I was nervous now because I did not wish to get Angelina into trouble, but I had no choice but to tell the truth as I saw it.

... and so I was watching out of the window of The Grange when they arrested Jamal. He was only coming to see me to give me an update on Gerald's whereabouts. You see, he's discovered that Gerald is alive, but I don't know if he's found out where my husband is as yet.'

There was a pause as Cathy tried to internalise this turn of events. I could see that she had no idea as to how to proceed.

'Would it be possible for me to see Jamal do you think? I'm sure I could get him to explain.'

'That seems a way forward. I'll go and discuss this with DS Brown. Would you mind waiting in the lobby?'

I nodded in affirmation and was led out of the room, cup and unfinished sandwich in hand. From where I came from, every morsel of food was vital.

It was not long before the duty officer answered the phone and I was led down to the place where they held Jamal. In truth they were alcoves in the crypt which had plaster board walls erected for security and privacy, for the rare occasion that they held two people in custody at one time. Ideal, if not a bit primitive as makeshift police cells, I thought.

Jamal was sitting on a bench staring dejectedly at the floor. At first he didn't look up, but when he caught sight of me he rushed to the bars,

'Oh Auntie,' he exclaimed.

I was let into his cell, Cathy almost forgotten at my side as Jamal started to babble on.

'Oh Auntie,' he repeated. 'I'm so glad to see you. I didn't know what to do. I was so scared. I couldn't tell them anything because I wanted to protect you. How are you?'

'Jamal I'm fine. Don't you worry about me. You need to tell DC Peterson here about why you were at The Grange and what you've discovered about Mr G. I'm not even sure that you can be charged for trespassing, but I do believe that it is only if you intended to do harm, like damage or steal things. I think *I* was doing more wrong in the eyes of the law by squatting,' I paused. 'Which means I stayed in the old house overnight when I shouldn't have done.'

'Oh Mrs G. What a mess!'

'Jamal, I'm going to ask if I can be taken over to Westgate Farm to explain. I only hope that the farmer's wife will not be in too much trouble either.'

'Oh Auntie. Don't worry about me.' I don't think he realised that he had repeated me parrot fashion. 'You know I'd do anything for you and I'll do as you ask.'

'I'll be back to see you let out of here and we'll have a long chat. Everything changes now I'm afraid.'

'I'm so sorry Auntie, that I've *blown your hide-away.*' His eye brows raised as he caught my eye.

'Yes Jamal. The expression we usually use is *blown my cover.* Anyway, that's the least of my worries, but before I go can you tell me one thing. Have you found out where Gerald is?'

'I'm afraid I haven't seen him but I was working in the north-west again and so located the estate agent, who in turn directed me to a solicitors' office. Of course they wouldn't talk to me; client confidentiality and all that, but I was coming to see you today because The Red Cross have some important news. A person at the Bedford office wants to speak to you in person, so I was going to arrange a time when we could go there by bus together. I thought you'd like the company.'

'Thank you Jamal. Now, you must tell this constable anything she wants to know. She can be trusted to help us. You must believe that.'

'OK Mrs G.'

'Now, I promise that I'll be back soon and I'm sure I can see you're released from here.' I smiled reassuringly at him as I was let out of the cell. Glancing over my shoulder before I mounted the stone stairs I saw a far more relaxed young man from the one I'd found twenty minutes earlier. Jamal smiled back at me and I was gone.

CHAPTER 26

I WAITED IN the lobby for half an hour after which Cathy Peterson arranged for PC Harper, the constable on the duty desk, to transport us to the farmhouse. He occasionally glanced at me in his wing mirror and smiled, but otherwise our journey was silent. My stomach fluttered with anxiety as we approached the gates. Whatever happened here would determine both mine and Jamal's future.

As we drove into the yard, the sound of wheels on gravel heralded our arrival. We were greeted by the tethered Alsatian, who growled at our vehicle as it came to a stop.

Jonathan, the farmer, came out and barked an order at his dog, who in turn fell on to his haunches and whimpered, keeping his eyes on his master. As he came striding towards us I could see a blotchy red eyed Angelina appear at the farmhouse door. Farmer Jonathan and DC Cathy Peterson shook hands perfunctorily, and he nodded for us to follow him. I looked into Angelina's eyes as I passed and I could sense that she had told her husband everything. Her last look was a warning shot as she headed for the kitchen but that placed me in a dilemma. I felt that I could only tell the truth.

Jonathan Barton gestured for us to take seats on the well-worn sofa and he cleared his throat.

'You must understand why I'm taking this matter very seriously. Firstly, there have been several burglaries in farms across the Home Counties. It is impossible to secure all of our equipment in locked barns and I can't afford any major losses. It could ruin the business. Times are tough enough as it is. Not only that but, with the terrorist threats we have been warned to be extra vigilant. Who knows what damage a farm vehicle could do in the wrong hands?'

He looked a little embarrassed at DC Peterson, who seemed to take it in her stride, but I was sure she was refraining from making a remark about possible racist attitudes.

'Mr Barton. You had every right to call us. The gentleman in question, who was trespassing on your property, refused to leave and began yelling at you in a language you didn't understand. It was understandable that you were upset, and we were glad that you called. You can rest assured that we will do everything within our power to check the young man's background and will report back to you shortly. Even though he did no damage to your property you were correct in contacting us.'

At that moment Angelina appeared with a tray of tea. Her eyes smiled shyly at me in a way that was imperceptible to those around us.

'.. but we also have the intrusion of Dorothy Gibbons to discuss,' Cathy Peterson nodded in my direction, 'which has complicated matters, but if she is to be believed then neither she nor Mr Hussain had the intention of causing you or your family any harm.'

'She was a squatter!' Jonathan spluttered out a shower of tea drops. He glared at his wife. 'She had no right to be there. It might have put my family – my daughter in danger.'

'With due respect it sounds as if she had the permission of your wife, Mr Barton, even though you knew nothing about it.'

'That may be the case but she didn't have *my* permission. I am the owner of all of this – the custodian. Surely it is I who needs to be consulted and to give my consent or otherwise...' The look he gave his wife at that point made me shudder and regret that I had ever laid eyes on this refuge. I would have been better off remaining at The Ark for the winter months.

Being so little used to company, my mind drifted. I thought of my time in his library and the good I felt I'd done. It had certainly been a healing time for me, one that I shouldn't show remorse for, although I deeply regretted getting Jamal and Angelina in trouble.

I came to as Cathy Peterson was summing up the situation.

'I'm sure that Dorothy Gibbons and Jamal Hussain will promise never to come near your property again. We will investigate the young man to see that there were no ulterior motives and report back the outcome. Do you still wish us to pursue the course of prosecuting for *loitering with intent?* We understand the disturbance that this intrusion has caused?'

'You have to understand that if we are soft on them,' with that Jonathan Barton coloured somewhat. 'I mean, we have to give out a message that we are tough, otherwise they will believe that they can get away with anything.' At no time did he even glance in my direction. It was as if I was as silent and as deceased as the trophy stag's head, which was an odd decorative feature on a Bedfordshire farmhouse wall.

'Who might *they* be, Mr Barton?' asked DC Peterson.

'Terrorists of course!'

'Now, I know that these occurrences have caused you distress, but please let us carry out our investigation to ascertain what the actual motives of both Mrs Gibbons and Mr Hussain were first, and then we'll speak again. Would you be satisfied with this as a way forward, Mr Barton?'

Farmer Jonathan nodded the affirmative although his eyes sent a different message.

Finally, in the silence, I plucked up the courage to speak out.

'I'm so sorry Mr Barton. I meant you no harm and I was so grateful for a roof over my head last winter that I did not think through the implications. I should never have come here.' I hesitated but decided not to mention the books or his wife. 'It is also totally my fault that Jamal was in your farmyard this morning.' Was it really only a few hours ago I wondered with dismay? 'He was looking for me to give me news of my husband who went missing two years ago. Jamal was my foster son you see.' I liked using the word son and decided at that moment that I certainly felt maternal towards the lad. I continued, 'I don't have a phone and so there was no way he could contact me otherwise, but that doesn't excuse our trespassing. I take full responsibility for this mess and I apologize. I assure you that neither of us will set foot on Westgate Farm again.'

At that point I saw Angelina take a step forward and tried to warn her to keep quiet but her eyes were shining and I could see that she felt passionately as she spoke.

'Jonathan, I can't remain silent. If it wasn't for your own kindness when we first met I might have ended on the streets like Dorothy here. What's your English expression *there but by the grace of God,* or something like that?'

Jonathan glared at his wife and was about to respond, but Angelina wouldn't be deterred. In fact her voice, at first shaky, grew with confidence.

'In my eyes Dorothy has been a Godsend and we have so much to thank her for. The cataloguing she has done in the library will make so much money that it will bolster the business and keep us afloat through these difficult times. I could never have completed the task so quickly or efficiently without her help. What harm did she do to us really? In some ways we should be paying her for her work.'

'..but you had no right to trust a stranger on our property,' the farmer spluttered.

'Once I had heard her story from the librarian in Drumford, that Mrs Gibbons used to be a librarian there too, I knew that we were safe and that our books were in capable hands. Have you no compassion?'

I felt moistness in the corner of my eyes. Angelina had been brave to defend me against her husband, but the last thing I wanted to do was to cause a marital dispute.

'No, Angelina, I was wrong to seek refuge without permission. What I did was carried out with thankfulness and my reward was to enhance my own feeling of self worth, which had reached its lowest point. I apologize and promise I will never trespass again.'

'That is no excuse for the, er, lad.'

'I am certain, Mr Barton, that Jamal will heed my warnings and keep away too. He will have no reason to return if I'm not here.'

Cathy Peterson glanced around at us all as if summing up the situation in her head, second guessing what we were thinking and allowing a few moments of reflection.

Farmer Jonathan did not want to concede to an outcome of forgiveness. Principles were at stake. He had to protect his family and property. Even if he trusted me, how did he know I wouldn't alert other homeless people to The Grange, or that Jamal wouldn't bring *God knows who* to hide here?

The farmer frowned. Neither, however, did he want the hassle of a possible court case, especially one which could be costly and he may not even win. The publicity could be damaging too. He imagined the headline *Farmer Sues Homeless Lady and Refugee.* That wouldn't reflect too well on his good name, would it? Finally he looked at his wife. His frown softened just a little as he thought of how he had been blessed since meeting Angelina. He would not have coped without her.

'I'll think about it,' he finally acknowledged. 'I'll show you out because I have work to do.'

We drove in silence back to the station. I was deep in thought, wondering what story lay behind Angelina's eyes. If only I had the opportunity to thank her personally for defending us. It took great courage to do so against her husband, who in turn had every right to protect his property and family from intruders. What had I been thinking of?

Cathy Peterson looked over her shoulder as we neared the outskirts of Drumford. 'I think that encounter went as well as could be expected Mrs Gibbons. Where would you like to be dropped off? We need to be able to contact you and I'm not sure that we have finished with Jamal as yet. The terrorist division may have to question him again, what with his links to Syria.'

I didn't want to have a long conversation; in fact I needed to be alone. I spent so much time in my own company those days that I was suddenly overwhelmed by a feeling of claustrophobia.

'You can drop me off here,' I said. 'I'd like a walk, but I assure you that I will stay at The Ark for the next few nights so that you can contact me there. If I don't hear from Jamal later on today then I will come by the police station in the morning.'

'I shouldn't think he will be held in custody over night Mrs Gibbons, unless more evidence comes to light.'

Somewhat reassured, I thanked her and began walking away, soon finding myself on the footpath along the river. I sat down on the dry grassy bank and watched the ripples in the water. The occasional fish jumped in the unsettled water. I sighed, clearing my head. A thrush was singing overhead in the branches of a young rowan tree. Remembering that I had hardly eaten all day I pulled out some biscuits, brought from The Grange in my hasty but final retreat. I sighed and began to nibble at the edges, taking intermittent gulps from my bottle of water.

Soon two ducks had waddled to join me and I shared some of my hoard with them. When I saw another family of feathered friends making its way towards us however, I decided that it was time to move on and collected together my trusty rucksack, ambling along and meeting no one. I had the ability to turn my thoughts to a blank peacefulness and was aware that my demeanour and my steps had lightened. It had been a very long day.

Feeling calmer I took a left fork in the path and negotiated the turn gate which would lead me towards Drumford. Once there I headed for the cafe where Jamal and I sometimes met. Enjoying my tea sitting outside in the far corner, the only place I was allowed to sit, I waited. The kind waitress refilled my cup with hot water leaving a watery liquid in my hands but I was truly grateful. Jamal didn't appear and so by five I headed to The Ark; now my only safe refuge. Laura and Orla were tidying up but they always found time for me if they could. We sat down in the ageing leather armchairs, which sagged even before our weight and bore several tears and scratches, not to mention stains – tea or coffee hopefully. I shuddered to think of the alternative.

Orla was distraught at first but after hearing my story she left with a determined expression on her face. Having shared my story my energy was spent and so Laura took me out to the hut where only a few sought a roof over their heads since the weather was so good. It was only when I had settled in my bunk that I began to think about the day and its implications and I remembered Jamal's message about Gerald. I was too exhausted to dwell on the possible outcomes of such a meeting or to analyse my feelings, compartmentalising those thoughts in a deep drawer in my brain to retrieve, perhaps, on another day. My only immediate concern was for Jamal to be released without charge. In time other matters would be brought into the light. With my priorities clear I fell asleep, totally oblivious to the sounds around me as several other inmates settled down for the night, some more clumsily than others.

CHAPTER 27

THE FOLLOWING MORNING I was woken up by Orla who explained that Jamal was waiting for me in the client lounge. I was about to ask questions, but her look of relief reassured me that all was well.

'He'll tell you everything Auntie,' she said before leaving me to rush to the washroom, a luxury I usually savoured, but this time I had a cursory wash, dressed and was soon greeting Jamal. Orla brought us tea. I smiled. She didn't have to.

'Well Jamal?'

'Orla came to vouch for me last night and waited for me until I was released. The police set me free at around nine o'clock and I stayed at Brian's. DC Peterson doesn't know whether the farmer is going to charge me as yet, but she seems fairly confident that I am no longer seen as a threat to security. His eyebrows furrowed. I knew he was thinking of Ahmed.

'You are not your brother's keeper,' I said keeping my voice gentle. There was a moment of quiet.

'Anyway, I'd like to take you on the bus to The Red Cross in Bedford today to hear their news. They won't tell me anything and have no way to contact you in confidence.'

'Are you sure you're not too tired after your ordeal?'

'I'm fine Mrs G. Things have been far worse you know.' Looks of understanding were passed between us.

I had nothing planned and was just relieved that Jamal was out of custody. My spirits were so lifted by the thought of spending a day with him that I did not dwell on what news I might hear. We chatted at the bus stop about my book.

Jamal had word processed my manuscript so far, but was enthusiastic that I should focus on getting it finished.

'I wish you could move in with us,' he said, 'but I'm sleeping on Brian's sofa as it is. I'm saving as much as I can though. Maybe one day I can rent a couple of rooms for us both.'

'Oh Jamal! You mustn't worry about me. I'm not your responsibility. Since the weather is good I'll be fine. I'll have to be like an artist and write out in the open. I can't stay at The Ark all the time. I would find it suffocating after a while, but Orla is negotiating with the Social Services to find me a room in a women's hostel. I'm not sure how I will cope there, and I might still sleep rough when I can, but it will be a base – an address. I will be a person in the eyes of the state again and will be able to access the small funds left in my bank account. Anyway, in three months time I will be sixty and will be entitled to a small librarian's pension too.'

We had arrived at our stop in Bedford and there was only a bit of a walk to the Red Cross Centre where we were ushered into a small interview room, reminiscent of the police station.

'Do you have any form of identification on you Mrs Gibbons.'

Jamal had had the foresight to rummage through the few possessions he still looked after for me and handed over my shabby and bent at the edges driving licence.

'Thank you,' the man said as he scrutinised the photo and then looked at me.

'I know I've changed,' I said. 'I was only forty five when they issued me with that credit card type photo one.'

'It's OK,' he said. 'Now, we have been carrying out an investigation as to the whereabouts of your husband Mr Gerald Gibbons. Can you confirm that he is your husband?'

'Yes he is still officially my husband,' I conceded.

As silently as he could, Jamal rummaged in his carrier bag and produced our marriage certificate. I smiled my gratitude.

'That's perfect.' The man glanced at the aged document. 'Well, after being given the information uncovered by your friend here, Mr Hussain, that Gerald Gibbons spent some time living near The Lake District running a small pub restaurant, it was not difficult to track him from there. He has changed his name a couple of times of course and we are not at liberty to tell you what he calls himself now, but we *can* tell you that he is living in a region of France where people dwell in caves. Troglodytes I believe they are called, in the Loire Valley. He has been renting a room and working in a local bar. One of our counterparts in France has approached him but, as yet, he does not want to be contacted or found. Life has been quite tough for him since he left you and he is just finding his feet again.'

At that point my shock at the news turned to anger and I exploded, 'Does Gerald have any idea how *I've* lived since he left and chucked me out of my own home without the courage to face me? Did Gerald experience living a life with *no* roof over his head when he disappeared, with the meagre remainder of our life savings, the rest of which he squandered on a whim?'

I would have continued with my rant but the poor man put his hand up to halt the flow. 'In situations such as these, and we deal with many, your husband cannot come to terms with his own plight. He has no idea and is too riddled with guilt and regret to deal with yours too Mrs Gibbons. I know that it's impossible for you to comprehend, but you'll have to come to terms with this and respect his decision, I'm afraid.'

'So where does that leave me? How does this help?'

'Firstly Mrs Gibbons, it will take away the uncertainty about your situation. I hope that, given time, you will feel relieved that he is safe. It does, however, mean that you will not be able to make a claim for any life insurance your husband may have had.'

I was speechless. My husband had lied to me. He'd stolen my life from under my feet. He had a home. I did not. How was I supposed to feel? Should I feel grateful to him for being alive? Should I feel relieved? I felt none of those things. In fact, I felt numb with emotion. Totally drained. The healing process for me had only been skin deep. Gerald still had the ability to inflict a deep and sharp pain.

Jamal filled the silence, looking almost embarrassed by my inability to respond positively. He thought I'd be relieved to hear proof that Gerald was alive. He did not understand – or was it me who had no understanding?

'Thank you for all your help. Is this the end of the process or is there any more we can do?' Jamal asked, his voice stuttering, unable to hide his confusion.

The man smiled at Jamal. 'I'm afraid that, if Mr Gibbons has no wish to be found, then we have to respect that. We have no right at the Red Cross to say more. In fact, he has agreed for us to pass on this limited amount of information because he felt that Mrs Gibbons would be reassured by it.' A frown appeared momentarily on his brow as he glanced at my scowl, but it was soon replaced by a caring, albeit forced smile. 'What you *can* do, if you wish, is to contact your husband through ourselves. It will be the old fashioned snail mail I'm afraid, unless it's very urgent, but we *can* offer you this service free of charge – unless of course your circumstances change and you are able to give us a donation.'

I did not return his smile but, coming to my senses, I had the presence of mind to mutter a thank you for his time before being ushered out of the room and the building. Jamal popped a few coins in the collecting box as we left.

We walked to the bus stop. The silence a stone wall between us as solid as the one by which we stood. Taking seats on the upper floor of the bus I gazed out of the window, feeling a moment of guilt as I spotted Karen's bungalow. How long was it since I had visited? Had my courage failed me? I had abandoned a friend who had so few people in her life. The word 'friend' is such a loaded word, 'husband' similarly, I mused.

Jamal cleared his throat. 'Auntie, you know how I respect you, but at this point I don't understand you. If I had heard that Ahmed was safe I would be, how do you say it, *over the moon,* even though he did not wish me to find him.'

I did smile then at Jamal's attempt for colloquialism. 'Yes, that's a perfect phrase for how you'd feel Jamal.' I paused. 'I can't explain my reaction to the news. I know that it seems irrational and uncaring to think this way about the man I shared so many years of my life with. Sad to say any sentiments I had for Gerald were buried when he left me.' I noted that I resisted mentioning the word *love.* 'I am going to shock you here but in some ways it would have been better if he had been found dead.'

Jamal looked horrified and I softened a little. I did appreciate that he'd tried so hard to please me. We were silent for a while longer. I broke that silence. 'At least we know the truth now. In time I may see this as a blessing. Our search has ended and I must thank you for all your sleuthing.'

'Sleuthing?'

'Ah, that means an investigation into a mystery or even a crime and tends, but not always, to be associated with someone who is an amateur; who is not in the police force I think. I'll have to look it up. I'm not sure come to think of it.' Jamal's face had slipped into the boyish smile I knew so well and I in turn smiled back.

'I will never forget your patience teaching us English in your kitchen Mrs G,' Jamal's voice was warm and soft.

'Over many cups of tea,' I added, the tension between us finally dispersing.

'I don't think so Mrs G.'

'You don't think what?' My eyebrows lifted.

'The Red Cross Man explained that their investigation is at an end but it doesn't mean we should stop looking.'

I frowned. 'I expect they get a back hander from the life insurance company.' I could not help but allow cynicism to colour my tone. This was lost on Jamal who probably didn't understand what I meant by *back-hander*, let alone the implications of an insurance company. 'I think you should just let the matter drop now Jamal. You have your own life to think about. Your own future. My life will change once I've got a base again and maybe I can get a part time job too.'

It had been a huge step for me to agree to be assessed by the Social Services. Firstly I always thought that there must be cases more deserving. After all, I'd found occupation at The Grange and for a while I'd had a roof over my head. I also had allies in Jamal, Orla, Laura and Angelina. Was I too proud? If so then it had to stop. Tomorrow I would visit my new home, although I was a touch afraid, having been influenced by hearsay of druggies, loose women and maybe worse. Who would my neighbours be? I shuddered.

Thinking I was feeling chilly Jamal retrieved my coat from the top of the rucksack and draped it over me. He lifted the bag on to his own shoulders as we alighted the bus and he walked me to The Ark for possibly my last night there ever.

'Thank you Jamal. I don't know what I would have done without you.' Feeling a touch self conscious following our misunderstanding and also aware that we were standing in the street, I refrained from hugging my 'son', but instead I grasped his hands in mine.

'Shall we meet at the cafe in a couple of days? I'm working tomorrow but Friday I'm free – say three o'clock?' he asked.

'Yes that would be lovely,' I replied as we parted.

As I drifted to sleep that night I was searching for something. I was at Tintagel Castle Cornwall investigating Merlin's Cave. Taking the steep stone steps with wooden balustrade downwards to the beach, I admired the waterfall and the face of Merlin carved near the cave's entrance. The path, at first sandy, was soon strewn with rocks and pebbles and then I was climbing over the rocks themselves avoiding large pools; a warning of the need to be vigilant. I paused for a few moments to gaze up at the crystal seams in the grey granite rock face and patches of damp glistening with spring water from above. Looking over my shoulder the sandy beach, was now framed in jagged light; waves rolling in. As I turned my foot slipped and caught between the rocks and for a while I struggled to free myself. Once free I noticed the pools filling up, but ahead I caught a glimpse of light. Choosing each step with care I walked on. I knew time was precious. I gave myself only a few moments to gaze on the ocean at the other side of the island before turning to retrace my steps towards the light from whence I'd come. Soon I was up to my knees in water, although unsure of my footing I waded on, now afraid for my own safety.

At that point I felt a hand on my shoulder. Disorientated, I opened my eyes to see Orla standing over me.

'Come and have a cup of tea Mrs G. Your cries are disturbing the other residents.'

Dazed and groggy I followed Orla out of the hut and back into the lounge. She placed my rucksack at my side and I was grateful for her presence of mind to retrieve it. Who knows whether my sleeping neighbours were trustworthy? Probably not.

Once seated I shared what I could remember of my nightmare with her.

'I'm no expert Mrs G but I'd say that it was a good sign that there was light either end. Whichever way you choose, your way may be tough, and at time fraught with danger, but you will get through.' She smiled.

We drank our tea quietly together for a while after that, before she left me to my thoughts.

CHAPTER 28

I DOZED IN the lounge until the following morning, but as soon as it was light I left to have a walk over the fields around Drumford, glancing over my shoulder one last time at The Ark, my refuge. After clearing my head I retraced my steps to take the steep climb to Drew Street in a northern suburb of the town. I was shown into a single room by a kind matronly lady with an East London accent who called herself Bella.

'I'll leave you to settle in,' she said. 'When you're ready, come down to my office and we'll complete the paperwork. Then I'll give you a tour of the shared area and brief you with Health and Safety Instructions.

I frowned.

'Yes I know. It sounds a bit officious but those are the rules. I'm sure you'll find your feet Mrs Gibbons and you can have as little or as much to do with the other residents as you'd like. We have a variety of self help groups and craft activities, even a creative writing workshop.'

My eyes lit up.

'Yes,' Bella said. 'Many of our folks here find creativity a way of healing. Some describe their experiences. Some write poems but others find writing stories takes them to a place which they can control. Anyway, I'll introduce you to the tutor, Jill, if you are interested.'

'I think I know Jill.'

'Ah, she teaches at The Ark too. That's right. I'll give you some peace for a while now though. '

'Thank you,' I said as the veneered light wooden door, which was slightly scuffed in places, closed behind her.

It was quiet. I barely moved a muscle. Then my hearing tuned in to the sounds of the hostel which would soon become familiar. Muffled music. The thump of a low bass. Someone singing. A door closing. A car starting up outside my window. I was alone inside my own room for the first time since I'd left home; that is if I did not count The Grange.

I observed my surroundings like a stranger, feeling detached from my body. A single bed with a burnt orange bedspread; a grey padded plastic chair, like a cheap office armchair; a tiny desk under the window with two drawers and a wooden chair pushed right in to give space to move past. The windows were framed with burnt orange curtains and old fashioned nets. There was a small sink in the corner of the room with a broken mirror above and next to that a door leading to the water closet. Ah, I thought, that's another word for Jamal. Yes, in layman's terms there was just enough space for a toilet. A small oak wardrobe with a large base drawer filled the spare corner of the room and that was it. But it *was* my space. I sat at the desk. Enough light to write for hours. I smiled. So this was to be my new home.

I reached for my rucksack and pulled out my notebook, pens, pencils and the precious reams of scrap paper and laid them out neatly. Then I spread my few clothes on the bed, most of which had been donated by Angelina and all had been washed for me at The Ark last night. Two changes of underwear, two tops and two pairs of trousers, those jersey kind which don't need ironing – vital when you are sleeping rough; my waterproof coat and lastly my pink hat, both of which I hung on the back of the door. Orla had even kindly washed my burgundy coat which had seen better days, although my hat looked even more battered and smelt a bit musty. She hadn't dared wash it in case it fell to pieces. Nevertheless it was mine and had been my companion all these years. For a moment I felt a pang of longing for my special clearing, air filled with butterflies and bees and the scent of lazy summer days. Resisting the temptation to escape back to the familiarity of life on the road I picked up my notebook, locked the door behind me and went in search of Bella.

Her instructions were simple and common sense really. I had no need for notes:

If there is an emergency after ten o'clock at night, pull the panic cord.

Don't wander through the building at night.

No music to be played after 11 pm.

No shouting at anytime or running for that matter.

Don't call on your neighbours unless invited, but meet up in the public areas and not in your rooms.

Respect each other's privacy and don't pry.

Keep your own room locked whether you are in it or out of it.

Keep your own room clean.

Cleaning agents and cloths can be found in the cupboard in the kitchen which is locked at 10 pm.

In case of fire leave your belongings and quickly evacuate the building by the safest fire exit, at either ends of the corridors on both floors. Break the fire bell glass if you discover the fire.

I'm sure there were more rules but I switched off after that and longed to be free.

'Let's show you around then,' Bella said as she got to her feet and I noticed that she locked her office after her too. It didn't take long to show me the small lounge which contained a few old armchairs, a red melamine table and red metal dining chairs to match. There was a small kitchen which was spotless. The fridge was like none I'd seen before because it contained eight drawers like a freezer but each was locked. Bella pointed out the tiny key on my key ring for my compartment labelled eight. A wonderful aroma of chicken curry made my mouth water. Various condiments were in the door of the fridge for general use – tomato and brown sauce, mustard, salad cream and such like and two four pint containers of milk.

'The residents all contribute towards those items because there wouldn't be room if everyone had their own,' Bella explained.

Finally there was another room on the other side of the corridor and this contained semi comfortable chairs, like the one in my room but spaced in a circle, and also a couple of desks with very old PC's on them.

'We do have Wi-Fi here. If you want to book a slot then you need to sign up on the chart on the door.' One woman looked up from her computer and smiled tentatively. The other ignored us, staring grimly at her screen. 'If anyone hogs the computer time then they are banned for a few days. We try to be as fair as possible. This is also the room where the group meetings take place, including the creative writing. That's tomorrow night if you'd like to join it. You can sign up on the back of the door too.'

'Yes, I'd like to very much thanks.'

'It's good to join in to activities if you can. Now where was I? Ah yes, this board here is for notices of events at the hostel.' She paused, smiling at me.

Having people around me suddenly made me feel a bit claustrophobic and I must have frowned, echoed in the hesitancy of my voice. 'I'm sure I'll be fine.'

'Well Mrs Gibbons give it time, eh. I know that you're older than all of our current residents, but can we call you by your first name rather than Mrs Gibbons? It seems a bit formal for a home like this.'

I thought about it for a moment, realising that the two ladies at the computers were listening. Most people call me Mrs G, I replied, 'but my name is Dorothy,' I conceded.

Bella smiled with a warmth that shone from her eyes. 'Well Dorothy, I'll leave you to settle in. If there's anything you need or want to know then please come and ask.'

With that she left me. Suddenly embarrassed I scuttled back upstairs to my room. All of the bedrooms were on the first floor. Relieved I locked the door behind me and flopped down on to the bed. I must have slept because I suddenly came to wondering where I was and remembered that I was to meet Jamal at 3 pm. There was a helpful clock on the wall; I would buy a new battery for my own watch when my social security money came through. I shuddered at the reality of it but then snapped myself out of my indulgent self pity and looked out of the window. It was a sunny afternoon so I grabbed my small purse and left without the encumbrance of either rucksack or coat. It was a sense of freedom with a difference as the realisation that I had a more permanent base became a reality.

Jamal beamed at me. 'You look so different Mrs G. Sort of carefree.'

'Thank you Jamal. I think I'm going to be OK.'

CHAPTER 29

MY DAYS FELL into a pattern. I would write in the mornings and then after a simple lunch I would go for a wander, if the weather was favourable. On those days I would love to roam around the paths and lanes I had come to know so well and call my own. It uplifted and revived my waning creativity levels.

If it was wet I would have a small break and continue to write all day, or find another resident to talk with. One young girl was very lonely and appeared constantly on edge as if she were scared of any noise or new intruder to her space. I shall call her Samira because that is what she named herself, although we both knew that it wasn't her real name.

Samira jumped whenever the door opened. One day she told me her story.

'I was in love with a young Bengali lad but my family didn't approve. I had known him from primary school and we'd always been close, playing together in the playground and sitting together in class. At Comprehensive School it was harder because we were in different classes and our meetings, which were in fact innocent, could be over dramatised by our friends. We were always afraid that this gossip would get back to our parents. Instead, we contacted each other on line and sometimes talked on Skype when we could. We even met occasionally but our parents couldn't know. Unfortunately, one day my cousin snitched on us and we were in big trouble. I was just seventeen and had started a catering course at the local College of Further Education. I swore to my parents that no harm was done and that we wanted to get married anyway. They were furious.'

'You weren't pregnant were you?' I asked.

'Oh no, nothing like that Auntie.' I smiled at her use of 'Auntie'. She continued her story. 'We had only held hands a couple of times, but we *were* in love; truly we were.'

'So what happened next Samira?'

'Well; my family stopped speaking to me and took away my phone and laptop, confining me to the house when I wasn't at college. They drove me to the door each morning and picked me up the moment classes finished. I couldn't breathe. One day I heard them plotting to send me away to Pakistan to get married. I didn't know what to do. I was desperate to finish my qualifications. I adore cooking you see. Well, my girlfriend encouraged me to go to the student's services at college and ask for counselling. One day, in strictest confidence, I shared my story with a kind lady who gave me options.'

'You had a difficult decision to make then Samira.'

'Yes Auntie. I could do what my parents wished me to do or I could agree for the authorities to help me to run away. It wasn't that simple a choice though. I knew that, if I chose the latter, then I would either be searched for or rejected totally by my family. If I chose to do as they asked I would probably have been married to some old man in Pakistan, a widower with lots of money no doubt, just to teach me a lesson.'

There was quiet between us as I realised the enormity of this vulnerable girl's situation.

'You were brave Samira. So you chose to run. That must have been hard.'

'I had so little time to think, Auntie. I had been told that I would be taken to a safe home in a different town if I chose. I won't tell you where I've come from or which college I went to. No-one knows. Safer that way. They counselled me over several days explaining that to run away would not be the easiest option.'

'Have you heard from any of your friends or family?'

'No Auntie. I was warned not to. Not even my best friend. I don't think any harm would come to me but I've heard such bad stories. It wasn't worth the risk.'

'Do you feel safe now you're here though?'

'Safe, yes I think so. I can't deny that I'm lonely at times, but everyone is so kind. I miss my mother though, so very much. It's a pain right here.' Samira held her hand over her heart.

'Oh bless you child; I know exactly how you feel.'

'I'm not a child,' Samira said with a voice of defiance. 'I've nearly finished my course and will apply for jobs working in a hotel on the coast. It is my dream. It will be my life and I will love it.'

'And your boyfriend?'

'I can't contact him either Auntie.' For a moment Samira looked wistfully out of the window, her eyes a reflection of her great loss and sacrifice.

I reached out and held her hands in mind. 'You're so strong Samira. You'll get through this. If ever you want to talk, then just knock on my door. Don't hesitate.' I knew that she had taken on a different identity, and would have to refrain from using Facebook or any social media which could be traced. It would be certainly be extremely lonely for her.

The following afternoon I met Samira in the day room. She smiled up at me from her book, a large tome of the technical language she would need to learn for her trade.

'Would you like me to make you a cup of tea, Auntie?'

'That would be lovely,' I replied. 'I'm not disturbing your studies am I?'

'No Auntie, I could do with a break. Anyway, it's nice to have company and I'm thirsty too.'

Samira made some milky tea for us in the kitchen, showing me how she would have made it at home. Once we had settled down in the armchairs she continued her story as if she had never broken off,

'You see, Auntie, I was told that, if I really wanted to escape.' She paused a moment or two. 'If I was absolutely sure, then I was to give a signal. I can't even tell you what it was. I worried and fretted, making myself ill with the decision I had to make. Either option made me shudder. Life was so unfair. Until one day I overheard my mother and father whispering about booking a flight for me to go to Pakistan the following weekend and so I felt I had no choice. I made the secret sign in college the next day. A Thursday. At home I gathered together a few belongings, not many, in my carpet bag and waited.

A police car came to the door and asked to see me and they took me away in their car and into custody, initially. I'm not sure what they said to my brother but my parents were out at the time. Mum and Dad had already confiscated my mobile and laptop so I took nothing that could be traceable. Later that night they brought me here and I was introduced to Bella. The journey was a long one and it was dark, so I didn't know where I was being taken. Even here I have been banished from the computers. That was nearly six months ago.' Her face suddenly brightened. 'I love the catering course I am doing though. It's a challenge but it's the only thing I cling on to.'

As I glanced at Samira I noticed that her face had a serene glow of acceptance. It was a story which moved me greatly as I compared it to my own circumstances.

'Don't you want to contact your boyfriend, even now?'

'I have to be strong Auntie, and follow my rescuers advice and not contact anyone.'

'You are an amazing young lady Samira and I'm sure your dreams will come true. You deserve it.' We smiled at each other.

As I thought about Samira in my room later on, I believed that her total surrender to her current situation gave her the peace and strength to carry on with optimism and good grace. For me it was still *a steep learning curve* and I had great admiration for her fortitude and resilience.

On another occasion she told me about Ali and once more she showed a strength of character well beyond her seventeen years.

'Auntie, I believe in fate. If we're meant to be together, Ali and me, then our paths will cross again. Meanwhile I am working towards a better future for me and my future children.'

I was truly humbled by her story.

Another young lady I met there had been verbally and physically abused. Janet had a deep scar on her face where her partner had attacked her with a kitchen knife, jealous that she had spent an evening with her best friend. It was all about control. Her partner Alec was a control freak who was possessive to the nth degree. Yet again Janet had changed her name for her own safety and had been brought to Drumford Refuge, miles away from home, in the hopes that she could begin to build a fresh life for herself.

Other neighbours were more reticent to talk about themselves and I respected their privacy. One of these ladies was glued to the computer when I first arrived. Back in my room that night I reflected on my own circumstances. I was so fortunate to be able to gain solace from my writing and the countryside. I was also blessed with a network of support at The Ark, and I had Jamal of course. I wondered how Angelina was. I had not heard from her but one day I hoped I would, having so much to thank her for.

CHAPTER 30

THIS WAS A period of calm and stability in my life. I neither dwelt on the past, nor dared to think too far into the future. I aimed to make each day count and to strive to achieve something to be proud of in my writing. I watched the relationship between Orla and Jamal grow, comforted by the knowledge that Orla's sister condoned it. Like Samira I endeavoured to trust to fate for all of our lives, especially my own; escaping in my story was my true refuge.

Jill's monthly session focussed on harnessing the power of hardship to colour our writing. 'You have to feel deeply to write about intense feelings,' she said and she read out some pieces to inspire us. My experience living rough in winter certainly prepared me for the chapter ahead, big time.

The Nun's Tale Part 4

To Bonnie Scotland

Maud and Archie endured a punishing journey across the Pennines. After two days they had reached Lockerbie and found a barn in which to shelter for the night. The following day they were forced to turn back when snow drifts barred their way. They found sanctuary in the same old barn where they had slept the previous night and were forced to remain there for two more days. Clouds of snow flurried like feathers from gaping holes in the straw roof, blown into heaps against the rafters and the barn door. It was this water source, in fact, that saved them from impending death. By filling their old water bottle with snow they were able to melt it between them under a pile of sacking. It was worth the sacrifice of a few moments heat loss. They still had meagre rations which they had squirreled away at the farm; dried biscuits and hard stale bread which they softened in the water. Likewise they soaked rolled oats, making it more palatable to swallow; only just keeping thirst and starvation at bay. To avoid frostbite they huddled even closer together, periodically rubbing each other's hands and feet. Even so their hands were achingly numb and they could barely move their fingers.

The following day was brighter and so they walked on, the air thinning and the track ascending. Maud had never seen such beauty and wondered if she had, in fact, died in the barn and gone to heaven. The sheer majesty of snow covered hills contrasted against the clear blue sky, glorious and yet impenetrable. Later that day the stillness was replaced by squalling gusts and the wind chill factor encouraging them to walk faster. Soon a large dark cloud sped across the sky and loomed above them, an ominous portent of their future and perhaps a warning to retreat. They paid no heed of it and continued to trudge on.

Thankfully the cloud passed over with only a flurry of sleet. Maud shivered although warm inside from their exertions, her arms swinging at her side. Her fingers tingled; a pain-pleasure feeling, not totally unpleasant. The trick was to let them thaw slowly, she could almost hear her friend Emma whispering in her ear.

Maud smiled. Archie glanced in her direction.

'What you grinning about?'

'Oh, I was thinking about Emma. I doubt if we'll ever see her again.

Archie frowned. They continued in deafening silence.

They passed a ridge of hills on their right, which appeared like the mountains Maud had seen in sketches at the convent. There she spotted a bird, larger than any she had ever seen. It soared in the air. She refrained from smiling this time but remembered a verse from the bible which gave her comfort.

'Those with hope in the Lord will renew their strength. They will soar on wings like eagles, they will run and not grow weary, they will walk and not be faint ..'

Maud's spirit was uplifted with the memory and she caught up with Archie, who was racing ahead of her, wishing to reach the end of this leg of their long trail before the final rays of sunset dissipated. They reached Beattock before total darkness and stumbled on towards Moffat. Maud was able to buy some scraps to eat just before the market closed. They were desperate to find somewhere to stay for the night but could not afford a room. Maud was extremely tired and so she sat down in a porch way to a guest house while Archie searched for shelter. Visitors returning from the spa thought she was begging and handed her a few coins and to her surprise, amongst the farthings was a shilling. She looked up but her Good Samaritan had disappeared.

It was the first time Archie had smiled for days and they found a cheap boarding house on the northern outskirts of the town where they were shown to a room no more than the size of wardrobes she had polished at Belmont house, and as dark too. From the light of the moon spilling sparingly through the dirty window, they shared their limited refreshments and, exhausted, they fell into a deep sleep, only to be awakened by their landlady the following morning.

'If yous don't leave in the next ten minutes I'll be charging yous another days rent,' she yelled.

'How many miles is it to Glasgow?' Archie ventured before they escaped.

'Why do you want to go all that way?' their landlady retorted.

'That's where we're headin,' replied Archie, even now unwilling to divulge any personal information.

A moderately dressed middle aged man with a beard and hat came out of the door behind them. He smiled, a look which Maud thought was familiar, but she was not sure.

'It's about sixty miles,' he said.

From their crestfallen glances the gentleman took pity on the pair. 'If you'd like to sit atop my carriage you're welcome to travel wi' me', he said. 'My man is just fetching it from the stables. The journey will take us at least two days, possibly three, but the weather looks fair for now, so you'd better make up your minds quickly.'

'Yes, that would be kind of you,' Archie replied for both of them.

'At night you can sleep in the stables with the carriage. You can be a guard while my man sleeps. What do you say?'

'That's more than generous,' Maud said.

Once the carriage had arrived, Archie and Maud climbed up, huddled between two trunks, some tarpaulin to shield them from the worst of the cold.

'Try to cover your faces and get some sleep if you can,' the gentleman said before settling himself inside the carriage below them.

Maud and Archie saw little of the remaining landscape. The temperature was below freezing and so they kept well hidden from the frosty air. The road was, in all honesty, smoother with the layer of compacted snow than it would have been pitted by rains and storms. By night they took it in turns to remain awake to repay the man's generosity. He asked for no money and ensured that they had bread and cheese or gruel each morning and night, even a bottle of beer for Archie.

Their final journey took them into the centre of Glasgow one late December afternoon. Their benefactor would take no payment but had the forethought to drop them at The Old Green in Great Clyde Street; the location of Glasgow's Poorhouse. He also slipped a few pence into Archie's hands as they parted. For a few moments Archie and Maud stared at each other in almost disbelief. Their wedding coats had done them a great service in giving protection from the worst of the weather and they had secured transport when they needed it most.

'We made it then,' said Archie. 'Let's see what Glasgow has to offer us.'

The initial euphoria at reaching their destination was short lived. After a few hours trudging the streets looking for work and food, with not enough money in their pocket for even one night's lodgings, Archie and Maud felt totally defeated. No choice was left but to retrace their steps to the poorhouse for shelter, but the couple were even turned away from there. The Inspector of the Poor took down details and noted the date of their request of entry, stressing that meanwhile both should do their utmost to secure employment and accommodation. The rules were that folks had to be in the vicinity for at least six nights before admission and, since Maud and Archie were strangers to Glasgow and had no recent residency in the city, they had no other option but to wait.

Downhearted and exhausted they turned along a side street and huddled together on a doorstep of a tenement building. This first night in the city didn't bode well for the bright future of their dreams. Neither spoke.

Occasionally they were shoved out of the way as men, usually drunk, tried to climb over them to access the building. This would be followed by yelling and screaming from within. Then all was quiet once more.

As Maud tried to sleep she could not help but think of how far she had fallen in pursuit of happiness. She could have been warm, dry and respectable as a nun had she not succumbed to temptation. Evie was on her mind once more as she drifted in and out of sleep.

The following morning a young woman in a long grey cloak shook them awake and handed them some bread, wholesome albeit a bit stale, before disappearing into the mist.

'I'm gonna find my way to the docks to see if there's work. You must look too. See what you can find out about this place and I'll meet you back here at sundown,' and then he was gone.

Maud waited where she was, in the hopes that a resident might help her. Soon the door opened behind her and a pair of youngish ladies brushed past. She plucked up courage and raced to walk beside them. Their pace quickened, noses upturned.

'Please, can you tell me where I may find work?'

One of the lassies, a dark haired girl with a plait just showing from under her hooded cloak, paused and looked at her friend. She shrugged her shoulders and was about to walk on when her companion, a fair haired lass with a shawl wrapped tightly around her head stopped, remembering her mam's premise, 'Treat strangers as you'd wish to be treated yusel.'

'Well,' she said.

'Come on Aggie, we'll be late for work.'

The dark haired lass pulled Aggie by the sleeve of her coat but the girl looked over her shoulder and called out, 'Look, I canna stop the noo but if yer here when us cum home then we'll talk to yous,' and off they went, walking at a pace.

Maud drifted through the day, never too far away from Clyde Street. Neither her experience at Grange Farm nor Belmont House had prepared her for the life she saw before her. She was filled with sadness verging on despair as she was turned away from a dress maker, a laundry and several small shops. She passed several beggars on the street and shivered. How could she ever have reached so low?

The secret she held became a heavy burden. Her glimmer of hope that Archie might find work was short-lived when his crestfallen face summed up their situation.

'So what have you done today to get us out of this mess Maud?' spitting out the words.

'I tried all the places locally and they aren't taking on new workers. I've been on my feet all day. A lady from inside,' and she flicked her eyes in the direction of the upstairs window, 'has just spoken to me. She's a weaver but they only

need skilled workers. That's no good for me. I can sew pretty well but I can't weave. What about you?'

There was silence for a while and Maud wondered if Archie was even going to bother to reply. 'I met this chap who told me to try the engineering works at Tradeston. I'd do anything,' he paused struggling for words, 'but there was nothing. Then I walked back along the river to the Queen's Docks. I was far too late. They queue to be stevedores early in the morning, so this Jock said mebbe tomorrow.' The inflection in his voice tried to portray optimism when he felt none.

They ate the rest of the bread which Maud had kept deep in her pocket. Both were ravenous and it did little to stem the tide of hunger pangs which kept Maud awake most of the night.

The same lady gave them more bread the following morning just before daybreak and grabbing the majority of it from Maud's hands Archie was off. 'It's up te you te find food for tonight,' he called back over his shoulder.

This was the pattern for the next two nights. They found no work, although Maud was given some bread by a lassie from a baker's just before they closed; a place she had enquired about work with no success. Despondent, they were just snuggling down for the night when it began to snow. Out of the flurry came a man of the cloth who beckoned them to follow him. He said little but led them to the porch of a church which would shelter them from the storm that was to come. Maud was beyond gratitude to be sharing this refuge with half a dozen other folks, especially when the parson's wife came out with platefuls of a hearty potato soup. Much to Archie's annoyance Maud shared the bread between their companions. Sulking, Archie turned his back on her as she tried to curl up and sleep that night and in the morning she

*found herself close to a girl a few years younger than herself.
Archie had long gone.*

*'Ah'm fair scunnered!' Aggie's broad Glaswegian accent
woke Maud up with a start. Not understanding a word the
girl had said Maud didn't answer. 'Where yer from then?' she
added.*

*'We're from England. What did you mean just then –
Scunnered – is that what you said?'*

*The girl laughed. 'I'm right fed up, that's all. Lost me job
yesterday and was thrown ooot the hoos I was in. Lucky the
pastor found me. I was right cold.'*

*'We're looking for work too. Heard Glasgow was a good
city with lots of opportunities.'*

'Yer heid's full o'mince. Gud fer some no dout.'

'Mince?' Maud frowned.

*'Nonsense!' the girl replied hooting with laughter until
her belly ached.*

'Me name's Aggie.'

'I'm Maud.'

*They sat in silence for a moment or two. Meanwhile the
parson's wife brought them a pot of porridge to share in their
licked-clean bowls from the night before.*

*Once they'd had their fill Aggie said, 'Come wi me,' and
they walked together in the winter sunshine, arm in arm.
Together they trailed the streets locally but found no work.
Nevertheless Aggie did take Maud to a back street behind a
large hotel where they waited for over an hour. Their patience
was rewarded because a young lad sneaked out and handed
Aggie a couple of scones and some old cheese before rushing
back inside.*

*'That's me wee brother,' Aggie said by way of
explanation. They rushed around the corner and out of sight*

before heading back to the church porch, the sky having turned an ominous dark grey.

Archie arrived back as grumpy as ever. There was no point Maud even asking what was wrong but Aggie said, 'Who stole yer scone?'

At which point Archie's anger exploded and he yelled. 'I haven't got any scones. What the hell are you talking about?'

If Maud had been on her own she would have been mortified but Aggie's mischievousness was infectious and Maud found it hard to suppress a giggle. She handed him one of the scones at which point Aggie was fit to burst once more, when the parson came out to see what the noise was all about.

In a quiet voice, almost a whisper, he explained, 'Yer cannae be making a noise like that in the hoos of God. Yer must move on the noo.'

And so they were back on to the streets once more, all three of them. Archie didn't speak to Maud for the remaining two days as they huddled in their previously found doorway. The following day he even came back worse for drink and Maud knew that he'd spent the last few pence that they had had been given. They were destitute.

The following morning was their sixth day in Glasgow. Maud and Archie returned to the poorhouse, with Aggie tagging along. The Inspector of the Poor, a portly man with a severe demeanour, signed papers declaring them paupers and signalled that they should proceed to the gatekeeper. There Archie and Maud were separated at the threshold. Aggie and Maud were taken to a side room, along with a large group of women also being admitted. They suffered the indignity of being stripped and checked for diseases but it was wonderful to be bathed, albeit in tepid water, and given clean skirts and smocks, both scratchy on the skin but at least they were dry.

'They'll wash yerr clothes and keep them for yer. Dunna yous worry.'

Maud didn't see where her husband had been taken. Archie was no longer at her side for the first time since they had left Drumford, because men and women slept in segregated dormitories. They had no way of communicating and she had a great deal of time to reflect on their misfortune. Sleeping rough would have been the death of them for sure as winter progressed. At least they now had a roof over their heads and some food each day, as gruel was served each morning.

Three days later, before they could become too comfortable in a routine, if comfortable was the right word for their harsh life, they had a surprise. It was after Sunday prayers that a well-to-do man visited the poor house. His air of authority was heightened by his attire; a ruffled silk neckline showing above his double breasted woollen coat which went down to his britches. The gentleman asked to see the residents and so they were all lined up in the great hall. He walked up and down the lines staring at each in a sombre albeit kindly fashion. On his second walk around he pointed to twenty of them, and the House Governor, who had accompanied him, indicated that these inmates should step aside while the others were ushered away.

Maud glanced up and caught Archie's eye. She could see that he was pleased to see her and felt a mixture of relief and fear that they had both been chosen. Archie hoped it was for work of some kind, after all he noted that those chosen had been young and fit. Anything to be free of this prison-like existence, he thought.

All were given their own clothes to change back into and, as Aggie had predicted, they had been steam cleaned. Maud and Archie's clothes were fresh, albeit a bit ragged after their *travelling. Soon they were ushered to waiting carts, the first time they'd seen the light of day in three days. Maud was pleased that Aggie had been chosen too.*

'Do you know where we're going?' she whispered to her new friend.

'I think the posh man is the owner of a mill. I've heard rumours that he wants workers out' the city and if that be true then we're blessed indeed.' She smiled at Maud.

Their fellow companions were equally excited and nervous as to their fate, especially as they headed out into the open countryside. For some it was the first time they had ever left Glasgow, but for Maud and Archie it was just another step on a long and arduous journey into the unknown, from which they now had no alternative but to travel. The buggies appeared to be heading south east, and Archie hoped that they were not being returned to England.

It took two hours but eventually they were heading down a steep track which disappeared into a ravine. It was beautiful in the snow and occasionally the wheels slipped on the ice, unnerving the horses. Nothing prepared them for the sight which was to greet them next.

CHAPTER 31

DAYS PASSED QUICKLY in The Refuge. Hours writing, interspersed with talking to the other residents, carrying out mundane tasks of shopping and cleaning for myself but also collectively. Each of us had our chores to complete. Mine was to keep the kitchen spotless, a task I found strangely therapeutic. Talking of therapy I also had a fortnightly session with Bella. She helped me to think about the next stage in my life. After all, I couldn't remain there forever. I had five months before my 60th birthday and so our timeline worked towards that point, when I would finally be entitled to my small pension from the council for my work in the library. This gave me even more incentive to complete my novel.

By now Jamal was passing back chapters for me to proof read and improve and so gradually a pile of almost complete manuscript was growing on my chair. Jamal kept a copy just in case. I was excited albeit a little nervous about the next part of my story. Having visited New Lanark Mills on a couple of occasions on holidays to Scotland, I was fascinated by its history and in awe of its authentic restoration.

The Nun's Tale Part 4

Lanark Mills

A huge mill and stone buildings several stories high, flanked by rows of tiny cottages, surrounded us in all directions. A tiny church stood strategically visible on an outcrop. There was a grocers shop for our needs and a washing area down by the river where women were singing. Other couples were taking a stroll between the newly planted trees. The place was like a miniature city within a valley - everything was so clean and new. The day was Sunday and the mill was eerily quiet.

The group alighted from their buggies and were ushered into a hall where they were registered by two clerks sitting at carved oak desks. Husbands and wives were reunited and given a hearty vegetable soup and bread for their nourishment before being shown to the tall stone tenement building opposite and allocated quarters.

Archie and Maud were to share a room with another couple of a similar age. Maud had been separated from Aggie but she hoped to find her friend again one day.

'How are we all to sleep in here?' asked Maud, since the room was small and the furniture spartan. Two single slatted wooden beds were pushed to the wall with a curtain for a modicum of privacy. These were either side of the fireplace over which hung a large cooking pot with a kettle at the side. The grate was clean and blackened and a tiny bag of coal sat on the hearth. A small table near the window, a wooden bucket, chamber pot and a tin beside the kettle, in which was a tiny amount of leaf tea, completed the furnishings. All was

scrubbed spotless and a clean pile of ticking, with the earthy scent of hay, lay on one of the beds.

The other lady bent down and, to Maud's surprise, she pulled out another slightly smaller wooden slatted bed on wheels.

'There's y'are,' she said. 'It's called a Hurlie bed. I'm Brenda by the way and this here's Duncan.'

'I'm Maud and my husband is Archie,' Maud replied shyly.

'Yous not from these parts then?'

'No we're from England. It's a long story but we were searching for work.'

'Looks as like yous fallen on yer feet then.' Brenda smiled.

Maud was too tired to try to puzzle out what her new companion meant and frowned.

'We've all bin lucky,' Brenda said more gently. 'I've heard rumours about this place and they're all gud.'

Maud smiled.

The men began to lay the fire while Brenda and Maud investigated a water source. It wasn't hard to find. They followed a few women to the outskirts of the village and waited in line to fill their bucket from a well. Retracing their steps they noted the foul stink from the rear of the buildings, which they knew they would have to visit later.

By the time the four of them had brewed some tea it was dark and time to settle for the night and so, lighting their way by tallow candles, and by their sense of smell, they found their way to the nearest midden; earth closets where they were able to carry out their ablutions before returning and retiring for the night.

The following morning Archie and Duncan were taken up river where work was still being carried out laying and maintaining paths. They were also shown where they would be labouring for the stonemasons who were building Double

Row and Wee Row, the first of cottage style terraced housing on the edge of the main development. Both were put to work there, a gruelling long day of hod carrying, especially in the winter months, and at night the men moaned incessantly to Maud and Brenda.

The women's lot was more pleasant, since they were both trained as spinners in the mill itself. Maud only caught glimpses of Aggie, who had been put in a different department due to her proficiency in weaving. Not long after that Maud heard that Aggie had returned to Glasgow to look after her siblings, since her Ma had passed away with pneumonia.

'Stop yer moaning,' Brenda exclaimed to the men one day. 'We have work, a roof over our 'eds and two hot meals a day. Millie's a dab hand at cooking too. The beef broth we 'ad today was the best I've tasted in me life and that's a fact! Stop yer complaining, will yer!'

For a while it was quiet. The men slouched on their beds while the women swept the room and cleaned the hearth between them.

'While you's rest we women still work, 'n that's after a fourteen hour day in tut mill. Tomorrow the Bug Hunters are aroond and we'll as like as not have our wages cut if we're found wantin.'

'Bug hunters? Whet yer on about woman?' said Duncan.

'These men come aroond and check that we keep the place clean. If our cleanin' isn't up to standard we could be thrown oot, rumours have it,' replied Maud.

Duncan frowned at Archie, who winked and then closed his eyes. That's women's work as far as he was concerned. Mebe they had a point, thought Duncan, but he wasna going to admit it.

The women finished their chores and went downstairs to the midden to ablute. Each held a tallow candle for the *other as they found their way in the dark. Maud sighed as they settled down for the night. Life wouldn't be so bad from now on, would it? she thought. Tomorrow she would tell Archie her news. Maybe?*

Did Gerald try to tell me the truth? I wondered. How hard did he try? Was he frightened as to what my reaction would be for his betrayal of trust? Almost certainly. Would he have contacted me if the business had been successful? I wasn't sure.

In spite of unbidden questions invading my sense of calm, I gradually found a sense of freedom and renewed purpose to my life. Apart from writing in the mornings and editing in the evenings, I volunteered at the soup kitchen one lunch-time a week, feeling that I was 'giving something back' to the community which had sheltered and rescued me. I spent most afternoons walking unless it was wet. Then I would find someone else to talk to in The Refuge, saddened by their tales of abuse, whether it was physical or mental. For the first time in my life I realised that it was the mental abuse which was the most intolerable. The men who used psychology to make their wives or partners feel that they were somehow ill or going mad, almost goading them to lose their minds. The Refuge was the silken spider's thread which bound all of us women to our sanity and self belief. Many of them had fluctuating hormonal issues to deal with too. Did Gerald show similar symptoms? I wondered. Was it some kind of mid life crisis or was it premeditated? I had no idea. Or was it a case of 'shit happens' as one of the residents kept repeating. I smiled. Seriously though, I was a great believer in everything having a reason and maybe I was being tested.

Of one thing I was certain, that this was a time of reflection for me and when enjoying solitude I continued to meditate, in my own fashion.

CHAPTER 32

I REMEMBER THERE was also a period of about two weeks when I became so absorbed in my story that it was a period of healing; not a time to mull over my own burdens, but instead to reflect on the suffering in the lives of my characters. I slipped into my other world and it gave me brief solace from reality.

The Nun's Tale Part 6

The Dire Consequences of the Truth

'You can't be with child!' exclaimed Archie after Maud had confided in him. This had followed a rare moment of intimacy between the pair one Sunday afternoon when Duncan and Brenda had accompanied them for a stroll in the spinney surrounding the mill. After the walk Brenda and Duncan chose to go visiting, allowing Maud and Archie a modicum of privacy. Maud had been lying contentedly in Archie's arms and had felt it to be the perfect moment to share her hitherto secret.

'It must have happened on the journey up here. One of those nights you'd had a drink or two and we'd paid for a night at an inn.'

Archie was silent, his body tense.

'Maybe it was our wedding night or the night of celebration at the end of the neeps harvest.' Maud prattled on, nervous of the cavernous dark shadow which had crept between them. In the end he grabbed his clothes and marched the two steps to the door.

'I don't remember any of that. Are you sure I'm the father?' he said as he stormed out, leaving Maud reeling in shock, remembering the rape. She hoped to God that the mite had been conceived on a happier occasion; otherwise its future did not bode well.

Maud dressed and busied herself with preparing vegetables, her head bent low, her heart heavy. Archie didn't come back for supper but, just as she ventured out to the midden before settling for sleep he came up behind her and, *catching her arm, he dragged her into the shadows behind the buildings. He pulled her up the slope, drink on his breath, her feet catching in brambles and her face grazed by twigs. Only the moon lit their way, dappled through branches which brushed against her. At a clearing Archie stopped and pushed Maud to the ground, tearing her skirt before he raped her. The more Maud struggled the more pleasure he seemed to gain until she hung limp in his arms, her energy spent as he gave one last thrust before slipping off her and lying still.*

'Your precious Evie was more to me than you'll ever be,' he spat.

At the mention of her sister's name Maud tried to sit up. Archie was already striding back down the slope.

'What do you mean by that,' she called after him.

Archie turned, the sharp features of his face stark in the moonlight. 'She hung herself, didn't she?'

Maud gasped. 'What are you talking about?'

'She hung herself out of shame; didn't even give me a chance to prove myself. I'd have stood by her and the baby, you know.' Archie turned his back on her then. 'I loved her,' he ended in a whisper before stumbling down through the trees, falling into his cot fully dressed and inebriated. Looks passed between Duncan and Brenda but they said nothing. As they settled for the night Brenda fretted about Maud but knew she could do nothing until the morning. She slipped into a restless sleep until they were woken by a banging on the door before sunlight.

Maud lay there, her blonde hair now loose and returned to the colour of her birth fell like threads of gold over her face. As she drifted in and out of a fitful sleep the snow came. Outside she was so cold but inside she was burning in her own hell. Memories drifted like snowflakes through her mind forming vivid images of the past; the giggling in the woods near The Grange, her sister's reticence to talk about anything private; Evie's happiness as if she was blooming with a secret which Maud now knew to be love. If only they had confided in each other, she agonised.

As the cold seeped into her very being, her mind, body and soul became the Millie she had left behind in Bedfordshire and no longer the Maud she had become. Thoughts of Evie became more intense; her quietness before Millie escaped and the silence, never returning Millie's notes or the occasional letters while Mille was working at Belmont House. Snow settled on her face, melting at first until crystals of ice formed on her eyelids and she could open them no more. Millie's mind wandered to her little boy, his home and his adoptive parents. For the first time she felt glad that he was safe and loved, a reassurance which comforted her as she drifted in and out of consciousness.

Snow began to lie shroud-like over her. She had never been Jack's at all was her last thought as life left her and her soul lifted into the ether.

Early the next day a body was recovered from the woods above New Lanark and Archie was arrested. He hadn't fled. He'd had a lifetime of running. There was nowhere for him to go.

Name,' barked the sergeant at Glasgow police station where he had been taken.

'Jack Watt, he answered.

'You are not Archie Dowling then?'

'No, I'm not,' Jack answered.

'However, you are charged with murdering Maud Dowling. Have you anything to say?'

'Her name is Millie .... and she is my wife.'

'Are you pleading guilty or not guilty?'

'Not guilty,' Jack mouthed.

'Louder please. We didna catch that.'

'Not guilty sir. My wife was alive the last time I saw her.'

'And when and where might that be?'

'We had a walk in the woods and had an argument, but she was speaking when I left her.'

'Your wife was found with her skirt torn, lying under a drift of snow. Did you just leave her there after your ...,' the sergeant paused, 'argument?'

'She was alive when I last saw her. That is all I know,' and Jack would say no more. He refused to answer questions as to why they had changed their names or travelled so far from where they were born. His silence condemned him.

Jack was hanged a week later. He spoke not another word, even to the priest who came to absolve him of his sins. In his heart he knew he was as guilty as if he'd rung her neck. The only words which came into his mind before his head went into the noose were, 'Why? Why did we go to all that trouble to escape? Why did I blow our chance of happiness with a fit of temper? Why?'

I felt drained, bereft almost, as I imagined that my novel was now complete having killed off my main characters. Reluctantly I passed the remaining chapters over to Jamal. It was November 4th. Tomorrow was my 60th birthday – a milestone in anyone's life, particularly my own. I would move out of The Refuge, rent a furnished room in a shared house not far from Jamal and make tentative steps toward normality, whatever that maybe. The small party Orla and Laura put on for me at The Ark, sharing with the other guests, was lovely. I was one of their success stories. I'd been pulled out of poverty, resisting the lure of alcohol or drugs to ease my pain, and had turned a negative into a positive like a developed photograph. The shadow of my former self had emerged in full technicolour, well nearly.

While we were at the party Brian had kindly moved my few belongings to my new home. He was one of those silent heroes, never asking for thanks or praise and I vowed that I would make it up to him as soon as I could. Bella had been invited to the party so that I could thank her personally. I would visit Samira and Janet another day, but otherwise I had no reason to return. Although full of hope, my happiness was tinged with a momentary pang of emptiness; a sudden fear of the future, especially since I thought that I had completed my manuscript. It was as if I had lost a great friend. Yet, I was a believer in the saying '*as one door closes another opens,*' so I'd just need patience to find out what the next stage in my life might be. Mind you, my novel was one step ahead of me and was already plotting, as if it had a mind of its own.

Orla had kindly framed a photo of our group - me, Jamal, Orla and Laura - and it had miraculously appeared on the bedside table in my new room. They all piled into the house on Dormer Street leading me blindfold up the staircase.

Room 4 was full of flowers, fragrant pink carnations which I breathed in as I was led inside. When they removed the scarf, the first thing my eyes set upon was the photo; my new family. Each day I would wake to see all those who had truly cared about me. I was humbled by their generous natures. When I was alone later that night I stared at their faces in the photo and felt truly blessed.

The following morning, Sunday, I went to church, something I had rarely done since Gerald left. After all I hadn't even begun to unthread my confusing spiritual background. I couldn't face St Mary's, Gerald's church though – the interminable questions and the looks of pity, so I slipped in unnoticed, or so I hoped, into the back of Orla and Laura's church, St Mark's. As an outside observer I listened, partly with curiosity, as the not too dissimilar morning service was unfolding. There was swinging of incense and a few more chants than I was used to, but otherwise an atmosphere of moving tranquillity pervaded. A calmness seeped to the depths of my being as the congregation sang *'Make me a channel of thy peace,'*...during the Eucharist. The haunting melody made my eyes well up and silent tears fell as I knelt. I didn't participate. I wasn't sure of the protocol, and as the service neared its end I slipped out of the back and headed for Belmont Park where I enjoyed my own meditation on all that had happened to me over the last two years. Jamal and Orla found me there and sat quietly on each side. I took each of their hands in mine.

Eventually I broke the silence between us. 'So you knew I was in church then.'

'Yes Auntie. Orla squeezed my hand and nodded in your direction as soon as you entered the back. We thought we'd find you here.'

'Do you go often Jamal?'

'Oh Auntie. We have so much to tell you. What would you say if you heard that I was having lessons from the priest in Catholicism? The faith isn't that much different to mine anyway.' His voice trailed into uncertainty, questions highlighting his eyes.

'Jamal, you must find your own way in life. I have never tried to influence you in any way. Your roots are important to you, but so is your future.'

Orla blushed.

Jamal continued. 'It's the only way for Orla and I to have any conceivable future together Auntie. I've seen so much evil coming out of my religion too.'

'Oh Jamal, you mustn't think like that. There's bad in any group of people. Islam is no different to Christianity in that respect. There is good, too. Think of all the mosque does to support the poor in the Muslim community. Many people who follow your faith have such a generous spirit.'

'I know Auntie but The Ark is Catholic and it respects people of all backgrounds. Homeless people are given help irrespective of their faith.'

'That's true Jamal. I'm just afraid that you are turning your back on your own faith because of what your brother has done.'

Jamal's face clouded over with thoughts of Ahmed. 'If I could've brought him back Auntie I would've burnt down every mosque in this country, but I know that it wouldn't have done any good.'

Orla, up until this point, had remained thoughtfully quiet. 'A bitter heart has no place in Catholicism either Jamal. You'll have to forgive your brothers in Islam with sincerity, if you wish to become Catholic. Dot's right. There are so many similarities in our faiths. The roots are exactly the same. It's only twists of fate which made each path diverge from the true faith, whatever that might be, and Catholicism doesn't hold all of the answers either. There are always a few who distort the truth and corrupt the very essence of what we believe in. I know that for a fact.'

'I agree with you Orla,' and we smiled at each other. 'There's a saying in English *two wrongs don't make a right* and it's so true. I would become a Quaker or some such religion if I had the courage, where all faiths seem to merge and be accepted. I'm not sure I know enough about it, but it certainly sounds a very peaceful religion, finding all war abhorrent, I believe.'

My eyes drifted towards my old house between the larch trees on the hill. The lady was just pulling the pushchair inside her front door. Life had certainly moved on.

'Orla and I want to get married Auntie. I know we've only been seeing each other for a few months but we love each other.' It was their turn to gaze into each other's eyes in a way I could only describe as genuine love.

'I give you both my blessing, of course,' I said and I paused a while.

'I can hear one of your buts Auntie.'

I grinned at both of them. 'I doubt if you've told your parents yet Orla,' I said, replacing my smile with an expression which I hoped looked appropriate for the occasion.

Orla looked embarrassed, which was not my intention. 'They wouldn't understand Auntie. Do you mind if I call you that too?'

'Not at all. I think you're both right to explore options which might smooth the inevitable storm.'

'I don't understand Auntie,' Jamal said.

'I'm sorry Jamal but it's likely that Orla's parents might not take too kindly to a Muslim boy, however lovely you are,' with which he blushed, 'asking to marry their precious daughter.'

'We're not in a hurry to tell them Auntie. Jamal needs to find a steady job, but since he's been coming to church with me, our priest suggested that he have a weekly session with him; lessons in what it might mean to change his faith. He's quite open minded about it, is our priest.'

'I expect he is,' I exclaimed, 'thinking he has a conversion in the palm of his hands.'

'No, it's not like that at all, Auntie. I'd like you to meet him. You'd like him.'

'I'm sure I would Orla, but I liked the Imam too. In the time Jamal was living with me I never once tried to convert him.' I could see this building into a full scale argument and that was far from my intention. 'Anyway,' I softened the tone of my voice, 'I am fond of you both. You mean everything to me and I would love to see you happy. I just want to be reassured that Jamal is not thinking of converting just to please your parents and to marry you. Many couples go down that route I know. Love is a strong motivating factor, but you need to be sure.'

'Oh Auntie, I didn't want to upset you. I won't make this decision lightly but Orla and I feel destined to be together.'

I took a deep breath. 'Can I let you into a secret, both of you? I was born Jewish. It was Gerald who was Church of England.'

Orla and Jamal gasped. 'So you understand; truly you do, Auntie.' Jamal exclaimed, smiling.

At that moment they stood up and Jamal put his arms around Orla and squeezed her tightly, oblivious to passersby. They looked so genuinely happy that I felt guilty that I'd tried to unravel their chosen path, to highlight its flaws and the hidden dangers awaiting them.

I stood up too and put my arms around them. 'I wish you every happiness; you both deserve it,' but before my eyes welled up I began to walk away towards the gates, turning only once to wave to them before disappearing from view.

After that it became a nightly ritual for me to say a prayer for them as I switched the light off, their photo being the last sight as I plunged the room into darkness.

CHAPTER 32

I NEEDED A new purpose but had no idea where to turn. Unlike The Refuge, the residents of this house in Dorma Street were all young, what we used to call white collar workers. They were ladies in clerical work who liked a bit of independence from their parents, now that they were earning a regular wage. Two had taken a job away from home. A couple had boyfriends and I found the racket they made in their bedrooms at night quite embarrassing. Surely Gerald and I never made noises like that, or maybe that's where we went wrong. Even in New York we put music on to hide our modesty.

I found myself a job at the nearby newsagents behind the counter three mornings a week. They were turning it into one of those open plan post offices but I avoided being trained. I didn't want the responsibility. I also volunteered for a day a week in the Oxfam bookshop, which I loved. The former fed my need for the occasional treat by supplementing my meagre pension and the latter fed my appetite for books, undernourished since my unceremonious departure from The Grange.

It was while working in the bookshop that Angelina came back into my life. One day she was walking past and saw me arranging the window display and came inside. We agreed to meet for coffee during my lunch break in half an hour and met in the corner cafe, where they treated me a bit like a celebrity. 'Local tramp turned her life around!'

'Oh Dorothy,' Angelina said as she joined me as I sat, out of habit, at my usual corner table. 'It's so good to see you again. I never did have time to really thank you or even to apologise.'

'There's no need to do either, Angelina, and call me Dot please. Everyone except Jamal and Orla do.'

'Except the children. They still call you Lady Pink Hat!'

'Oh I know.' I smiled. 'Coffee?'

'Yes, please. I'll pay. It's the least I can do. How long is your break?'

'Half an hour but I'm afraid I've had ten minutes of it already.'

Oh,' said Angelina, unable to hide her disappointment. 'We've so much to talk about. I'd like to hear all that's happened to you after you left The Grange.'

'And I'd like to hear what happened to the books in your library,' I answered.

We smiled shyly and then ordered our drinks.

'You start,' we both said simultaneously, and then laughed.

'Maybe we could meet up when I come into town,' Angelina suggested. 'If I know you're in the Oxfam Shop on a Wednesday then I'll wave at you through the window to let you know I'm about. If you could give me a sign; wave if you can meet me or shake your head if you can't. How about that?'

'Sounds perfect,' I said, but realising that time was running out I added, 'a bit of intrigue in my life at last,' I grinned.

'I'm so sorry Jonathan threw you out of The Grange. You were doing a fantastic job cataloguing the books for us. I certainly didn't have time to do it myself and I hadn't a clue as to what I should do anyway. Following your methodical procedure I was able to finish the task in no time at all after you left.'

I felt momentarily bereft to think of the library at The Grange now empty. 'What will you do with The Grange now?'

'We're going to refurbish it for David, our farm manager, and rent out his cottage in the lane to make a regular income. Funds are quite tight. There's no way that Jonathan would rent out The Grange, even though it would make more money. '

'It's a bit close to your farmhouse I should think.'

'Yes there's that. Jonathan couldn't abide strangers,' and she coloured at her faux pas. 'Not on a permanent basis anyway but he's softened in other ways Dot.'

'What do you mean?'

'Well Evie, our farm manager's wife, is going to run a B&B there in the summer. In fact, we are going to run it together using the rooms in the eaves of the old house. It's far too big for one couple.'

It was like someone had *walked over my grave* when I heard the name *Evie*. It seemed too much of a coincidence and I wondered how the ghost of Evie, Millie's sister, would cope with the intrusion. My mind drifted back to the sound of the swinging from the rafters. I shivered.

'Are you alright, Dot? You've gone very pale.'

'Oh, yes I'm fine,' I stuttered as I re-entered the here and now. 'I'm afraid I have to go back to work now.'

'Oh that's a shame, Dot. Can we meet up next Wednesday?'

'That would be lovely.' I shook her hand and left, glad to be back surrounded by the comfort of novels and busy enough to distract my spiralling thoughts and questions.

It's just a coincidence; surely it's only a name, kept running through my head.

The following Wednesday I told Angelina my story, bringing her up to date with where I lived, giving her the address and a contact number, Orla's iPhone, in case she needed to get in touch. I still didn't possess a mobile myself and thought that giving her Jamal's would not be very diplomatic.

'I'm so glad that Jonathan decided not to proceed with a legal case against either of you Dot.'

'No more than I am!' My shoulders tensed a bit but Angelina continued regardless.

'To be honest with you, I don't think he wanted the publicity.'

'I expect he didn't,' I replied trying to think more philosophically. 'Don't worry about it. I only wish I could have helped you more, but I don't think I would have been very welcome if I'd appeared back at Westgate Farm, do you?'

'Oh no, Dot. You couldn't have done that.' For a moment Angelina's face showed lines of fear, but then they cleared. 'But it's lovely that I've found you again.'

Yet again the time ran out and I rushed up the street. I hated being late anywhere and took my obligations, even as a volunteer, seriously.

The following week I asked one of my burning questions.

'Where did you sell all of the books?'

'We found *The Eagle*, a reputable bookshop in Bedford which deals in old and antique books. For a small fee he took most of them off our hands. They made good money; enough to furnish the house afresh anyway, and do the limited amount of restoration needed.'

'The Grange has kept in relatively good condition.'

'Yes, fortunately Jonathan's grandfather had the foresight to leave money in a trust fund for its upkeep. If it wasn't for the fact that we've had a few poor years of harvest and margins of profit have been down to next to nothing, it might have remained like that, in our lifetime anyway. We had no choice. We had to diversify with the farm. We didn't want to convert a barn but felt that the empty house was brooding beside us and needed to be brought back to life.'

'It is certainly broody,' and I paused replacing a frown which had crept over my demeanour with a sunny smile, 'but it has a lovely atmosphere ... and did you sell all of the books?' I asked, hardly daring to imagine the reply.

'No, we kept any of those which related to the history of The Grange. They're part of Jonathan's family history after all.'

The relief which flooded over my tense features must have been transparent because Angelina smiled. 'I know you were fond of reading them Dot. Sometimes you left them open at the page you were reading. I was the person who would close the books and place them carefully back on the shelf; not before glancing at the fascinating diaries though.'

It was time for me to go once more but before we said goodbye Angelina added, 'Would you like to borrow them Dot? I know that you would look after them. I can see by your smile that you would.'

I didn't have time to tell Angelina about my writing. The anticipation of holding those tomes in my hands once more made me as excited as a small child before an impending birthday. I could hardly concentrate or sleep.

I saw Orla and Jamal occasionally in the weeks that passed, but they were preoccupied with each other. I felt joy for their happiness, for Jamal securing a full time job at the yard, and his search for meaning in life through his meetings with the priest. I was also nervous for them too, anticipating problems which had not as yet surfaced. I tried to dismiss these negative thoughts in a flick of my head and focus on the warmth of their presence; smiles of genuine love and affection.

The following week Angelina handed me the first of the three diaries of The Grange; one I had pored over many evenings until the light had grown too dark for me to read. Next I plucked up courage I didn't feel and told her about my writing.

'Jamal and Orla are paying for it to be professionally proof read before sending it off to publishers. I couldn't handle any of that. I couldn't take the rejection.'

'I can imagine that it might be tough. I'm so excited for you Dot. I really hope you're successful.'

'Angelina, I'm going to have to ask you a favour. It might be difficult but I can't really publish a book which has The Grange central to the plot, without Jonathan's permission. It was inspired by his family's history after all. I know it will be tough for you but what do you think he will say?'

Angelina frowned. 'I really don't know Dot. He softened in his attitude when I showed him what you did for us, especially now that the sale of books has saved us from possible bankruptcy. He even knows about me bringing this diary to you and he's OK with that,' Angelina's face relaxed. 'Leave it with me. I'm sure it'll be fine.'

I was extremely nervous whilst waiting in the cafe for Angelina the following week. Jamal had begun to send a synopsis and the first two chapters to publishers and agents but we hadn't heard anything as yet. We probably wouldn't but I had no regrets of writing the story.

'You'll never guess my news Dot,' Angelina sat down excitedly, the waitress serving our usual coffees.

Expecting an answer to my question about The Grange I was taken aback when Angelina continued. 'Well, Evie slept at The Grange for the first time last week and she thinks the place is haunted.' Angelina looked up at me. 'You knew didn't you?'

'Yes, I did actually. I heard the sound of swinging in the rafters while I stayed there and it was, in fact, one of the inspirations for a twist in my novel.'

'You didn't say,' Angelina's voice unusually brusque.

'I was a little concerned that it might affect your plans for a B&B and was nervous to put the dampers on your idea.'

'Evie's quite excited about it actually.' She paused. 'I had a word with Jonathan about your book and he's fine with it, as long as you give us some anonymity; also that we have a chance to read it before it's published.'

'Of course Angelina. Thank you so much. You don't know how much that means to me. Of course I'll change the location; in fact I've already made the main places in my novel imaginary, so no one will guess The Grange is real.'

'Jonathan even mentioned a friend of his who's had a novel published and is writing a series; a humorous take on the life of a farmer I believe. My husband has promised to talk to him about it, to see if he has any advice.'

'That's wonderful. I couldn't have asked for a more positive response, could I? I'm so grateful.'

'It's the least we could do Dot. I'm so glad you found us. Truly I am.'

The following afternoon was my creative writing class which I returned to The Ark for, not being too proud to meet with my fellows from my itinerant days. Back in my room later that evening I thought about a conversation I'd had with Jill on my own at the end of the session.

'I've read the end of your story Mrs G and I loved it. I even shed a tear or two when Millie passed away. What a tragic life.'

'I can hear there's a *but* coming next,' I said, amused at Jill's reticence to upset me.

'There are a few loose ends you need to deal with. It's up to you to find them but the biggest one is Millie's promise to return to her son.'

'but how is she ...'

'I know. How is she going to do that now she's dead? Well, that's your problem.'

'What should I do?' I said in an almost inaudible whisper of self doubt.

'What I do is sleep on it. Leave it a while; a few days or even weeks. Listen out for clues in your life and the answer will come to you.'

'Are you sure?'

'Positive. You'll see.'

That night I reran the conversation with Jill in my head and allowed the nagging doubts I'd been having about the last chapters of my novel swirl around in my mind, like the snow over Millie's body. I was unsettled; that feeling akin to displacement when you lose something precious and have searched high and low. Even in your dreams its location is just beyond reach. With a few novels I've read, authors have left unresolved issues. I, in my amateur way, had tried to follow the rules, writing about what I knew with research either online or in the Bedford archives. I had been hampered by having no resources to travel further afield but Jamal had helped enormously by rescuing a box of leaflets, books and pamphlets I'd collected over the years. They were safe in the small store of effects Brian's father's company still held for me and I had used them to verify many facts gleaned on the Internet.

In confusion I decided to read through the whole manuscript once more and subsequently realised that Jill was right. There were a few key anomalies to deal with; and as Jill had pointed out, the most glaring was that Millie had promised to return to find her boy. How could I resolve this now that both Millie and Jack had died in Scotland?

That following Friday afternoon I was passing the Catholic Church when I noticed that the door was open. I crept inside, only to see a few people waiting for confession. I sat at the back of the church absorbing the atmosphere; religious pictures and artefacts of Jesus and Mary his mother, not to mention numerous saints adorned the place, but I could not help but notice the presence of Mary in particular. Her eyes were upon me and as I walked to the chapel at the side of the church to burn a candle, her kindly gaze bore into my back; the mother of all mothers; the mother of all sons and daughters too for that matter. Clearing my head I lit three candles; one for Gerald, one for Ahmed and one for Jamal and Orla. Did Mary really smile when I turned and glanced up at her before leaving? A dove of The Holy Spirit painted in bright white and gold above the doorway took my breath away. I paused a moment before continuing on my way.

A question popped into my consciousness unbidden. Could Millie return in spirit? I wondered. Do ghosts travel, if they even exist? I was pretty sure that they did, thinking of Evie at The Grange. For fun I called into Drumford Library and logged on to a computer that very afternoon, typing 'can ghosts travel?' I was surprised by the plethora of replies from all backgrounds and faiths. Once back in my own room I mused on my findings and began to jot down a few ideas.

That night I had a dream. It was as if my mind was solving the plot discrepancies while I slept. My memories were muddled but the following morning they gave me glimmers of ideas as to how to rescue the end of my novel.

I arose quickly and, without dressing, sat at my desk while the muse was fresh. Where the words appeared from I had no idea.

The Nun's Tale Part 7

The End and the Beginning

1781

Snow began to lie over Millie's, shroud-like form. She had never been Jack's at all, she thought, as life hung in the balance, her soul shifting as if attempting to break free. Her mind turned to Evie and she thought she could hear the sound of her beloved sister swinging to and fro, to and fro.

As the cold took her last breath Millie looked down on her earthly body. There was no return, try though she might. She hovered over New Lanark Mills long enough to see Jack arrested and protest his innocence. She had no desire to see him hanged. She had loved him once.

Millie didn't belong here. Her eyes searched for Brenda and Duncan. She floated for a while watching the day to day life at the mill return to some form of normality and another family take over their home. There was Brenda welcoming the new strangers and Duncan grasping the man's hand. They had a wee boy too who was so sweet and Millie became wistful; her desire to see her son heightened once more. She was determined to retrace her steps, but how? Her mind skimmed over images of her life, folks she had met along the way and all the promises she had failed to keep in her lifetime. Was it possible to atone for these misdemeanours even in the afterlife?

Her thoughts turned to Glasgow and her friend Aggie. She drifted, for what felt like a lifetime. Hours, days, weeks and even years were meaningless in her transient state.

1810

One night Aggie looked up from her favourite armchair by the fireplace. She had put her grandchildren to bed while her daughter was out at work in a local hotel and she was oh so very tired. Millie floated above her. Aggie sighed with contented exhaustion. It had not been a bad life. Having returned to Glasgow she had supported the family for a couple of years, being lucky enough to be given her old job back. Then she had married her neighbour's son, who had always been sweet on her. Jimmy had been willing to take on her brother and sister too. Her daughter was their only child.

'We've had a braw lif and me grandchildren are adorable,' she spoke aloud as if to no one. As she slipped into the sleep which ends sleeps, Millie was there to greet her; her finger reaching out towards Aggie's.

'I'll take you to your beloved husband,' Millie said.

Aggie smiled up at her friend.

At that moment Aggie left her mortal life, her arms lifting towards Millie, whom she knew of as Maud. They needed no explanation. Millie led Aggie through the misty void until there was a piercing light ahead. They beamed at each other; Millie letting go of Aggie's hand, her index finger directing Aggie onwards.

'Jimmy'll be there for you Aggie, please don't fret,' she reassured her friend.

Seeing Aggie's puzzled expression Millie smiled, 'I have to abide here a while my dear. Don't you worry about me.'

Having fulfilled her promise to Aggie to keep in touch it was time to be gone.

Millie floated endlessly in that in between state until her thoughts focussed on her son. His image in her mind was so faint; there were still so many miles between them. She flew through swirling snow above The Pennines, her form creating a drift of snowflakes floating this way and that, like a flock of starlings; ever changing patterns in the sky. As she reached the borders the sky cleared and Millie glided under a blanket of stars, her light twinkling across the sky like a shooting star.

1820

The next vivid image in her mind was of her marriage and she found herself above Gretna Green where, wistfully, she watched a couple tying the knot. Then, as time flashed by in lightning strokes, she was drawn to a courthouse in nearby Carlisle, which was still in session late into the night.

'I declare your marriage null and void,' proclaimed the judge, 'since you married under false names.' He was speaking to the couple whose nuptials Millie had just witnessed in what seemed like minutes, but in truth had been a couple of earth years before. The young lady looked dumbstruck as her young man was led away to a cell to await another trial for theft. It was during that investigation that his change of name had come to light.

Millie winced, now knowing full well that she would never meet Jack to be with him in spirit. What he had said was true; he had never been hers after all.

She continued to watch as the woman, whose name was Rose, was led to the workhouse, obviously heavy with child. Her heart went out to the lass as she watched the rough treatment Rose was subjected to as she awaited her time.

Millie hovered over Carlisle long enough to see the girl, relieved though bereft of her burden. She stroked Rose's hand at the birthing and gave her comfort as best she could when the little mite was taken away from her. Rose was then taken into service and a few years on she married the

butler. They had a child together, in part lessening her loss.
her work in Cumbria was done.

Millie felt an emptiness as she drifted, dealing with her
mixed worldly emotions; loss, heartache for a love that was
never meant to be and her wasted life. Where could she find
peace?

I was feeling quite despondent about my story and Millie's haunting discovery and so I decided to go out for a walk to clear my head. I found myself, yet again, in St Mark's, the Roman Catholic Church next to The Ark. This time, as I sat mulling over my life and Millie's story ,a priest came and sat beside me.

'Can I help you my dear? Are you in trouble in some way?'

'I am not really of your faith Father. I'm a non practicing Jew but have attended C of E most of my adult life.'

The Father raised his eyebrows and smiled. 'My question doesn't change, whatever your background. Do you still want to talk about it?'

I paused a moment. 'I have a great deal to be thankful for Father. I was homeless but now I have a roof over my head and friends who care about me.'

'And?'

It was my time to smile. 'I have two mutual friends Father, Orla and Jamal, but they are not really who I'm fretting about.'

'Ah I see, and so ...'

'Do you believe in ghosts father? Do spirits walk this earth?'

'Oh, that's a big question I didn't expect. Would you like the official line or my personal views?'

'Both I think, if you don't mind giving me some of your time.'

'It would be a pleasure but where to start?' He paused, his brow furrowed for a few seconds. 'Well,' he continued, 'the official line is that there are no ghosts. When we die we go to either heaven or hell. Our loved ones do not return to either haunt or comfort us.'

'So what actually is haunting us then?'

'The argument is that they are the devil's helpers come to cause mischief.'

My face must have been a picture of disappointment.

'...but I have my own views. I can't believe God does not welcome comfort to the bereaved whichever way it comes. Please don't quote me on this, but there are even groups within the church who believe that some of us go through a sort of purgatory on earth when we die.'

'That's interesting, and do they appear to people?'

'Many believe they do, especially in the churches of some of our American cousins. Why do you ask these questions?'

'To be honest with you father I'm writing a book; a novel, and I didn't want to upset people in the church.'

'Ah,' and the Father laughed. 'You're writing a novel! Well, anything goes in fiction doesn't it? You can let your imagination fly!'

We shook hands then and I apologized for wasting his time.

'Not at all,' he said; 'Now, if you'd asked me about Angels,' he called after me his eyes twinkling.

'Next time Father,' I said smiling as I turned to leave. Orla was right, I thought. I did like her priest.

That night, with greater enthusiasm and confidence I continued Millie's story:

The Nun's Tale Part 8

The Long Return in Search of Peace

1830

Millie continued floating southwards in years and miles of equal proportion and there appeared beneath her a newly formed canal from Kendal guiding her way. After a while she seemed to recognise a lady below, who was the image of her friend Emma, handling a barge as if she were a natural. Maybe it was Emma's grand-daughter, she thought. The name 'Emma's Afloat' on the side of the barge all but confirmed her guess. So the family had returned to a life on the water after all, Millie mused.

She followed the barge for some time, playing a few tricks on the woman, Pippa; a jolly portly lass with a wonderful laugh. She enjoyed moving things about and appearing as a cloud, moving in unnatural ways and making faces in the sky. Pippa just hooted at her antics but soon Millie knew it was time for her to continue her journey, assured by the knowledge that Emma's kin were fine. After that she was shunned by other spirits who haunted those stretches of water. It was time to move on.

1891

Disoriented at first, Millie continued to follow this route south until she reached a branch in the canal going eastwards. Sensing that this was the direction she should be heading, she followed this waterway until she noticed familiar places around Leeds. The imposing site of the working mills along the banks near the town led her onwards. She recognised Water Hall Mills, and a man who they called Joshua Kay caught her attention as he welcomed beggars and itinerants to his home, giving out food and old blankets. She remained there for some time until, in fact, the kindly gentleman passed away. There was no pause for reflection on his life though. He winked at her as he shuffled passed, throwing his walking stick aside before passing through the tunnel of light.

Gliding ever eastwards, Millie was just smiling at the remembrance of this man, and the tableaux of benevolence she had witnessed, when a horrendous noise and a sharp whistle passed beneath her; a steam engine chugging across farmlands sending grey smoke upwards which suffocated her very soul. Her form hovered ever higher to avoid this affront to her being, as it sped like a scar across the fields below.

She remained in that state of suspended animation, her vision inward looking, unwilling to assimilate the changes beneath her, until her essence was brought alert once more. She spotted a newspaper headline sold on Leeds Station giving the date 1890,

'Gas Workers Strike for Eight Hour Day.'

Over a century had passed in meaningless moments since she had left New Lanark Mills in Scotland and she reminisced of the times when her working day had been long but enjoyable as her fellow women had lifted their spirits in song.

Fewer barges floated along the canals now, much of their work replaced by the trains which now criss-crossed the countryside. She watched the demise of canal life, as she knew it, with sadness. For a while all but the major canals became overgrown and uncared for. The roads, often taking a nearby or parallel course, had carriages with engines which moved along at a great pace when the surface allowed.

Millie continued floating ever eastwards through time and space, until some of the once thriving industries on the *canal-side began to look derelict too. The world was changing beneath her, beyond recognition. Nearing Hull she sensed a presence which pulled her in and she caught sight of a group of barge folk. The man appeared to be mooring his barge, The Merry Maid 2, in a basin not far from Hull. It seemed like a funeral as the man, with features not dissimilar to Alf, led his family away.*

1915

At Hull, however, the waterways were as busy as ever as she headed towards the port. She was curious to see new buildings; a Picturehouse and Pavilion in the city, which drew people to the town for their pleasure. Looking closer at their expressions she noticed underlying grief as couples parted, as if for the last time, before the men embarked on the waiting ships. There was a flurry of activity as a multitude of naval officers and crew arrived in trains to join those already waiting at the quayside. They were off to war. She thought of joining one of the ships but many an unfriendly ghost chased her away.

Returning to the Humber she located the mouth of the River Trent, and for a time explored small tributaries; quiet waterways now undisturbed by humankind. Millie found amusement by mimicking the kingfishers as they dived towards the river, before skimming the surface. Her drooping hands made a gentle draft, enough to send pond skaters into a spin, turning upside down in the disturbed airflow. Eventually, tired of her play, she headed southwest, following the main river once more. Ever searching, she swooped silently owl-like above the rolling fields of the Midlands. Earth years passed.

1945

As huge bird-like beings thundered overhead, disturbing her reverie, she was aware of another change to the folks on the canal barges on the Trent. Crews of predominantly women appeared to be transporting coal, also large smooth wood-like planks which she heard called 'steel' and white powder which made the girls cough if disturbed. Written on each bag were the letters 'CEMENT'. Millie wasn't sure what that was. She travelled with three of these girls for a while, keeping them company, listening to their talk of men folk at war over in France. It was all quite baffling, but she enjoyed their conversation.

She felt a particular affinity to a kindly lass who wrapped her fair hair in rags each night to make it curl, then pulled it back with a red scarf, showing off her perfect complexion. Lizzy was her name, and it was Lizzy's task to stand on deck and handle the tiller, skilfully navigating their barge safely along the waterways. Folks they passed by called them the 'Idle Women' as they waved and laughed at their own joke. Millie didn't understand this at first, but nevertheless was amused by their banter. She stood next to Lizzy for a while as the summer breeze blew in her face as she smiled at each passerby. Millie knew, however, that the girl's inner turmoil was well hidden. She had spied her reading a letter from her fiancé Stevie who was a prisoner of war and the letter was dated nine months previously in September 1943. It was not Millie's way to intervene in the lives of those people her being brushed upon, but her instinct knew that Stevie was well and that the pair would be reunited at the end of the war. She was pleased that the girls moored for the evening near a village fair at Winthorpe. She willed Lizzy to visit the tent of a fortune teller and Millie whispered words of encouragement to the old lady within, who looked the part with her glass ball, large *hoop earrings, beads, rings and trinkets in abundance and a long flowing scarf over her head.*

Totally unaware of the source of her words, Old Nell reassured Lizzy,

'Well lass, with your silver I can tell you the truth. Your young man will return one day. Be patient. His injuries are minor and he's in good spirits. Don't fret.'

1950

Pleased to have achieved some good in her 'in between life' state Millie continued on her way. She noticed a broken sign on the river's edge. 'Inland Waterways' it said, followed by the initials, 'I.W.' and she laughed as she suddenly understood the play on words. Idle Women, she grinned. The women including Lizzy, who wore blouses with the same initials embroidered on them, had hardly been idle.

Nevertheless, much of the industries, which had made these canals vital in their day, were all but gone and for a while the tributaries were quiet and had returned to their natural state. It was disorientating but also comforting as Millie drifted aimlessly for a while. Suspended in time, she was swept by a contentment that her son was closer still, but she knew she needed to be patient in her wanderings. Their time would surely come.

I, too, was overwhelmed by a sense of peace that my scribbling was heading in the right direction. Sometimes it was as if my pen was writing by itself. At a book sale I was drawn to a novel which I bought for thirty pence. It talked of life between lives, when you were able to make sense of your current life after you die. Its argument explained that this earthly time was not the end, but only one stage in a series of existences. It was revealing to read that there might be a chance to make amends, or at least to understand the reasons for events in each life, even after you have passed away. At each level it said that you were learning, and it was the learning whilst on the journey that mattered. I was not sure where this book fitted into the teachings of the Jewish or Christian Church, or any other faith for that matter, but, like Millie, I found it comforting and it filled me with a reassuring warm glow for my personal self and the way my writing was being guided.

The Nun's Tale Part 9

Nearly Home

1964

Finally Millie recognised the outskirts of Nottingham and the West Bridgford Farm where she and Jack had worked. The folks on the barges seemed to be no longer from the working classes, but families and couples enjoying a jaunt. It puzzled her. The women appeared to be wearing either extremely short dresses, or trousers like the men, which were so full around the ankle that they looked a bit like long skirts at an angle - and the colours; they were all bright rainbow colours and flowery too. Millie loved them.

The farmhouse itself had altered little since Millie and Jack's time, so long ago, although not far away was an enormous complex. 'GEM SUPERSTORE' was emblazoned above giant sized glass doorways, 'THE FIRST EVER SUPERSTORE IN THE UK' a notice said. Intrigued, she investigated closer and slipped inside. It was cavernous and eerily empty of life. There were vast displays of everything you could think of for the home and many she could never have imagined. The food stuffs too were so numerous that it was overwhelming; some kept in large cool glass boxes and some in stacks of metal tins.

It was not a place Millie wanted to dwell in for long, in fact its newness and unfamiliarity unsettled her. She knew that she should now leave the River Trent and head south, but had no idea which way to go. There were no familiar landmarks and for a time she drifted above, lost to the world in endless indecision. Disorientated and confused, sensing her son as far away as ever, Millie stumbled upon Rockingham

Castle. In fact, so demoralised was she by this time that she cowered at the base of one of the castle's towering walls where she remained for many nights.

Several moons passed before she dared lift her head and then she noticed the ghost of a lady floating behind an old yew hedge, then disappearing through some elaborate wrought iron gates. Gaining in confidence she began to explore further and entered the building through the thick walls, only to catch site of a Cistercian Monk disappearing through wood panelling ahead of her. This only made her longing for The Grange and Drumford even greater.

Nevertheless, in her time at Rockingham she gained in strength and understanding of her limitations. By thinking herself back in the gardens she found herself floating between lavender beds and under arches of blossom, the smell of which she found intoxicating but also healing in the early summer evening. One windy night she thought of the protection of the long panelled corridors and realised, without effort, she had found herself within the castle walls once more. One night she followed the lady in white through the iron gates. Just as her companion disappeared, the light from the moon caught her gown in a translucent state, so that it glimmered like a falling waterfall. The lady smiled before disappearing from sight this time, but in that moment realisation dawned on Millie that the moon could give her direction too. The following night she watched with awe as the moon rose and fell on either side of the castle, reaching its fullest height at midnight. If at night time she followed directly through the moon's path she would be heading southwards and her memory of the similar trajectory of the moon above The Grange gave her renewed confidence.

1974

Her thoughts turned to her journey and she remembered the farm where they had worked in Northamptonshire. Immediately she was transported above a place which seemed vaguely familiar. Unlike the Nottinghamshire farm though, the whole area of fields, where she and Jack had laboured, was covered in small buildings; little boxes of houses where families came and went. She hovered too close to the patio windows of one house when a cat spotted her and hissed, its hair standing on end and its eyes wide and disbelieving. The curtains were quickly closed and peace was restored.

1980's

For a while she sought quieter places for refuge, finding fields of sheep and corn more reassuring. On one occasion she paused in woodland, remembering her close call with capture and the hunting hounds, but now she only had squirrels and the occasional fox as company. The latter respected her presence, with no need to give her whereabouts away. She did not remain too long in the shadow of the trees because on clear nights she always liked to keep sight of the moon. Her next thought was of Belmont House and instantly she appeared over an area with recognisable features. The lake and folly were still there, as were the rolling grasslands and oak trees, although they were so much larger than the ones she remembered. She flitted amongst the ruins and then up to the folly, enjoying the novelty of sitting on the green dome looking out over the path. Millie's expression became wistful as she noticed lovers strolling hand in hand in the moonlight and then she spotted a middle aged woman sat alone on a park bench. Her heart leapt although she had no idea why.

She remained there for some time, thinking of happier times when she had been in service and had been given a second chance. She forbade the memory of Master Belmont's attempt to rape her from filling her mind as she stood beside the lake, her reflection barely leaving a shadow on the glistening water. Drawn into the town of Drumford she sought familiar places. Drumford had changed but many of the buildings were recognisable, including the imposing structure of the workhouse. It loomed above her but by day it was full of tiny offices where people worked, rushing out after their toil to return to their homes and families. Night-time took on an ethereal quality as many resident ghosts drifted in and out; an alternative world which never embraced the other. Young, old, children and babies; all who had lost the struggle to survive; so harsh had been their hardship. She shivered, remembering the night she had given birth to her son. She sensed his presence with her now, almost as deeply as she had felt that night, and was overwhelmed by longing and an urgency to find him.

2015

Savouring each memory Millie took her time to follow the river and fields towards Canbury, enjoying the familiarity of the landscape although watching out for clues along the way. An earthly part of her was also preparing herself for disappointment. Millie's imaginings turned to her last moments in Canbury and she was desperate but also excited to be floating above the house where she had last seen her beloved son. It was still there, but hovering in front of the windows she could see rows of elderly people sitting watching a box of light, hardly moving and certainly not conversing with each other. Frustrated, she visited the graveyard and spent weeks scanning each gravestone. She danced to avoid resident spirits who spent their time frightening old ladies who were bent down arranging spring flowers in pewter pots or spooking local children playing dare.

Finally Millie found her son's grave, tucked under some trees deep in a far corner:

> *"On 10th March 1845 Thomas Croft passed away leaving a beloved wife, seven children and ten grandchildren who loved him dearly."*

For days and weeks Millie hovered over this grave, hoping that her son would find her there. The grief she felt overcame any sense of time or a need to move on. She was in limbo between this world and the next until she could fulfil her promise. The brown stems of old flowers, crisp in their deadness only added insult to her grief.

2016

One day though, when the nights were drawing in early, Millie appeared as the evening sunset was still amber on the horizon. She noticed two ladies walking towards the grave to lay fresh flowers. A little girl held on to the hand of her mother, in all probability. The other lady was holding a bunch of bright orange and purple carnations.

'Why are we putting flowers on this grave, mummy,' the child asked.

'Well Greta, Dot discovered that this is the grave of Evie's ancestor and this is the anniversary of his death.'

'10th of March, one eight four five, Thomas Croft,' Greta read.

Yes, that's right Greta. It says eighteen forty five. That's the year Thomas died, one hundred and seventy one years ago.'

'Wow! That's a very special birthday then.'

'That's not his birthday Greta. That's the day he died.'

'Is Thomas anything to do with the nun we hear at The Grange mummy?'

'We think so, Greta. We are hoping that the ghost Evie, my namesake, might rest in peace if we care for Thomas's grave, knowing that Thomas is loved.'

'Was Thomas her son then?'

'No Greta, we think she was his aunt.'

'So where is his aunt's grave then,' asked Greta, more puzzled than perturbed.

Evie looked over Greta's shoulders at Angelina. 'That we don't know I'm afraid.'

Millie seeped into the sunset, creating misty purple clouds which formed patterns on the amber sky.

'Look at that mummy,' Greta gazed up in awe of the beauty around her. 'It looks almost like a heart.'

The three of them stood in silence enraptured by the glorious sky, Greta holding each lady's hand.

Greta glanced down. 'Look at the flowers Evie. I chose the same colours as the sky.'

Without waiting Millie knew where she should go next. Finally her mind returned to The Convent and the last vision she had experienced at New Lanark Mills, as she had drifted away from this world into the next. It was of her sister Evie swinging to and fro from the rafters in the attic above their tiny room in the eaves of The Grange.

The appearance of the outside of the Georgian house had barely changed since it had been her home. She entered at the kitchen door and her form quivered as she recognised the fireplace surround with the bread oven still intact. She inspected this closely. In her day it had always been warm with enticing aromas, but today it was cold and although blackened it held an air of neglect. Her curiosity was roused by the shiny cooking surfaces set into the range and the sparkling brass knobs. Her hand brushed though them as she moved on. Other rooms inside The Grange were less familiar, with classic but twenty first century furnishings. She could not shed a habit of servitude formed all those years ago as she chose the back stairs rather than gliding up the centre staircase, with its polished mahogany rails and deep pile burgundy red carpets.

Millie paused a while in the room she had shared with her sister. It had a single chintz covered bed and a door at one corner which led to what was obviously the midden, although it smelt of lavender and the pine, familiar smells she remembered from her Scottish life; very strange.

Hearing a groaning noise and noticing the stars through the curtained windows revealing the dead of night, she hastily took the laddered way up to the attic door, which her form slipped through.

'Oh no!' she gasped as she found her sister still swinging to and fro from the rafters.

Recognition flashed across Evie's pained face. In spirit Millie held out her hand to her sister. They were reunited at last, Evie finally released from her waiting vigil, both smiling as they embraced and walked towards the distant light. Evie hesitated a moment as she caught a vision of Greta in the graveyard below. They flew to the churchyard hand in hand where, instinctively, the sisters paused, watching and waiting for the moment when the little girl was in tune with their presence. Suddenly the child looked up and seeing the pin pricks of lights dancing in the shadows, Greta ran after them. Gently they led the child to a piece of untended scrubland behind a hedge where there were three overgrown graves; the one in the far corner bore Evie's name.

'Come and look at this,' Greta called out to her mother and Evie, the farm manager's wife. 'I've found a grave with your name on it.'

Angelina followed her daughter and knelt to brush grass and moss from the stone. 'Your namesake,' she smiled up at Evie. 'We must come back with some gardening tools and tend to it.'

Angelina, Greta and Evie knelt side by side; three people joined by fate and reverence to the once occupant in the earth below.

Evie read aloud:

'Here lies Evie Jameson who took her own life on

August 1st in the year of our Lord seventeen eighty.

May she be forgiven for her most grievous crime.'

'Why was she buried here and not in the graveyard?' asked Greta.

'It was against the law to take your own life Greta,' her mother explained. 'This is called unconsecrated land, which means it's not been blessed by a vicar or priest.'

'Is she the lady who plays on a swing at night time in the roof of The Grange?'

'Yes that's right Greta. She's my ancestor. Her name was Evie too.'

'Is that why you've called The Grange *Evie's Place,* after her?'

Evie and Angelina glanced indulgently over Greta's head, trying not to laugh at her serious expression. Greta, on the other hand, smiled up at two lights in the shadows, which momentarily showed their form as they waved to her. Greta waved back as they disappeared into the misty evening light.

'I know that she's OK now though,' continued Greta. 'Your relation Evie is back with her sister now. I'm sure she'll not return to the Grange anymore or come to disturb your guests.'

The Nun's Tale Part 10

With Forgiveness Comes Peace

2016

The sisters, Evie and Millie, rose towards a compelling light. Their work here on this earth was done for now. On the other side of the long tunnel they were first met by their loving father and then Millie turned to see her son Thomas greeting her with joy. To her delight Thomas was holding out a tiny child to his mother.

'My brother, your other son,' he said.

Millie experienced moments of pure happiness as she held the bundle of life she had never had a chance to birth into this world. With Thomas's arm over her shoulders she embraced her sons, one for the first time, enjoying the warmth between them. This perfect moment might have spanned to eternity if she had not noticed her sister Evie looking uncertain. The sisters paused simultaneously, turning back towards each other, sharing such a feeling of mutual love in the moment. They looked down on the earth, each knowing that they had one more task on that plane to fulfil before perfect peace and final healing awaited them. Millie handed her second son, whom she named Peter, to Thomas for safe keeping until she returned.

... Jack was in that dark red space between the moment of death and what was to come. It lasted a timeless age as if he was suspended. Waiting. Reflecting. Occasionally a spirit came to speak with him but he brushed them away. Finally he saw two glimmers of light and was not surprised to see both Millie and Evie coming to greet him. They smiled and spoke kindly to him but still he showed no remorse. In the end

they had no choice but to turn their backs on him and leave him to a darkness of his own making.

Millie and Evie experienced a moment of earthly sadness at Jack's demise. 'We gave him one last chance Millie,' Evie reassured her sister, her face glowing. 'You need to let go of your earthly life now and we'll move on together. Don't you agree?'

'Yes I do.'

But, as they turned and began their journey upwards they heard a familiar voice behind them. Jack, who was frightened at being abandoned to an eternity of darkness, called out, 'I'm so sorry. Please forgive me.'

Evie was the first to turn back and to embrace Jack, leading him onwards and upwards. At that moment Thomas appeared with Peter at Millie's side and she was thankful as they followed the pair through the tunnel of light.

'It's never too late to be forgiven and to forgive mother.' Thomas explained gently as she battled with her final, but compelling earthly emotions.

At her son's words Millie's jealousy melted away, replaced only by pleasure as she watched the soul mates of Jack and Evie reunited. She was glad for the lesson she had learnt about her own relationship with the man who had never really been her husband. Thomas was leading her onwards and she held Peter close.

As they walked hand in hand back upwards, Millie's face glowed as a reflection of her beloved sister's. Jack turned and she smiled up at him and they were all at peace.

Contented I dropped into a deep sleep.

CHAPTER 33

JAMAL RUSHED EXCITEDLY to Dorma Street. The farmer had sent details of his friend's publisher through Angelina and had kindly mentioned my story and novel to his agent, Coleman and Martin's. A few days later Jane Coleman contacted Jamal asking for my complete manuscript. He was so excited to share the good news with me.

'But I've altered the end,' I explained, nervously.

'Don't worry Dot. Give me the new ending and I'll update the manuscript before sending it off. Brian's read it through too. He's a great reader and linguist and he's given me a list of errors to amend. Leave it with me and I'll sort it.'

It was a tense few weeks before Mrs Coleman wrote back to say that she had agreed to take the novel on, but only if I was prepared to write my memoir too. She had heard my story and felt that the two publications would do very well launched, if not simultaneously, fairly close after each other. The letter also said that she would be happy to act on my behalf if I would agree to those terms.

A few days later I met Jamal again.

'Jane Coleman phoned me yesterday asking if she could meet up with you, Dot. This is so exciting. She suggested that I should come along too.'

'Where does she ask me to meet her?'

'In London, Dot. She's even offered to pay our expenses, knowing your circumstances. She asked if we could meet her tomorrow.'

'No time to brood then and get so nervous that I'll call the whole thing off.'

'Come on Dot. Have confidence in yourself. You'd only say the same to me.'

The following day the three of us sat having a light lunch at Cafe Rouge near Charing Cross Station and The Embankment.

'It's more of the length of a novella but it's very special nevertheless. I have a publisher in mind but we have a lot of work to do first to get it into shape for submission. Are you prepared for that Dot? I'd be giving you strict deadlines.'

'That's no problem. One thing I do have is an abundance of time.'

'Quite. And you agree to writing your memoir?'

'Of course, but I can't see why people would want to read it.'

'Are you crazy! Readers love those kind of stories; especially if they're true. Even if you managed to get a standalone book deal, which is rare these days, the one book will help to sell the other.'

'I'll start straight away then. I go to a counsellor and I asked her advice. She thinks it might be cathartic.'

'Yes I should think it would be. I'll get my secretary to write out the terms and contract. Dot, do spend time looking at it carefully and ask if there is anything you don't understand. I suggest involving your good friend,' and she smiled at Jamal, 'to scan through it with you before you sign it and then my work will begin. There is no certainty in this industry but I have a hunch about this one, and my hunches are usually correct. It might take a while though.'

I nodded, bemused by it all. I did not want to repeat myself but time was certainly not an issue. My life was quite comfortable as it was and I had learnt the lesson to be content in a state of *wanting for nothing*. One day I might like a flat of my own maybe, but that could wait and possibly would never materialise. Who knew what lay in the future?

We parted amicably.

On the way home Jamal said, 'Orla might be more helpful than me Dot. She'd be happy to take a look at the contract. After all, thanks to you my English is OK but Orla has a degree in English.'

'I'd appreciate you both looking at it Jamal and I'm so grateful to you. How is Orla by the way?'

'She's preparing for a trip over to Ireland. She's hoping to talk to her parents about me and she needs all the courage she has in her.'

'It's so sad that it should be like that, and is there any news of Ahmed?'

Jamal brought his face closer to my ear and his voice turned to a barely audible whisper, 'That man arranged to see me again Auntie. Did you know that he helped in releasing me from the police station after I was arrested?'

I shook my head slightly, my eyes frowning.

'Well, Ahmed was detained trying to find his way back through Turkey and he is being kept in a detention centre there.'

'At least you know he is alive and well Jamal. What next?'

'The man I know is trying to negotiate for me to go over and talk to him. I suppose they think he might divulge more to me than he would to them, under interrogation.'

My face must have been a picture of fear because Jamal's voice softened further, 'Don't worry Auntie. The English have promised to protect me if I'm allowed to go over there. It might take months, or even years though.'

After the train we found a bus from Bedford Bus Station to Drumford, but spoke little during the journey, each in our own thoughts.

'It's been an exciting day Auntie,' said Jamal as we parted. He smiled but his eyes were tinged with sadness. I held his hands in mine for a couple of moments hoping that the gesture conveyed the hope I had no words for.

I had a great deal to think about as I settled down that night.

CHAPTER 34

IT WAS MUCH more problematic to tie up the loose ends of my own life than it was to complete Millie's story to my satisfaction. I spent the next year in a routine of writing my memoir in some sort of coherent form, but you know the details already and so I won't share them with you twice.

I met Angelina regularly, forming a close bond with her, also enthusiastic to hear second hand news about The Grange; a place which still held happy memories for me. The time for Greta's departure to boarding school was now imminent and so I was relieved that her mother had a positive shared venture to focus on.

Jamal, on the other hand, was busy working but he was also furtive about his other activities and I didn't pry, even when he went away from time to time. Sometimes I met him alone, but most frequently I met Orla and Jamal together, when I felt privileged that they confided in me their tentative plans for a future life together. I heard no more from my wayward husband, but that was fine.

I remained in the shared house but, strangely, I was less able to build up any relationship with these girls than I was at The Refuge, or The Ark for that matter. I returned to see if Samira was still there but she and Janet, like myself, had moved on with their lives. It was only meant to be a staging post, to wait, reflect and begin to plan before stepping on to the next part of our lives. I never returned, preferring to meet up with my creative writing teacher, Jill, at The Ark. I often left her sessions experiencing a confused sense of despair at the ever diverse tales of adversity that the members of the group shared with us. Yet most of the accounts were tinged with a silver tasselled edge of hope, a balance of nature as the strength of human resilience and fortitude overcame the devastating effect of their loss. We were all survivors, that's for sure. There appeared to be three groups; those who accepted their lot unquestioningly but tended to turn to cheap alcohol to deaden the pain of life; there were those who sought solitude and through self reliance and sheer determination they survived as they trod the countryside, only taking shelter in the worst of weathers; and finally there were those who were fortunate to be blessed by a gentle guiding hand and sank their pride, reaching out towards a new life. I suppose some, like me, were a combination of each. I felt fortunate, though, that I had never found the pleasures of alcohol appealing and so easily resisted that temptation.

And so, by the close of the year, I had written my own story and carried out a multitude of sensible amendments to my Nun's Tale, prompted by my agent Jane Coleman. I still enjoyed long walks when the weather was fine, often taking a picnic to my favourite clearing, which had taken on a new meaning since Millie came into my life. There was an extra special day when I really did find Evie's grave. The affinity I felt to the two sisters grew as I dug in snowdrops to bloom each year, rather than flowers to brown, crisp and die.

My walks evoked recent times but also brought back memories of long strolls with my grandma when I was a child and teenager, at a precious time when our bond was strongest. With each step came the healing of my mind, in a way medication could never have reached me.

I know it was wishful thinking but oddly I sensed Millie watching over me and sharing my sense of peace. Angelina assured me that their resident ghost had moved on. Had she been waiting all those years for someone to take an interest in her tale and set her free? Who knows?

Time passed quickly. I still didn't own a mobile and so, one memorable day, Jamal came in search of me to let me know that I had been awarded a book deal for both of my books. The moment was magical and we dropped our reserve and gave each other a hug, as mother and son would. We celebrated in style by buying cream cakes to share with those visiting The Ark that lunch time, and with all of the staff too. This was reminiscent of birthdays at Drumford Library, only all the more poignant.

I found it extremely touching that Old Ben approached me before he left, cake crumbs escaping from the corner of his mouth. He'd never uttered more than a grunt to me in all the times we had sat at tables side by side eating lunch, but today he astounded me.

'Dot,' he said. 'Please write my story?' and then he scuttled off. I knew that he was a creature of habit, like me, and came each Tuesday for a change of clothes and a hot meal. I vowed I would ask Orla about him, discretely of course, and also come in on Tuesdays to see if he said any more. I knew it would take courage beyond words to open up to me, but I was flattered that he had taken that first step. I would have to be patient and wait for his timing, even if it never happened. The following Tuesday he smiled. Just a tiny lift of the corners of his mouth, but the gesture made me glow with happiness. I believe though, that when or if he opens up to me, it will be impossible to pause the flow until his message is shared.

It was nearly a year to the day of this celebration that I sat alone at the Vintage Books Awards Evening sipping my drink. I'd been shortlisted for their debut author prize and thought I had no chance of winning. After all I'd gone through in the past few years this environment seemed alien to me, more absurd than my meadow clearing, where I had been at one with nature.

I reflected on my change of circumstances, inadvertently feeling in my pocket for my familiar dice. My new friends Angelina and Jonathan, the farmer and his wife, had been more than kind to overlook my trespassing over those months. They invited me to their farmhouse one afternoon, which was a total surprise, and I reminisced as I walked from Drumford. As I sat down in their lounge Angelina disappeared.

Jonathan cleared his throat. I was aware of his embarrassment but nothing would draw me to speak first.

'I need to say I'm sorry Dot. Can I call you Dot?' The normally self assured man fiddled with the edge of his shirt. I nodded and tried to smile.

'I hope you can understand my dilemma though,' he said, his head at first drooping, suddenly alert.

'There's no...'

'Anyway I'd like you to know that you have helped to save our farm Dot,' he said, interrupting as he struggled to put his thoughts into words. 'It was as serious as that. I was so stressed by money worries at the time. No excuse I know.' He paused.

'I understand, Mr Barton. You were only protecting your family and property, rightly so. There's no need to apologize.'

At that point Angelina brought in a tray of tea and smiled at me.

'Oh yes there is Dot, because I asked him to,' and she winked at me and then smiled at Jonathan.

'If not to apologize I must say how grateful we are for all the work you did for us and we'd like you to have this small cheque. Can you take a cheque?'

I paused, taken aback by this unexpected gesture and swallowed. 'It's my turn to say thank you then, not just for this money, and yes I can now access my bank account, but also for the opportunity of working in your library.'

'What do you mean?' asked Jonathan.

'Well, it was a pleasure and more than that, it helped to make me a whole person again.'

'Let's have tea,' said Angelina, wanting to defuse her husband's anxiety, 'and I've made a cake for the occasion.'

'Oh how lovely,' I said.

'I hear that congratulations are in order too,' said Jonathan, his smile now reaching his shoulders, and his hands finally still.

We toasted our tea cups, momentarily the embarrassment dissipated slightly and I continued,

'I'll always remember my time here with fondness; it literally changed my life.'

'I don't know about that but without you and your story, Dot, Evie would still be here causing us grief,' said Angelina, unable to contain a giggle.

We all laughed and then talked of Greta and how she was doing before I made my excuses to leave. That was a *five* I thought and smiled. They were both due to come tonight but after the milking was finished.

Jamal would also be arriving as soon as he had finished work. He had only returned from Turkey the day before. It had taken so long to obtain the legal authorisation between Turkey and the UK for Jamal to travel, let alone to visit his brother. We hadn't spoken since his return so there was a lot of catching up to be done. His personal life was fraught with difficulties too, since Orla's parents had initially refused to meet him, but neither he nor Orla had given up on their love for each other. I admired them greatly, even though I could see that it might be misguided loyalty in the long run. I hoped with all my heart that my fears were proved wrong. They were children ahead of their time and I prayed to our mutual God to shine favourably upon them.

Music began; a Big Band Sound which reverberated around the auditorium. The theme was retro and there was to be dancing, with intimate candlelit tables for four or six dotted around the ballroom. There were more on shallow stepped levels throughout the hall, much like in the old Ginger Rogers and Fred Astaire movies. A huge disco ball sent star like light flickering around the hall, and on a raised dais at its centre. A waiter in a dinner suit and crimson bow tie paused in front of me to offer a drink. I chose the orange juice, my hands shaking as I lifted it to my dry mouth. The place was filling up. I looked around enjoying people watching and admiring the dancers, already waltzing to some Glen Miller. I wished I had arranged to arrive with someone rather than on my own.

I reflected on my publishing deal, not enough to retire by, as the saying goes, but enough to ease my immediate financial situation certainly. Wanting a distraction I threw my dice; careful that it would land on the table. It was a *six*. Yes, this was certainly a *six* and I was proud that my dice adorned the front cover of both my novel and memoir, in different backgrounds. I glowed in joy at my achievements.

Bringing me out of my reverie I noticed someone edging towards me on my left. I dare not look directly at him but was aware of his shape in the periphery of my vision; a man with long straggly grey and white hair wearing an old tweed jacket. An arty type, I thought; maybe even a writer too. He sat alone at an empty table next to mine. I prayed that he would not ask me to dance; sensing his tension I was determined to hold my gaze away from him. Having learnt to tune into my environment I analysed the atmosphere. Was it fear? His aura was certainly a nervous energy in shed loads. Out of the corner of my eye I could sense this man's attention. He seemed much older than me, but that could be the lights. He was bearded, a fashion which can sometimes but not always age a man beyond his years, or maybe he had something to hide, I mused. I tensed up as I felt him glancing my way. Oh no, I thought. I hope this elderly stranger does not start to speak to me.

With relief I saw Jonathan and Angelina being led by Jamal towards me, Angelina beaming brightly. As they reached my table I stood up but so did the man, who must have been only ten feet away. Determined not to be fazed by this I kissed Angelina and Jonathan in welcome and held out my hand to Jamal to shake his, still sure that closer contact would be seen as inappropriate in such a public place with cameras about.

To my surprise Jamal turned to the stranger.

'Mr Gibbons, can I introduce Mr and Mrs Barton, the farmer and his wife I was telling you about the other day.'

My face turned white, life draining from me sending a shiver through to my very soul. I sat down, Angelina fussing over me. I dared not even look up to this man's gaze; this stranger.

'Are you OK Dot?' Angelina frowned. 'Take a sip of your juice. I'll pour you some water too. Or something stronger?' she glanced up at her husband for reassurance and guidance.

I could hear a bit of a shuffle and Gerald's voice, clearly shaken too, talking to Jamal. 'I shouldn't have come Jamal.

It was wrong of me to barge in on such a special occasion for Dot without giving her warning. I'll go.'

'I'm sorry Mr G. It was my fault. I thought that it would have been a nice surprise but I guess I was wrong. It must be quite unnerving for her.'

'I must go. I should never have come back or even thought that I would have a place in Dot's life again. I've hurt her too much already.'

'Stop this moment,' I exclaimed. 'You're both talking about me as if I'm not here. Yes, it's given me quite a turn. I can't grasp the reality of it, but that's nothing new for me.'

Gerald winced at the barbed remark. 'I'll go,' he said. 'I'm so sorry Dot. I'll get out of your life forever now.'

'So you think you can just walk out of my life once more and that's going to solve everything Gerald? Is that all you can think of? Running away again. Can you never face up to your responsibilities?'

I realised that, by this time, my voice had risen to quite a high pitch and the people around us had silenced, listening intently to the actual drama before them. The music paused in sympathy.

'What do you want me to do now?' Gerald whispered, his demeanour turning from an old man into a helpless schoolboy.

'Sit down and stop making a spectacle of us all. After tonight we must arrange a time and place to talk. You have months of explaining due to me, but this is neither the time nor the place.'

Jamal looked at me with admiration as I took control of the situation, but he had the forethought to take his place between Gerald and me. I smiled at his wish to alleviate my discomfort and to keep peace.

I half turned to Angelina, who had settled on my other side and had grasped my hand; a sense of protection which I found most touching.

Gerald sat down again, grudgingly, leaving Jonathan the only one still standing, with a look of total bafflement verging on embarrassment. The music recommenced and this snapped him out of his reverie. He went to fetch a glass of wine for me giving me a few moments with Angelina. I smiled with gratitude on his return before he turned to his wife and asked her to dance. She glanced at me before standing up and I gave her an encouraging smile which said, 'I'm fine,' without words.

So, there we were, the three of us in a row, silence between us. This gave me a chance to catch breath but no time to assimilate the current situation. The pain which had surfaced was still too acute.

Relief flooded into me, however, as the music stopped and the proceedings began; a welcome distraction.

We clapped the third prize winner but my colour drained again as I was announced the second prize winner for the most promising debut authoress. In an absolute daze I walked up to the stage for my prize; a silver pen as a trophy to treasure, an envelope which contained a cheque for £500 and also the opportunity to attend a two weeks writers' retreat in the Cotswolds. I was thrilled. The thought of my dice popped into my head as I walked slowly back to my seat, the clapping still echoing around the hall. This occasion should truly have been the best *six* of my life so far, but had it been marred by the unexpected arrival of my missing husband? He officially still held that title I mused wryly.

I shook myself to live in the moment and enjoy the applause. Those thoughts were for another day. Tonight was a time for celebration. Light had shone through my personal darkness and I was so fortunate.

Next I concentrated on the winner of the first prize, feeling the joy for his success. I'm afraid I can't even remember his name though; such was the fog in my mind. Angelina, Jonathan and Jamal were all talking at once, congratulating me on my prize and admiring the pen, until the music began once more.

Even Gerald was carried away by the enthusiasm of the event as he exclaimed almost shyly, 'I'm so proud of you Dot.'

I couldn't help but smile my thanks to this man who had been my life for so long. Jamal was talking to both of us, speaking at double speed, his face bearing a frown.

'Auntie, this is such a special day for you; all that hard work. You of all people here deserve success and I'm so lucky to know you.'

'I couldn't have done it without you Jamal, or without the kindness of those around me. You are all part of this achievement.'

Embarrassed by my outpouring Jonathan took Angelina's hand once more and they headed to the dance floor for a jive, leaving the three of us yet again.

'Thank you Jamal. It must have been your sheer determination which brought Gerald here tonight. You've never given up and I'm so proud of you too. What news of Ahmed though?'

'He's still in the detention centre in Turkey but the British Consul is trying to extradite him. I know that many here will wish him to rot there, but he's so sorry about what he's done. He's been imprisoned for over two years now.'

'At least you know he's safe now. What are the conditions like?'

'Clean but bare Auntie. He's bored and fed up; angry even, although I tried to persuade him that his attitude may not be helping proceedings.'

'When did you get back to the UK Jamal?'

'Only last night but I'm allowed to talk to him every other day on the phone in the coming days.'

'That's promising news, and how's Orla?'

'She's over in Ireland right now but I spoke to her on my way here. She's fine.'

'..and her parents?'

Jamal blushed. 'They're coming over in a month's time to meet me. I can't really ask for more, can I?' I squeezed his hand, struggling to find the right words of encouragement. There was a pause. 'But those are other stories to tell Auntie. I think we should focus on your celebration tonight.'

'I'll drink to that!' said Gerald, calling a waiter over and passing a glass of wine to me and a glass of orange juice to Jamal, putting two more glasses on the table for Angelina and Jonathan. Sensing an anxious shyness I had not seen in Gerald since we were teenagers, I could guess he was wondering whether this night was going to be our last before the divorce. Could we ever conceive of a new beginning after what we'd been through? Were his eyes glistening or was it just the effect of the alcohol?

After we had sipped our drinks there was another embarrassing pause in conversation. I slipped into a world of my own, barely listening to Jonathan and Gerald trying to make polite conversation.

As if cutting into my reverie our favourite song, 'As Time Goes By,' filtered across the floor. Gerald caught my eye. He recognised it too. Our tune enhanced by one of the few series on the television we had enjoyed watching together. Our eyes locked for a moment. His conveyed a cocktail of sorrow, hope and fear. What message did my eyes give to this man who I once knew so well, but was part of my past – a time I had tried to bury in the depths of my memory?

As if in a daze Gerald plucked up courage he did not feel and stood up holding his hand out to me. Without hesitation, as if compelled by an unseen force, I rose and he took me in his arms to whisk me around the floor. He was always an expert dancer was my Gerald.

I tried to forget the questions. They must wait for another day. I also suppressed the multitude of mixed emotions from anger to sadness, from hatred to love as I glided around in the moment.

This may be the beginning of a new chapter or the beginning of the final end, but in that instant we waltzed around the dance floor in togetherness and forgetfulness...

... Oh dear! I do apologize for digressing into fantasy again, as I am wont to do. Reality does not allow us tie up ends in life like a Jane Austen novel, does it? So this is what really happened...

Just after the music started to play '*As Time Goes By,*' Gerald glanced at my silent retreating expression and took his leave; before turning his back on us however, he paused:

'Can I see you again for a coffee sometime Dot?' I could feel everyone around me holding their breath.

I nodded the affirmative, 'Yes Gerald, get in touch through Jamal.'

He turned and weaved his way along the edge of the dancers, head bowed low. After he had gone, the mood lightened and I had that dance, only it was with Jonathan, who kindly asked me, prompted by a look from Angelina, bless her.

CHAPTER 35

DS TONY BROWN arrived early for work to clear his head. The Friday before he and DC Peterson had been moved back to Police HQ in Kempston from Drumford in the cutbacks. Streamlining they called it, bringing a larger team together rather than being dispersed in the more rural towns. However, the front desk at Drumford's temporary station would still be manned five mornings a week between 10 am and 12 pm by two police constables and two community officers who would still work from the site.

Although the change appeared to make sense on paper, Tony was still irritated by it. He sipped his coffee, bought at the petrol station down the road. It gave him a kick for the start of the day that he knew he wouldn't get from the police station's vending machine, which numbed his taste buds. Slowly he opened his local paper, The Bedford Times and Citizen. On page five a photo of Dorothy Gibbons caught his eye, proud to be collecting her literacy award. Tony recognised Jamal Hussain and the farmer and his wife in the photo but there was a stranger hovering in the background looking uncertain, who caught his attention. He scratched his head and clicked on line to see if he could get a better look of the man. The image zoomed in and he clicked 'search' knowing that within minutes their almost infinite data base would scan for a likeness.

Three possible photos appeared within moments on his screen and one of them was none other than Gerald Gibbons.

'Well, what do you know!' he exclaimed to himself. 'There's another file to close after a courtesy visit to Dorothy Gibbons to confirm it.'

DC Peterson entered the room at that moment and Tony beckoned her to look over his shoulder.

'I wonder how she's taking it?' Cathy Peterson frowned as she turned, without taking off her coat, and headed for the door.

'Let's go,' she said.

READING GROUP DISCUSSION

- Do you feel that Dot reflects the homeless ness of our age or is she driven differently? If so why?

- Do you think that MISSING, Past and Present handles mixed marriage sensitively? Why?

- In our age of controversy over immigration and support for people driven to migrate due to the recent conflicts what did you think of the characters of Jamal and Ahmed?

- In what ways do you think Dot's influence on the two lads helps or hinders their integration into British society?

- Author Diana Jackson took risks at the end of the story, playing on the two stories and interweaving them. Did you think this worked or did it irritate you?

Review for Diana Jackson's *Mystery inspired by History* Series:

MURDER, NOW AND THEN

This book covers a number of genres, as other reviewers have commented. The murder mystery itself is well developed and crafted, leaving the reader guessing until the end and the family drama aspect is compelling and intriguing on a whole other level. I also liked the local aspect, being from Bedfordshire myself, although readers from outside the area would not be put off by this; rather, I think they'd be enticed by the fantastic descriptions and feel like they were here themselves! Highly recommended read.

Reviewed by Adam Croft
Best selling Indie Crime writer

Extract from

MURDER, NOW AND THEN

The Prologue

May 9th 2019

'I wouldn't kill my husband. How could you think such a thing?'

Joanna sat on the grey plastic bench, her hands in her lap, absentmindedly tearing tiny pieces from a ball of spent tissue and watching them drift down on to the brown tiles; droplets of tears joining the snow-flaked floor.

Even though Joanna was alone, she could feel the glare of DI Norton boring into her, willing her to confess. How easy it would have been to halt his incessant questioning and say 'Yes, I did it,' just to silence him? His voice still lingered in her head.

Numb with the enormity of her situation she closed her eyes and sat in a sleepless trance, her hands now motionless and her mind free–falling in a bottomless void.

May 9th 1919

"Sergeant Major Alfred Donald Keith Regmund appeared before the Bedford Division Bench on Wednesday morning. Crowds waited outside Shire Hall to see the prisoner arrive and depart, which he did in a closed cab. Three or four rows of public gallery were filled, as also was the grand jury gallery.

Mr P D Holmer presided, the other Magistrate being Mr A C Greenachre. Superintendant Patterson went into the witness box and gave evidence as follows.

'On Tuesday May 13th I arrested the prisoner at Haynes Park. He was conveyed to Bedford. On arrival I charged him on suspicion of murdering a girl, Lucille Vardon at Wilshamstead on 9th May. I cautioned him and he said,

'I understand my unfortunate position, and your justification for arresting me, but I am innocent, and I shall be able to prove my innocence.'

The prisoner was then remanded until 11.15 am on Tuesday next." [1]

1. Bedfordshire Times and Independent May 30th 1919 (names have been changed)

CHAPTER 1

July 2017   Joanna and Bob Thomas at Pear Tree Farm

JOANNA, A FARMER'S wife of forty two years of age, whose youthful make-up-free complexion was more like that of a woman in her early thirties, looked out of the yellowing UPVC faux Georgian windows of their old farmhouse. She smiled at the sight of the small herd of prize Jersey cattle her husband had purchased. They provided milk only sold locally. There had even been a revival in friendly milkmen due to the plastics scandal. Though in Joanna and Bob's case she was a milk lady called Fiona who called three times a week, a young lady pretty enough to pose for Hello magazine.

'*Coals to Newcastle!*' would be her cheery greeting to Bob, Joanna's husband, if she passed him in the yard returning from the milking barn to have a break before checking the Jerseys. It seemed ironic that they had their own milk delivered, but that was the law. Even for their own use, the unpasteurised milk needed to be checked, cooled and bottled in the normal way, for which the dairy charged Bob an astonishing 40p a litre for his own milk!

Joanna focused on the cattle. Was it their panda-like saucer eyes which amused her or their upturned haloed noses? Bob was experimenting with a new purely organic herd of Jerseys which provided delicious unpasteurised milk for his friends and neighbours. It was like a 'trendy' hobby for him, but he was astute enough to foresee this becoming a dairy product of the future. Their son Paul had even persuaded him to introduce the most innovative milking system of its day, where the cows choose when they want to be milked and are milked by a robot. It was the only time Paul had paid any attention to life at the farm and he looked with disdain on the old fashioned parlour they still used with the Friesians.

Joanna's eyes panned over the scene and focused on the wind turbine which stood boldly on the hillside away from the woods. What an outcry there had been when plans were afoot to install it on their land.

'Self interest!' 'Waste of money!' 'Useless and inefficient!' 'Vital for our future!' 'Beneficial for the whole community!' 'Low cost power!'

Whatever the arguments at the numerous meetings Joanna and Bob had attended, each side seemed to have reams of evidence to back their own case, but in the end it was government policy and that was that.

Bob thanked his good fortune that he only rented the land to the council and did not have to maintain the monstrosity. Rumour had it that, five years after installation, it was costing more to repair it than the electricity it produced. Such was the advancement in technology or was it just fake news.

It took a while for all factions in the village to speak to one another after that. In their local, The Greyhound, Joanna perceived a drop in temperature the moment she and Bob walked through the door. It was strange that there had been little or nothing like those levels of resentment when they had been approached to have a mobile phone mast installed just a few years earlier. In the end most understood that Bob and Joanna had little or no choice in either matter and certainly the phone mast helped to compensate for the ever low prices demanded by the supermarkets.

Joanna's daydream was disturbed by a movement behind her and she turned around, her face a mixture of surprise and concern. Inadvertently she flicked her shoulder length wavy auburn hair behind her ears.

'Hello Helen. I wasn't expecting you in today. You don't need to worry about us for a while if you'd rather stay at home.'

'Oh, I don't think so, Joanna. Best for me to be busy. Time goes quicker that way.'

'Let me make a cuppa then, and we'll sit down and have a chat. How are you coping?' Joanna's eyes were full of genuine concern.

Seeing Helen's startled face obviously fighting to hold back the tears, Joanna realised, too late, that she had said the wrong thing.

'I understand Helen,' she said gently. 'Just do what you feel you can cope with. Come and go whenever you want to, but I'm always here if you'd like company.'

Joanna did not add - like you've always been here for me - but hoped that Helen understood.

Helen just nodded and went straight to the broom cupboard and Joanna did not see Helen's almost imperceptible wince at her last statement.

'I've just got some paperwork to do for Bob and so I'll shut myself in the office for a couple of hours. Help yourself to tea Helen, and there's cake in the tin.'

'Ta, Joanna, but you get on. Don't mind me if I just need to be alone.'

Joanna walked sadly into the office, a muddled den she and her husband shared, and closed the door, carefully putting her hot mug down on a mat of St Aubin's Bay. They had honeymooned in Jersey, as Bob's mum and dad had also done years before. Bob had no wish to go abroad and Jersey was about as overseas as he would venture. Joanna had, on the other hand, spent all her holidays whilst at university travelling to exotic places like India, to do some voluntary teaching, and backpacking across South America from Argentina to Ecuador. Those were her Bohemian days when she had worked at a cafe all term and during the Christmas holidays to save for the long summer of freedom.

Joanna frowned as she stared at the screen coming to life. They had never found the money or had the inclination to update to the latest technology, like wall computer screens linked to gadgets she had seen in the homes of some of their friends. Their's was just the old familiar laptop, still with its reassuring wires leading to plug sockets; even though their son found it hard to hide his contempt at his parents' ignorance.

'Even your old thing is wireless, mum. You only need to recharge it from time to time. You don't even need trailing wires,' he had said pointing to the printer / cum fax / cum copier / come phone cum...he had helped his father choose during his last holiday.

Joanna picked up her mug and sipped. How could they help Helen? She had been such a friend and so supportive since Joanna and Bob married over twenty years ago. Through Helen, Joanna had got to know all the gossip about the locals and been guided as to the best way to win their hearts, even her mother-in-law Madelyn.

'Ask Madelyn if she'll show you how to bake cakes and make pastry,' Helen had said wisely. And she was right. Soon Joanna and Madelyn were laughing and sharing a kitchen as if they had known each other all their lives, Joanna showing obvious admiration for Bob's mother's skills in the art of cookery. For Joanna it opened up a whole new world. She had lived with a nut allergy and had to be careful all her life, but now they could be sure of the ingredients in their baking rather than scrutinising every single packet.

When Joanna moaned once that she still felt a stranger in their local pub nearly three years into her marriage, Helen had suggested,

'Ask for the same drink each time for a while and don't be too shy to use Bill's name.'

It was odd at first. Joanna was a free spirit and liked choice, but since the pub usually had a guest cider she opted for that. It worked like a treat. Not only did Bill, the landlord, have 'their usual' ready almost as soon as they appeared at the door, but after she had said 'thanks Bill' a few times and smiled at him shyly, he began to ask her opinion on the new brew.

'So Joanna,' he said one day with a wink. 'What's your verdict on this one? It arrived only yesterday,' and then he waited expectantly for her reply.

Taking a slow sip Joanna savoured the cider like she would a glass of her favourite Rioja. 'Umm. Bill. I think it's the best I've ever tasted.'

'You're not just saying that to please an old man,' Bill replied, his face beaming with pride.

'No, Bill, it's the truth. What's it called?' she peered at the pump label. 'Ah, Cibernicks. It's sweet and appley enough, but with a twang to make you smile.'

He had chuckled at her response and from then on he had always made a point of stopping at their table to have a chat.

Her thoughts switched back to Helen Carter. The once exuberant wholesome lady, full of mirth at the slightest notion that caught her imagination, once pretty in a charming earthy-countryside sort of way, had aged before their eyes. Two months ago her only daughter Kirsty had died of leukaemia at the age of 21. It was such a tragedy. Helen had brought Kirsty up on her own and had always been dismissive of the father and so no-one knew who he was. Many had wondered if he might reveal himself at the funeral, but no strangers had appeared. Of course it did not have to be a stranger, but the community did not like to look inwardly to seek the truth.

Anyway, Helen had always been adamant, on the few times she had been pressed, that the father was living abroad. Since Helen had once worked in Italy at a restaurant by Lake Como and had returned in the family way, they had no reason to doubt her. But, to the disappointment of some of the villagers, no olive skinned Italian appeared in Haynes churchyard two months ago at the funeral and so Kirsty's father remained a mystery.

Although Joanna's fingers hovered over the keys, her eyes had still not focused on the screen in front of her. She heard the sound of the Dyson overhead and wondered what Helen would do next. Since Kirsty had been born, Helen had been content to find numerous cleaning jobs in order to make ends meet, but a recent conversation over breakfast with Bob came to mind.

'It's a pity Helen can't find something a bit more rewarding now she's only got herself to think of,' Joanna commented as she served up the bacon and eggs.

'You'd be surprised, Joanna. Our Helen was always quite bright at school.'

'I don't doubt that, Bob, after all, you should know. You went to school with her but....'

'I'll have you know she even won several prizes for best pupil of the year and highest achiever in mathematics.' Bob interrupted without giving it a second thought.

'What happened then?' asked Joanna frowning as she stared down at her plate. It was one of those rare moments that Joanna had dared to ask, but was afraid Bob would clam up again, like he always did.

'Well, she'd planned to go to university but decided to have a gap year in Italy. I think there were some family connections, you know. There have been many Italians in Bedford over the last century, of course.'

Joanna waited. Maybe he would reveal something she did not know already, but unlikely.

'Then she came home...well you know... Is there anymore Daddies sauce, Joanna?' He looked up expectantly and Joanna realised that the matter was closed.

It made Joanna smile to think that Bob was unable to say that Helen was pregnant, even though he dealt with the facts of life every day on the farm.

Back to the present she heard the sound of the toilet flushing upstairs and the frantic scratching of a loo brush. Surely Helen could be free to do something special with her life now, if she could only recover from her overwhelming sense of loss. Joanna shivered. How would she have coped if she had lost either of her children? However annoying and worrying they were at times, they were adorable nevertheless and such a vital part of the life she shared with her husband, even though both of her offspring were now making lives of their own.

It was early days though, for Helen. She would talk when she was ready but she had to grieve first. It was not only natural but vital for her recovery. After about an hour there was a small tap at the door bringing Joanna abruptly to her senses. As Helen walked in without waiting, Joanna tried to look as if she had been busy rather than daydreaming, whilst Helen had strived so hard to make their home clean and tidy. Joanna turned a shade of pink.

'I'll finish for the day Joanna if you don't mind and do another hour downstairs tomorrow. There's a meeting of the Leukaemia Society in Bedford after lunch and I'd like to get involved. I've got to do something worthwhile,' she exclaimed with a determined expression in her watery eyes.

'Come whenever you want to, Helen, but don't worry if you don't feel like it. I understand.'

'Do you really?' Helen said, unable to hide the sarcasm in her voice, her eyes giving Joanna a piercing stare.

'I admire you Helen, for going this afternoon. I hope you get some support too,' Joanna replied, determined to ignore Helen's tone and to be warm and friendly in return. 'See you tomorrow then.'

Helen closed the door behind her without saying another word and Joanna heard the rattle of Helen's bicycle as she rode over the bumpy farmyard. Joanna switched off her PC. Now alone in the house she climbed the stairs and went into their bedroom to make the bed. Gazing momentarily out of the window on the south side of the house, she looked over towards a field of wheat, which shimmered like rippling sand.

......

Review of Diana Jackson's most recent publication.
A fantasy Memoir:

THE HEALING PATHS OF FIFE

'Mesmerizing and rejuvenating coastal path of Fife'

The Healing Paths of Fife is a memoir of Diana Jackson. A travel path full of fantasy encounters. She met significant strangers while walking the coastal paths of Fife and had equally special and strange experiences and adventures. Some are spooky and some are pleasant. Every new day of Diana's life is full of exciting adventures and with every day she understands what the time demands her to do. The Path proved to be a healing and self-discovering.

The story is a memoir with elements of fantasy. The book is a travel diary and a true account of Diana's life after relocating and settling down in her new life with her husband in Fife.'

Review by Surabhi on Amazon.co.uk

Over £500 has been raised by selling copies of 'The Healing Paths of Fife' for local charities in south Fife.

Reviews for Diana Jackson's *Riduna Series:*

RIDUNA

Riduna speaks volumes about the power of love and loss and is beautifully written with a fluidity that speaks to your soul. Author Diana Jackson's ability to portray the everyday ordinary yet life-changing events of those in a community is amazing; you get a true feel of what it must have been like living in Riduna during that era. Fans of *The Guernsey Literary and Potato Peel Pie Society* will fall in love with *Riduna.*

Reviewed by Angela Simmons from
The Historical Novel Society

ANCASTA ~ Guide me Swiftly Home

In first Riduna and then Ancasta, we follow Harriet and Edward, who always thought their path in life would be together, but the reality of life was that it was not meant to be. Finally, in their retirement years, are they able to realize that it wasn't them who changed but the world around them and that things happened to them to make the dreams change. Diana Jackson weaves a story that is real and true and makes you feel that you are right there living it. It is a wonderful mix of the romance and realities of life with some of the technological advances of the historical time period of the novel. It is definitely a novel of moving on and never giving up, one any reader will enjoy.

Reviewed by Michelle Randall for Readers' Favorite

Diana also compiled a memoir of an amazing 103 year old. Here's a review for:

THE LIFE AND DEMISE OF NORMAN CAMPBELL
(Norman's choice of title)

How to love and live life to the full!

The first of the copies I bought has been given and was thoroughly enjoyed. A very charming and uplifting book. The second has not yet been given as it is a gift for Fathers Day but I know he will also enjoy reading the book!

Review by Heidi G on Amazon

If you would like to find out more about Diana Jackson's writing you can check her website:
www.dianamaryjackson.co.uk

Her two blogs:
www.dianamj.wordpress.com
http://selectionsofreflections.wordpress.com/

Riduna on Twitter
and
https://www.facebook.com/DianaJacksonauthor on
    Facebook